RISING STAR

THE BELL FAMILY OF BLUESTAR ISLAND, BOOK 4

JENNIFER FAYE

LAZY DAZY PRESS

Published by Lazy Dazy Press

ISBN-13 (digital): 978-1-942680-19-2

ISBN-13 (paperback): 978-1-942680-20-8

Bluestar Island series:

Book 1: Love Blooms

Book 2: Harvest Dance

Book 3: A Lighthouse Café Christmas

Book 4: Rising Star

Book 5: Summer by the Beach

Thanks & much appreciation to:

Content Editor: Bev Katz Rosenbaum

Copy Editor: Lia Fairchild

CONTENTS

ABOUT THIS BOOK...

When Bluestar's hometown celebrity unexpectedly returns to the island, there's a heartbreaking scandal following her...

Country singer Emma Bell is finally making headlines—just not the right ones. Before she has time to heal her broken heart, her assistance is desperately needed. Bluestar's Concert on the Beach Summer Spectacular is in trouble, and her soon-to-be sister-in-law's job is on the line.

Financial investor turned carpenter, Noah Sullivan, has retired from his high-stress job due to health issues. He's moved to Bluestar Island for a quiet, healthy life, but when Emma blows into town, his days are anything but serene.

Everyone in the small town counting on them, Noah and Emma must work past their conflicts to keep a promise to someone special to both of them. Will the summer's sun soothe their tension and the sea breeze lull them into a peaceful surrender of their hearts?

*"Love comes as gently . . .
as a Bluestar breeze."*

Chapter One

Bang. Bang.

"Em, are you awake?"

Emma Bell groaned as she rolled over, pulling the pillow over her head. She didn't want to wake up. Not yet. She took a deep breath and then let herself drift back to dreamland.

She'd been having the most amazing dream. The images resumed playing in her mind. She could feel the warmth of the sunshine on her face. The light taste of the salty sea breeze on her tongue was so real. She was strolling along the beach. She felt the sun-warmed sand between her toes and then the rush of sea water.

She felt so at peace. She smiled and turned her head. There was someone standing just ahead of her, but she couldn't quite make them out. It took a moment for her gaze to focus. The man had his back to her. He was tall with short light-brown hair.

She was drawn to him. As she approached him, her heart beat faster. She loved him. But who was he? His brown hair and height were wrong for JT.

He started to turn to her.

Bang. Bang.

Emma sat upright with a gasp. The man's image vanished before she was able to see his face.

Disappointment assailed her. She knew it was just a figment of her imagination, but something about this particular dream had felt so real. But how could that be?

She'd already found her forever guy. Her thumb toyed with the diamond ring on her finger. It was still there. With a relieved sigh, she sank back against the pillows. How could she be dreaming about some mystery man when she was engaged to the sweetest, kindest man?

She glanced around at the beige walls and beige drapes. The hotel room didn't look familiar. She tried to remember the name of the city.

"Em, you ready to go?"

Emma cleared her throat. "Yeah. Be right there."

In that moment she regained her bearings. She was out on the road with her amazingly talented band. Her very first concert tour experience had been a whirlwind of events. And she had faced a steep learning curve. There was nothing to ground her—nothing to keep her from drifting off course.

She yawned as she stumbled out of bed and moved to the window. She pulled back the heavy curtains. The sun was just starting to rise. And as her gaze moved beyond the parking lot to the buildings across the way, she still had absolutely no idea what city she was in or even the state.

She couldn't keep going like this. No one had told her that chasing her dream of being a singer would be this way. She was the opening act for the opening act.

She wouldn't admit it to anyone but she was wearing out. Really wearing out. And that worried her.

Because not only did she sing country songs, but she also wrote and sold them too. At the moment, she didn't have a creative thought in her head. That had never happened before. She had notebooks filled with poems and lyrics. Some good, a lot not so good. But now when she stared at a blank page, the words didn't come to her. What was a singer without words?

If she lost her creativity—if she couldn't write the songs that evoked emotions—if she lost what made her her, then what was she doing all of this for?

Bang. Bang.

"Get a move on!" It was one of the band members. "The airport shuttle is pulling out in ten."

"Be right there." She turned, spotting her still-packed suitcase near the door.

During this tour, she'd perfected the five-minute shower, followed by pulling her damp hair into a messy bun.

Ding.

Ding.

Ding.

That many messages that close together piqued her curiosity. She retrieved her phone from the end table. It was there she saw a brochure that read Seattle. That was where they were.

With her phone in hand, she sank down on the edge of the bed. She swiped her finger across the screen. Her phone sprang to life and blew up with message after message. There were hundreds of them. What in the world?

Sympathies and virtual hugs abounded. Oh, no. Someone must have died to stir up this much of an outpouring. Her chest tightened. But who?

She clicked on the first link. It took her to a gossip site. Right there on the home page was a photo of her boyfriend, um, her fiancé, JT. He was kissing someone. And it wasn't some little kiss on the cheek.

The breath hitched in her throat. This couldn't be real. She blinked, but the image was still there—JT with his arms around someone else.

This couldn't be right. It had to be an old photo. Yes, that was it. This must be a relationship he'd had before he met her.

She desperately wanted that to be the case, so much so that she almost closed the screen. But a niggling bit of curiosity had her enlarge the photo. And that was when she saw it—his new tattoo.

They were supposed to get matching tattoos, but at the last moment, she'd chickened out. Her fear of needles won out over her disappointing JT. And yet he'd still opted for a new tattoo to add to his collection.

He'd gotten a star. He said it reminded him of her. She was like a star that guided him home. At the time, she'd thought it was the most romantic thing.

Now she wondered if he'd also used that line on the new woman in his arms. Her heart ached. Why had he done this right after proposing to her? Had it all been a lie?

As her gaze drifted down, she caught sight of a small photo of her. The image appeared to show her crying, but she didn't recognize the photo. She wasn't a big crier, not unless it was something really important—like your boyfriend kissing someone else. Where did this picture come from? She started to wonder if they'd done a bit of photo editing—make that a lot of editing.

And then she returned to her messages. There were also voicemails and texts. As she held her phone, it rang. Caller ID identified it as Razzled. A gossip site. The hottest site in Hollywood and Nashville. Their website didn't feature stories unless they were gossipy and messy stories about today's hottest stars. She wasn't a celebrity, but JT was Nashville's biggest star with a foot in both the music and film industries.

Emma shut off her phone. Her nice, quiet life on Bluestar Island had morphed into something so different since she'd won the television reality show Songbird. She'd become an instant national sensation. The only thing was once the show was over, her star had dimmed.

With only one song recorded, producers had been hesitant to take on someone new without a large social media following—well, that had been before her romantic relationship with JT. When their relationship had come to light, her social media numbers had soared.

Without JT in her life, her numbers would ultimately tumble. Just out of curiosity, she pulled up her social media. She did a double take. Her following had been in the four digits. This morning, it was in the five digits and rising quickly. And then she noticed her name was trending. In another scenario this would have excited her, but considering her personal life was on display for everyone to see and pick apart, she wasn't so happy. Not at all.

Buzz-buzz.

JT's image appeared on the screen of her phone. Tears stung the backs of her eyes. Sobs clogged her throat. How could he hurt her like this?

She refused to let him know how much he'd hurt her. And if she answered this call, she'd never be able to keep her emotions together. She pressed the decline button, tossed the phone onto the bed, and then headed for the shower.

Beneath the trickle of lukewarm water, she unleashed her pain. She cried for the fun times they'd shared that now felt like lies. She cried for the way he'd so casually broken her heart without the respect of calling her to say it was over before he'd rushed onto someone new. She cried for the pain of believing him when he'd looked into her eyes and said she was the only one in his life now and forever.

Minutes later, she gathered herself. She was still damp when she threw on fresh clothes and then put her hair up. She used her sunglasses like a hairband. The still-lose strands were damp to the point of dripping onto her neck. She hated that feeling. But she also knew airline flights waited for no one. After months of being on the road, they were at last headed home.

One last glance in the mirror had her noticing her blotchy complexion and her now red-rimmed eyes. She was a mess. Just as she reached for her purse to put on some makeup there was another knock.

"Last call! We're pulling out."

So be it. This was how she was going to look today—not that anyone would notice her. They never did—unless she was with JT. And they were never going to be together again.

She smashed her feet into her cowboy boots, grabbed her bag, gave the room one last glance to make sure she hadn't forgotten anything, and then headed for the door.

On her way to the airport shuttle, other guests of the hotel pointed at her. Luckily, she couldn't hear what they were saying, but when they pulled out their phones and started taking pictures, she lowered her sunglasses as she ducked her head.

When she stepped onto the shuttle bus for the airport, she spotted her lead guitar player. He was wearing a ball cap. She stopped next to him. "You wouldn't happen to have an extra hat, would you?"

He looked at her with sympathy in his eyes. "No. But here." He pulled off the cap and held it out to her. "I think you need it more than I do."

She wanted to argue with him but couldn't. She accepted the cap. "Thank you."

Emma pulled the cap down over her head and sank down into the first empty seat. She turned her face to the window and was relieved to see the people who'd been filming her had moved on. She should be excited to finally be heading back to Nashville. But it wasn't like there was anyone waiting at home for her, not even a dog or cat or even a houseplant.

When she'd first moved to Nashville, she'd been terribly homesick and still mourning the untimely death of her father, but she thought with some time that she'd settle in, and it'd be like home to her. And though the city was familiar to her, and she had made friends there, it just wasn't home—not like Bluestar.

Meghan Saunders, their tour manager, sat down next to her. "Are you okay?"

Emma turned to her. Meghan's brown bob always looked sleek. Her face was perfectly made up, as though she hadn't gotten to bed late or up early. Meghan was always poised and handled any situation with grace.

Though she was twelve years older than Emma, they still hit it off. It didn't hurt that they were the only two women on this particular tour. Meghan kept a close eye on Emma, and though at times it felt like she was being a mother hen, Emma appreciated the support.

"Do I look that bad?" Emma resisted the urge to pull the cap lower on her forehead.

"Let's just say I saw the photo this morning."

"Did everyone see it?" She glanced around to see if anyone on the shuttle was staring at her.

Meghan sighed. "Yes. I'm so sorry. Do you know the woman in the photo?"

Emma shook her head. "I've never seen her before."

"Is there anything I can do?"

Emma once more shook her head. "This is my problem."

"Just keep in mind that I'm here if you need anything."

"Thank you. I really appreciate it."

"By the way, the tour ended on a great note. You sounded awesome."

"If only I hadn't woken up to a photo of my fiancé kissing another woman splattered all over the gossip sites. Even some legitimate news sites are picking up the story." She just wanted to find a dark hole and climb into it until this nightmare ended.

"I know it hurts. And I'm so sorry. But you know what they say."

"What's that?"

"No publicity is bad publicity."

She frowned at Meghan. Surely she wasn't serious. "I definitely could have lived without this publicity."

"Have you talked to JT?"

She shook her head as her gaze settled on the five-carat diamond ring still on her finger. "No. I think the picture of him kissing someone else said everything."

Meghan briefly squeezed her arm. "Pizza and a gallon of ice cream work wonders for me."

"I'll keep that in mind." At the moment, she had no appetite whatsoever. In fact, she was feeling a bit nauseous. She just wanted to get to her apartment, curl up on the couch, and hide from the world.

Luckily, she didn't have any other obligations in the immediate future because she wasn't sure she could muster up that energy. As addictive as it was to perform, this revelation had leached away her enthusiasm.

She'd trusted JT. How could he do this to her? She'd been such a total fool.

Ding.

And yet another text message. She pulled her phone out of her pocket to turn it off. Before she could power it down, her gaze caught the name of her brother as the contact.

Hi, Auntie Em. It's Nikki. Guess what?

Emma smiled at seeing a message from her seven-year-old niece. Nikki obviously had borrowed her father's phone.

It felt so good to be distracted from the implosion of her life. Her fingers moved rapidly over the keyboard.

What?

Dash got loose again. Dad chased him around the yard.

Emma remembered the little goat that was born at her brother's farm a year or so ago. He was certainly a character.

Did your dad catch him?

We bribed Dash with cookies.

Emma smiled even though her heart was broken. For just a moment, she focused all of her attention on Nikki.

Good thinking.

When are U coming to visit?

Emma paused. She didn't know what to tell her niece. The last time she'd been home was at Christmastime for her mother's wedding to fire chief, Walter Campbell. It had been such a beautiful wedding.

And now it was already June. How had so much time passed so quickly?

She stared at her niece's words and then she typed... Soon.

Yay!

Love U!

Love U 2!

"Everything okay?" Meghan was lounged back, checking the messages on her own phone.

Emma slipped her phone back into her jean pocket. "Yep. The pet goat got lose again."

"Seems like he gets loose a lot."

"He does. My brother is always trying to outsmart Dash, but that goat is forever finding a way to escape."

Meghan smiled. "Your family sounds great."

"They really are." And she missed them a lot.

"Well, I just wanted to check in with you. And now I better go round up the rest of the crew so we don't end up missing our flight."

And then Emma was left alone with her thoughts—thoughts of home and her niece, her brother, her sister and mother, and that little goat. They all seemed so far away, which was probably because they were literally on the other side of the country.

Buzz-buzz.

Emma glanced at her ringing phone, hoping it was her niece again. It wasn't. It was her agent, Stan Morris. Her finger hovered over the red decline button. He'd want to discuss the picture and how they needed to make a statement. She hadn't even wrapped her mind around the image in that photo. How was she supposed to explain it to anyone else?

Still, Stan was a great guy. He was always in her corner, trying to get her more promotions while working to land her a recording contract. He had faith in her, even when she didn't have faith in herself.

She pressed the accept button and held the phone to her ear. "Hey, Stan."

"I've been trying to reach you." His voice was higher pitched than normal, and his words were rushed. "Did you see Razzled?"

"Yes." She slouched down in her seat. She didn't want to have this conversation.

"You're the headline!" He sounded so happy.

"Stan, I can't talk about it."

"Em, I have big news."

Was it possible he had news about her career rather than the dumpster fire otherwise known as her love life? She hoped so. She needed something positive to latch onto while she dealt with her broken heart.

She sat up a little straighter. "Good news?"

"Yes. I've been fielding phone calls all morning. They want you on all of the networks' morning talk shows."

"What?" It came out a little louder than she'd intended. "You mean like singing at Rockefeller Center?" It had been a dream all of her life.

"Well...um...not exactly."

Her body stiffened. "What do you mean by not exactly?"

"Well, they're interested in you and JT."

"No!"

"Em, you have to do this."

"No, I don't." Why did all of these people think she'd be anxious to cash in on her breakup—a breakup that she didn't know about?

"Will you at least think about it?"

She knew if she said no that he'd continue trying to persuade her to do it his way. So she took the shortest route to ending this phone call. "Yes. But I've got to go now. We're almost as the airport."

After they said their goodbyes, she powered off her phone. There was no one she wanted to speak to. She was talked out.

She slouched back in her seat and flung her backpack into the empty seat next to her. As the shuttle pulled away from the hotel, she turned her face to the window. She blindly stared out as her mind replayed the events that had led to her quick engagement and JT's subsequent betrayal.

Anger, sadness, and confusion all jostled for prominence. How could he have done this to her? Where had everything gone so wrong? Was it something she'd done?

She had absolutely no answers. And even worse, the questions kept coming one after the other. She swiped at her damp cheeks. How had she been so wrong about him?

Their first date had been arranged by their agents, who had hoped they'd do some social engagements together to create some publicity buzz. Both she and JT had agreed to meet, but it had to be private. If they didn't hit it off, they didn't want to be locked into this arrangement.

It'd been a Monday evening dinner. An exclusive restaurant had opened just for them. Emma had been so impressed that JT had so much pull to get a popular restaurant to open just for them.

He'd shown up with a single long-stem red rose for her. Her heart had pitter-pattered. She'd been utterly gob smacked by his presence and swept up in his compliments.

She hadn't realized at the time that his lines had been a little too smooth. Instead, she'd let herself eat up his sugar-coated words like they were cotton candy. Now she felt like such a fool.

The ride to the airport at that early hour didn't take very long. Emma knew she should have been over the moon. The tour was a success. It was her first time touring as an opening act for the opening act. Not exactly a headliner but it was a start.

There had been a couple of mistakes in the first few shows as she and her band got their bearings. But with some helpful advice from the star of the show, she'd found her footing. But JT had pulled the rug out from under her, and she was struggling to find her balance again.

In that moment, she felt the driving urge to see her niece's smiling face. She longed to wake up to the smell of her mother's fresh-brewed coffee and French toast. She'd had this sense of homesickness in the past, but she'd been able to stave it off.

This time it was different. This time she was questioning everything about her life. She wasn't so sure life on the road was for her. And if she didn't want to tour, no label was going to put money into backing her.

The truth was that she was a small-town girl at heart. There was a slower pace to life on Bluestar Island than existed in Nashville and when she was out on tour. But how was she going to achieve her singing dreams, if she couldn't keep up the hectic pace?

As they got inside the airport, her gaze sought out the board of departing flights. While the other people in her group searched for their flight to Nashville, she was searching for the next flight to Boston. And there was one in the next hour. What were the chances there would be a seat available?

CHAPTER TWO

T
ALK ABOUT A BEAUTIFUL June day.
   And for the first time that he could remember,
Noah Carson's flight into Boston had been on time.

His trip to Chicago—back to his old life—had been
brief, so he'd been able to pack everything he needed
into a carry-on. That meant he didn't have to linger by
the baggage claim. Instead, he could head straight for
a taxi and then on to the ferry. Soon he'd be home on
Bluestar Island and back in his beloved woodshop.

These days he didn't like to leave the island, but this
trip had been unavoidable. He had to settle things in
Chicago, as he'd made the decision to make the island
his permanent residence.

At the age of thirty-two, soon-to-be thirty-three next
month, he'd made a small fortune. Of course, the price
of earning so much had cost him dearly. But he didn't
want to think of any of that now.

Outside the airport, he hailed a taxi, but as he made
his way toward the lime-green compact car, a woman
with brunette hair and a ball cap pulled low and
big dark sunglasses race-walked toward it. Was she
planning to take his taxi? His steps grew quicker. She
was still in the lead.

"Hey!" he called out. "That's my taxi."

The woman opened the car door and glanced back at him through those dark shades that hid her eyes. "I don't think so."

"Well, I do. I hailed it."

Her head moved as though she were searching the crowd for someone. "Sorry. I'm in a hurry. Another should be along shortly." She sent him a small, forced smile that barely lifted her plump pink lips. Then she settled into the taxi and the door swung shut.

She wasn't the only one in a hurry. If he wasn't careful, he'd miss an important meeting. His stomach burned. He reached into his pocket and popped an antacid into his mouth.

Relax. It'll be all right.

He was attempting to take things easier these days and not get worked up. A slower pace was good for his heart health. And as he was finding, there was a certain freedom in going with the flow.

Suddenly, a large group of people exited the airport, making his endeavor to secure a taxi that much harder. But ten minutes later, he was at last on his way to the dock. He just hoped he'd make it in time to catch the ferry and not have to wait for the next one, as it wouldn't be back for a couple of hours.

Traffic was heavy leading out of the city. Noah tried not to but he kept checking the time on his watch. He'd learned the hard way that the ferries ran on a timely schedule. If he was even a minute late, he would have to wait for the next ferry. His go-with-the-flow attitude was losing out to his desire to nail down the sale on the perfect ocean-view house.

"Could you hurry?" Noah asked.

The driver wore a smoke-gray flat cap over his silver hair. He glanced in the mirror at Noah. "Sorry. I'm doing the best I can."

"I understand. I'm just in a hurry." His knee bounced up and down.

"You have someone at home waiting for you?"

"My real estate agent. I'm buying a house." And he couldn't wait. He was setting down roots on Bluestar Island. It was exactly what the doctor had ordered. Peace, sun, and relaxation.

While he was in the hospital following his heart attack, the doctor had told him he couldn't keep doing the things he was currently doing. His blood pressure was through the roof. His bad cholesterol was sky high. His body could no longer handle that amount of stress. He had to make some difficult decisions—decisions that saved his life.

At the time, the thought of giving up his career in investment banking had seemed incomprehensible. If he wasn't a hedge fund manager—the wheeler and dealer of fortunes—then what was he?

But he also was able to see that his career had cost him his marriage, including losing custody of his dog, Sammie. And then it had cost him his health. But he'd refused to give up anything else.

Now that he was officially retired from his former life, he felt a certain pressure to make a success of his new endeavor on the island. He knew his physician would lecture him about pushing himself. His doctor had told him to learn to relax. At one point, he'd even suggested that Noah take up goat yoga. He wasn't sure what goats had to do with yoga, and he was pretty certain he didn't want to find out.

But after nearly dying, Noah did see his life differently. His priorities had shifted. So instead of merely taking up a hobby as his doctor had suggested, Noah had taken the doctor's advice a step farther. He'd planned a move to someplace quieter and a change of careers to one that didn't have so much stress attached to it.

He'd forgotten how much he enjoyed working with his hands. The physical labor made him feel good, and the scent of the wood grounded him. These days if he made a mistake, it didn't come with the possibility of destroying people's financial futures. He simply picked up a new piece of wood and started again.

He stared out the window as cars converged at the dock from its many entrances. His gaze rose to the puffy, white cloud passing in front of the sun. And then his attention settled upon a lime-green taxi. Surely that couldn't be the same taxi with the mysterious woman who had snagged the taxi away from him.

Still, he watched as the car approached the dock. It was impossible to see the occupants. Noah checked the time. Two minutes until the ferry was due to sail.

Traffic was heavy at the dock. They were stuck a couple cars back at the intersection. Three lines of vehicles were waiting to merge into a single lane that led to the dock. Noah's knee continued to bob up and down as he glanced at the time again.

He thought of getting out there and making a run for it. But it was a long run, and he doubted he could make it to the dock faster than the taxi. And so he waited, hoping he didn't miss his appointment with his real estate agent. She was very busy and having to reschedule would mean having to wait days.

At last, they'd reached the front of the line, however the traffic on the cross-road was heavy. If there was an opening in one direction, it was busy with oncoming traffic from the opposite direction. And that other green taxi was waiting to make a turn in the same direction as them.

Noah's head turned left and then right, searching for the opening they needed to continue onward. And then at last a break in both directions. His taxi moved forward only to be cut off by the lime-green taxi. In a quick glimpse, he spotted the woman from the airport in the back seat. Noah's back teeth ground together as his taxi jerked to a halt. The force had Noah lurching forward, straining against his seatbelt before he fell back against the seat.

He groaned in frustration. A glance at the roadway showed another string of traffic in both directions. He glanced at the time again. He might as well give up on catching this ferry.

And then the taxi eased forward. Then again, he just might make it. He just had to hope the ferry was running a couple of minutes behind.

The car pulled to a stop, he paid, and then he stepped out.

Bwaa... Bwaa...

The prolonged blast from the ferry let everyone, including Noah, know that the vessel was about to pull away from the dock. He was too late.

He moved to the railing. He smacked his hand lightly on the rail as he sighed. He watched as the ferry pulled away from the gate. As he stared at the boat, he spotted the woman in the dark ball cap and big sunglasses. So he hadn't imagined her in the back of the other taxi.

She lifted her hat to comb her fingers through her brown hair with golden highlights. Then she removed her sunglasses. He was too far away to make out the color of her eyes, but he noticed the way she swiped at her eyes as though she'd been crying.

It appeared he wasn't the only one with problems that day. He couldn't help but wonder if she was headed toward a conflict on the island or running from her problems and seeking the solace of island life.

~ee~

Home at last.

Emma released a pent-up breath as she stepped up to the back door of her childhood home. She was anxious to see her mother. The six months since she'd been home felt like a lifetime.

She raised her hand to open the door but then lowered it back to her side. What if her mother had read the headlines? But her mother wasn't one to follow gossip sites.

Still, someone in town would have told her. What would her mother think of it all? Would she say that was what happened when you rushed into a relationship? No. Her mother wasn't the type to wag her finger at anyone.

Her mother would probably feel sorry for her. That was almost worse. Emma didn't want her loved ones to look at her with sympathy. She was strong. She could weather this storm. And in the end, she vowed to herself not to repeat her mistake by rushing into a relationship ever again.

With that thought in mind, she opened the door. "Mom?" She listened for a response. "Mom, I'm home."

Still no response. Perhaps she should have called ahead, but once she'd made the spur-of-the-moment decision to return to the island, she decided to surprise her mother and siblings.

And then she heard footsteps on the stairway. She spun around with a smile for her mother but the happy look faded when Walter Campbell stepped into view. He was her mother's new husband. And though Emma liked him, he just wasn't the person she wanted to see in that particular moment.

"Emma!" A surprised tone filled his voice. "I, uh, didn't know you were coming home. Your mother must have forgotten to mention it."

"Um, no. She didn't know I was coming." How did she explain this without creating more questions? She struggled to find the right words. "It was a spur-of-the-moment decision. I had a break in my schedule." Not exactly accurate but then again not exactly inaccurate.

Concern filled his eyes. "Is everything all right?"

Oh, no. Has he seen the headlines? Her chest tightened with panic. How was she ever going to explain any of this when she hadn't even made sense of it.

And then she thought of Walter reading celebrity gossip. The image filled her with a nervous giggle. There was no way he'd follow those sorts of sites. He was more of a Field & Stream or Reader's Digest sort of guy.

"Yeah." Not wanting him to worry about her, she sent him a reassuring smile that she didn't feel on the inside. "I just needed a break and couldn't think of any other place I'd rather be than here on the island."

Although, in her rush to get home, she'd forgotten about her mother's new marriage. Maybe she should stay somewhere else. She didn't want to intrude. She thought of staying at her brother's place, but Sam was busy creating a new life with Aster. She didn't want to intrude on their endeavor to form a happy family for Nikki.

And then there was her sister, Hannah, but she was so busy with her fiancé and her new bakery. Sure,

Hannah would make time for her and not say a word about falling behind on her work. But Emma knew how hard Hannah had worked to create the bakery of her dreams. And she didn't want to get in the way.

It seemed like everyone in her family had found their true calling in life as well as their someone special—everyone except her. Her special guy had turned out to be a toad instead of a prince. And as for her singing career, she wasn't so sure it was her calling after all. Maybe she'd just wanted it to be.

She didn't want to think about any of that now. She forced the disturbing thoughts to the back of her mind. There would be time enough for that later.

Walter sent her a warm smile. "It's great that you're here. I know your mother will be so excited."

"Speaking of Mom, do you know where she is?"

He nodded. "She's at the Welcome Center." He glanced at the clock. "She should be home shortly." Then he glanced at Emma's bag and guitar case. "Want me to take these upstairs for you?"

For the first time in her life, she felt awkward in her own childhood home. Because it was no longer just her and her siblings' home but was now Walter's home. When he'd married her mother, they'd opted to keep this house and sell Walter's place to his son.

Even though both her mother and Walter had assured Emma and her siblings that this would always be their home, it felt different now. Everything was changing around her, and she felt as though she were stuck in the same place.

"Do you mind if I stay here?" she asked.

His eyes widened as surprise reflected in them. "You don't have to ask me that. This is your home. It always was and always will be. My marrying your mother will never change that."

His reassuring words meant a lot to her. "Thanks, Walter. It's good to be home."

Buzz-buzz.

The phone in her back pocket vibrated. It'd been doing that a lot today—a whole lot. Most of the numbers she didn't recognize. She wondered how they'd gotten her number. And now she worried about having to switch her number. But like everything else that day, she decided to worry about it later.

First, she was going to get freshened up, and then she'd venture out for a stroll. It would help her clear her mind. She had a lot to figure out. Not only about her imploding relationship but about her singing career. She had so many decisions to make that it made her head hurt.

Still, it was good to be back on the island. The sunshine and sea breeze always made her feel so much better. Hopefully, the island would work its magic this time too.

CHAPTER THREE

A T LAST, HE'D MADE it back to Bluestar.
However, he'd missed his meeting with his real estate agent.

Noah stepped into his little apartment with its efficiency kitchen and small living room. It was fine for temporary lodging, but most of his belongings had to be put in storage until he found a bigger place.

The problem was that Bluestar had a limited number of houses for sale. Most of the properties available were rentals. And the houses he'd toured over the past couple of months were small one- or two-bedroom bungalows. None had a two-bay garage or room to build one for his woodshop.

And then, at last, the perfect house had come on the market. As luck would have it, he'd been in Chicago when the listing had gone live. He'd been selling his condo as well as doing some consulting at his old firm. By now there would undoubtedly be many bids for the ocean-front property, but if the seller hadn't accepted an offer yet, he still had a chance.

The asking price was a lot of money, and though he'd viewed the online photos, he needed to walk through the house before he could pledge that much money. He knew no matter what he did, it was a risk. If he made the offer sight unseen, he might end up finding the place in utter disrepair. Or, if he waited to make the offer until after the walk-through, they might already have accepted an offer.

Every time he tried calling his agent, his call went to voicemail. If it hadn't been for that woman with the ball cap and sunglasses, he would have made it in time for his appointment, and he would most likely be making an offer on the house of his future. But instead, he was stuck in a waiting mode.

On an island this small, there were only two real estate agencies. His agent owned one of them. In her office, there was another agent and two office employees. And from what he could gather, this was their busiest time of the year, handling both sales and rentals.

After pacing back and forth in his apartment, Noah decided it wasn't going to do him any good. He might as well head out. He needed to check on the woodshop he'd rented last month when he'd finalized his decision to remain on the island.

Leaving his bag unpacked, he headed for the door. His first stop was at The Lighthouse Café. He needed an iced coffee. The June sun on the island made it too hot for a warm drink.

He stepped inside the café, which was busy with tourists, and made his way to the counter at the back of the café. A young woman wearing a uniform and nametag that read Molly headed toward him. Her long red curls were pulled back into a ponytail. He'd frequented The Lighthouse Café many times while he'd been on the island, and he didn't recall seeing this particular server.

She stopped in front of him and gave him a friendly smile. "May I help you?"

"I'd like an iced coffee with cream and sweetener."

She rang it up on the register. "Will there be anything else? Perhaps a slice of peach pie?"

He shook his head. Though the pie was tempting, he wanted to get moving. "No thanks."

He paid for his coffee and moved to the side to wait. The place was hopping for it being almost four o'clock. But he'd quickly learned that summer on the island was a lot different than the other seasons. During the summer months, tourists flocked to the island. If it was this hectic year-round, he wouldn't have moved there. But he knew how peaceful it was during the other three-quarters of the year.

"Emma! Noah! Coffee is up."

He moved to grab his cup at the same time as the woman. Their shoulders lightly bumped. He pulled back slightly. "Sorry."

She apologized as well.

He waited for the woman to get her coffee first. After the woman took her cup, he grabbed the only remaining one. Before he took a sip, he noticed the name Emma written in black marker.

His gaze moved to the woman, who was already heading for the exit with his cup in hand. "Hey! Wait." She didn't seem to hear him over the noise of the café. He once more glanced at the cup in his hand. "Emma, wait."

That did it. She stopped and turned. As she did, he was struck by her dark ball cap and big dark sunglasses. It was the woman from the airport. He was certain of it.

He strode toward her. "It's you."

Color bloomed in her cheeks. "I... I don't know what you mean."

"We saw each other at the airport."

She shook her head. "I don't think so." And then she turned back toward the door.

He couldn't let her get away. "Hey, you have my coffee."

She paused. She removed her sunglasses to read the name on the cup. And then she turned around. The rosy hue in her cheeks deepened.

"Oh." She held the cup out to him. Her blue gaze met his, causing his heart to thump against his ribs. When he didn't move, she said, "Go ahead. Take it. I didn't drink from it."

He swallowed hard as he averted his gaze. As they exchanged to-go cups, their fingers touched. A jolt rushed up his arm and settled in his chest. He struggled to ignore the strange sensation. He swallowed hard. "I didn't drink from yours either."

"Sorry about that. I was in a hurry."

He couldn't help but wonder how many times she'd used that excuse to get away with pushing her way to the head of the line. Someone needed to call her out on it. "Just like you were at the airport when you took my taxi."

Her eyes widened, as though suddenly she recalled him. "That was you?"

He nodded. "And then your taxi cut off mine near the dock, causing me to miss the ferry back to the island."

A group of young people entered the café. Most of them were preoccupied with their phones. They stepped off to the side to let them pass.

A gasp floated through the air.

Noah's gaze moved around until he located the source of the sound. It was a teenage girl in shorts and a yellow tank top. Her gaze moved to Emma. She glanced down at her phone and then back at Emma.

"Can I have your autograph?" the girl asked.

Emma smiled. "Sure."

After the girl grabbed a pen and paper from her purse, Emma wrote a brief note before signing her name with a flourish. All the while Noah wondered who this obvious celebrity might be.

Emma returned the pen and paper to the girl. "I have to go."

Noah followed Emma out the door. He wasn't letting her get away. Not yet. But when a fresh wave of tourists came rushing through the door, he couldn't move. By the time he made it out to the sidewalk, Emma was nowhere in sight.

He stood there for a moment, looking up and down the walk, hoping to spot her. Somehow she'd faded into the crowd. How did she keep slipping away?

He paused to take a sip of coffee. There was some secret ingredient in the Lighthouse coffee. He didn't know what it was, but it was the best coffee he'd ever had.

And now he had to get moving because his new business, Noah's Woodshop, had its first contract. Aster Smith, Bluestar's events coordinator, had hired him to help with Bluestar's Concert on the Beach Summer Spectacular, which would lead up to the Fourth of July.

He was in charge of constructing the stage. It was a big order. And if he did it right, it'd provide his business with lots of exposure and hopefully it'd bring in more work requests. At least that was the plan.

ele

Who was that guy?

Emma walked quickly toward the beach. She couldn't get the man's image out of her mind. He'd been tall, just over six feet. His light-brown hair had been short and spikey on top, as though he took extra time to style it. His light-blue polo shirt was pressed and paired with khaki shorts.

He had to be a tourist because she didn't know any locals that dressed this nice unless it was a special occasion. Bluestar was a pretty relaxed place. And even though he seemed somewhat familiar, she was certain she wouldn't forget such a handsome face.

The thought of him being a tourist helped her relax. Soon he'd be gone, and their paths would never cross again. He certainly hadn't liked her. And even worse, he didn't even know her to form such negative opinion.

What was it with her? She seemed to attract man trouble, of one type or another, no matter where she went.

The crowd of people grew thicker the closer she got to the beach. The last thing she wanted was for anyone else to recognize her like that girl had done at the café. For the moment, she wanted to be no one special.

Emma veered away from the beach. She'd go for a walk along the shore later when there weren't so many people. This evening she could come back. Maybe she'd even indulge herself in a Whippy Dip's ice cream cone. The thought of ice cream with chocolate sprinkles definitely appealed to her.

But she needed something to do now to keep her from thinking of that photo. So, she headed toward The Elegant Bakery, owned by her sister. Hannah was always working, so Emma had no doubt she'd be at the bakery.

When Emma turned onto Main Street, she immediately spotted a line of people on the sidewalk in front of the bakery. Wow! Though, she shouldn't be surprised. She'd grown up eating her sister's delicious cupcakes and cookies. As kids, they'd challenged each other in the kitchen and then had their family do a blind taste test. Hannah won most of the time but not every time.

And that was okay with Emma. She had other interests, the number one being singing. Her father had been her biggest fan. Her mother was a close second.

When she was growing up, her father always asked her to sing him a song. Sometimes it was embarrassing, but he gave her the confidence to try out for the Songbird competition. Sadly, he never got to see her win the television competition.

Not wanting to get caught up in the sad memories, she pushed them to the back of her mind as she sidestepped the line in front of the bakery and made her way to the back door. There were definite advantages to being the owner's sister.

She let her nose lead her. The scents were amazing, from a spicy cinnamon to milk chocolate. She inhaled deeply, catching whiffs of butter and citrus. Her stomach rumbled in eagerness.

Her initial thought was to resist the temptation. After all, she'd been on a diet for months, trying to lose a stubborn ten pounds so she could fit into a smaller size. Her agent had told her the label heads wanted someone that not only sounded good but looked good. She wasn't sure what her looks had to do with her voice, but she'd been trying and failing to lose the weight. Well, that wasn't quite true. She'd go down a couple of pounds and then the next week go up three pounds. It was a constant roller coaster ride.

She wanted to tell them she was fine the way she was, but she didn't dare. She didn't want to be dismissed as uncooperative. And once she looked in the mirror, she started to doubt herself. Maybe losing a few pounds wouldn't be such a bad idea.

She stepped up to the door and pulled it open. Inside, she could see the half dozen staff rushing about, carrying trays here and there. She took a step inside, all the while her gaze searched for her sister.

"You can't be in here." An older woman frowned at her.

"It's okay."

"No, it's not. You have to leave right now."

"But if you could just tell Hannah that I'm here."

The woman's dark brows drew together. "I'm not her secretary. You'll have to go around front. Maybe then one of the girls can help you."

It appeared this woman was not going to let her take one more step inside the bakery. At least the woman hadn't recognized her as being the center of a romantic scandal. In fact, the woman didn't seem to care about her identity. She just wanted Emma gone.

"Maude, it's okay," Hannah called out from the other side of the kitchen. "That's my sister."

Maude sighed loudly as she frowned at Emma. "Well, you could have said so."

What? Maude was blaming her when the woman would barely let her say a word?

Emma swallowed down her frustration. "Are you going to let me pass?"

"No." Maude crossed her arms. "This isn't a café. It's a bakery. For employees only."

Emma glanced past Maude to her sister. Hannah wore an innocent expression as she rushed toward her. "I've got this, Maude. I'll be back later."

"Don't worry, Hannah. The bakery will be in good hands." And then Maude turned and sternly instructed someone that they'd put their tray in the wrong spot.

Hannah put a hand on Emma's shoulder and propelled her toward the door. "Let's go."

Emma practically tripped over her own feet as her sister pulled her outside. "Who is that?"

"Shh..." Hannah glanced over her shoulder, as though making certain they weren't overheard. And then she turned back to Emma. "First, this." She hugged her sister. When she pulled back, she asked, "When did you get back to the island?"

"I just arrived. I haven't even seen Mom yet. Now who was that?"

"It's Maude. She's my new manager, and she comes highly recommended. Ethan says I work too much and that I need someone else to step in so I can take some time off. And then he goes and lands a big contracting on the mainland for a relative of someone here on the island. And the pay was just too good to turn down. He says it's more money for the wedding, but it's hard because he's gone all of the time."

"Hopefully the job will end soon."

"I hope so."

Emma stepped back and took in her sister's exercise clothes. "So what's with the workout gear?"

"I'm headed to my first yoga class." And then her eyes widened. "You need to come with me."

Emma shook her head. "I don't think so. I don't do yoga."

"No time like now to learn." Hannah sent her a pleading look. "Please. Summer just started a new class at Beach Love Yoga."

"Summer did it. She opened her own studio?"

Hannah nodded. "I thought you'd know all about it."

Guilt settled over Emma. Summer Turner had been her best friend all through school and even after graduation. But everything changed after Emma won the Songbird competition and moved to Nashville.

The phone calls grew fewer and fewer. The text messages became infrequent. At some point, they'd gone from talking every day to just liking each other's social media posts, and even that fizzled out.

With a hectic schedule, it was so easy to let phone messages slide. And when she felt like her career was stagnate, Emma hadn't wanted to talk, because she'd felt like such a failure.

Emma shrugged. "We don't talk much these days."

"But why? You two were inseparable growing up."

Emma shrugged again. "Life got in the way."

"Well, I somehow promised that I'd come to this class. You have to come with me."

"I don't know."

"Emma." Hannah used her big-sister voice. "You have to come. If she hears you're on the island and didn't come, she'll be so hurt."

Emma wasn't so sure Summer cared any longer what she did or didn't do. The thought saddened her. If only things were different. And now with JT cheating on her, she didn't know what to say to people.

There had to be a way out of this. Emma glanced down at her jeans. "I can't do yoga in these."

Hannah waved away her sister's excuse. "We're still the same size. I have clothes at my apartment."

Emma wasn't in the mood to do yoga. "Hannah, I don't think so. I'm not in the mood."

"That's why this is perfect for you. It'll help put you in a better mood."

Emma's brows drew together. "You know, don't you?"

"About you and JT? Yes. My phone's been blowing up all morning. I messaged you. Didn't you get it?"

Emma shook her head. "There were too many messages, so I turned my phone off for a while, and now I'm totally ignoring it."

"I understand. Now let's get you changed. If anyone needs this class, it's you."

"Do I look that bad?" Were those extra ten pounds that obvious to everyone?

"No. But I know you and you're stressed. Afterward, I have a new cupcake recipe you can try."

Emma frowned at her sister. "Won't eating a cupcake undo all of the work we did at yoga?"

Hannah smiled and shrugged. "They'll just cancel each other out."

Emma sighed and shook her head. "How do I let you talk me into these things?"

"Because I'm the oldest and wisest. Now let's go."

Emma laughed as she followed her sister to her apartment, which was situated above the bakery. It was good to be home. The news of her cheating boyfriend may have followed her there, but the island breeze and her sister's smile would see her through this trying time. Bluestar was perfect. Or as close to it as one could get.

And then her thoughts strayed back to the stranger that she'd met at the café. Okay, maybe not perfect but it was close. She had no idea what his problem was, but she hoped their paths didn't cross again.

CHAPTER FOUR

HOME AT LAST.

Okay, maybe that wasn't quite accurate.

Noah unlocked the door to his woodshop and stepped inside. He didn't own the shop. It was in the backyard of a little old lady's house. She had strict rules about what he could and couldn't do in it. And he couldn't work past 6:00 p.m. She didn't want the noise to disturb her dinner.

Still, he couldn't deny the sense of peace he experienced during the time he spent there. He'd rented this spot on the edge of town after his doctor's earnest request for him to take up a hobby. Previously, his high-stress job had been his hobby—in fact, toward the end it had become his entire life. He couldn't let that happen again.

But finding a hobby—one that helped him relax was a job in and of itself. He'd tried golfing. It was okay but not something he could see himself doing regularly. Card games didn't interest him. And then a friend had asked what he'd done for fun when he was a kid. And that was when he recalled working in his father's woodshop that had been converted from a garage. The cars had been ejected, and in their place had been a wood lathe and table saw.

Noah hadn't been sure he'd still enjoy woodworking. It had been a lot of years since he'd done it. He started with the basics and made a stool. In the end, he'd found that he'd loved making things with his hands just as much now as he had when he was a kid.

He stepped into his shop, swung open the big door, which resembled a barn door, to let in the sunshine, and breathed an easy breath. As he placed his coffee cup on the workbench, his mind returned to the blue-eyed beauty that had made his morning challenging. He doubted he'd see her again. Many tourists were there and gone in a day.

Buzz-buzz.

He withdrew his phone from his pocket and found it was his real estate agent returning his call. "Hey, Madison. So sorry about missing our meeting. It was just one delay after another." Again, he thought of Emma and a frown pulled at his lips. "I was hoping you might be able to fit me in later today."

"Noah, I'm so sorry, but I have back-to-back showings all day."

"Oh." He had been hoping that wasn't the case. "What about tomorrow?"

"Tomorrow I have a closing in the morning and then one in the afternoon. But I could squeeze you at noon."

He didn't like the thought of wait to view the house that he hoped would soon be his home, but what other choice did he have? He'd signed an agreement with Madison, and up until now, she'd been great. It wasn't her fault he'd missed their meeting. That blame went to someone else.

"Has the oceanfront house sold yet?"

"They have a number of offers they're considering, but they haven't accepted any of them. In fact, I've been informed that with the family on the mainland, that an offer isn't expected to be accepted until next week sometime."

"Next week?" That was so much longer than the traditional forty-eight hours.

"I'd understand if you'd rather not extend an offer."

"No. I'm still interested." In fact, hope swelled in his chest. They were holding out for a better offer. "Is there any way you can squeeze in showing me the house today? I'd like to make an offer on it. I just need a quick walk through."

She hesitated.

"Please. I think the place will be perfect for my needs."

"Okay. Meet me there at seven."

"Thank you. I'll be there." And then he told her how much he was willing to offer so she could have the offer written up and ready to submit that evening.

He wasn't taking any more chances with this place. He was so close to having his home by the ocean, with his own woodshop that didn't come with so many rules.

"Sounds good."

After they disconnected the call, he paused and wondered if he should have saved time and extended the offer sight unseen. Part of him wanted to do just that, but the other part of him—the cautious part of him—reminded him that his savings had to last many, many years. After all, what were the chances the house would sell between now and seven o'clock?

Things didn't feel quite so bleak.

Emma couldn't remember the last time she'd attended a yoga session, but her body had been quick to let her know it'd been too long. She wasn't nearly as flexible as she used to be. Did that mean she was getting old?

At almost twenty-seven, she didn't think so. It just meant she'd been putting too much focus on her work and not paying enough attention to the other aspects of her life. It was time for more balance in her days.

Summer had been surprised to see her at the class with Hannah, but they hadn't had time to talk before the session, as they were running a little late after she had to borrow some of her sister's clothes.

Emma had been impressed with the studio with its pastel shades and the giant wall graphic of the beach. It was like you could step into the picture and let the water rush over your feet. Her friend had done well for herself—really well. And Emma was so happy for her.

It only added to her guilt over letting their friendship slip through the cracks. And it made her stalled career feel so much worse. Everyone had thought once she'd won the Songbird competition that her future was made. And even she'd gotten caught up in that thought.

They had been sooo wrong. Because once she'd arrived in Nashville, her reality television championship hadn't meant much. Sure it was a great way to meet people, but no one took her seriously. She went from being the big fish to a teeny tiny minnow in a great big sea.

That took some adjusting to, but she wasn't afraid of hard work. She'd been certain that if she put in her time growing her name and making connections that her next big break would come. And now nearly three years later, she felt as though she was in the same place she'd been in when she'd first arrived in Nashville. And now that the world was focused on her relationship with JT, her social media numbers were once again climbing, but it wasn't the reason she wanted to be popular.

During the class, she'd felt people staring at her and then whispering. She could only imagine what they were saying—how foolish she was for thinking that she could have a man like JT, that there was nothing special about her, that she was fooling herself to think she could be a country music star.

And so when the class ended, Emma was anxious to leave. Sure it would be nice to say hello to Summer. She missed her friendship. But she just didn't think she could take any more of the looks or the gossiping.

"Can we go?" Emma asked her sister.

"Give me just a minute? I see Jane over there, and I just need to have a word with her about a cake order she placed for her daughter's upcoming birthday party." Without waiting for a response, Hannah rushed over to her friend.

Emma was left to stand there with her sister's extra yoga mat in hand and a borrowed water bottle. She felt perfectly awkward. And yet she waited for her sister because, well, that was what sisters did—at least the Bell sisters. They didn't leave each other, no matter what.

"Hey, Emma."

She turned to find Summer headed toward her. Summer hadn't changed. If anything, she'd gotten prettier. Her strawberry-blond ponytail bounced from side to side as she walked.

"Hi." Emma forced a smile because on the inside she was nervous about seeing her former best friend.

She had no idea how Summer was going to react to her presence. "The class was great and your studio is beautiful. I'm so happy for you."

"Thanks." Summer glanced around at the studio. "It was a work of love."

People called out their thanks to Summer as they made their way to the exit.

"Sorry," Summer said to Emma before stepping over to have a word with some of the women who had been staring at her throughout the class.

Summer had grown from a quiet wallflower into a confident business woman. And people loved her. Her friend's life was perfect. Emma was happy for her.

"Sorry about that." Hannah stepped up to her.

"No problem. Are you ready to go?"

"Definitely." She started for the door.

She'd come out in public too soon. After all, the pictures just hit the internet that morning. What was she thinking?

Even there on small Bluestar, she couldn't escape the stares and the whispers. What had she done wrong? Why couldn't she hang onto her man?

"Emma, wait up," Summer called out.

She didn't want to stop, but she wouldn't be rude, even if it meant a chance for more people to stare. She leveled her shoulders and turned. Once more she wore her practiced smile, even though on the inside she was crumbling.

Summer stopped in front of her. "Since you are on the island, I thought we could catch up."

Apparently, Summer didn't read the gossip sites, or she would know everything there was to know about her life. But the thought of spending some time with her friend had her truly smiling and nodding. "I'd like that."

"Great. I have a couple of more classes today. How about we meet for lunch tomorrow?"

"Sure. What do you have in mind?"

"Tacos or pizza?"

Emma's mouth watered. For so long, she'd been denying herself both of those food items in her endless attempt to lose the stubborn ten pounds. If a cheating fiancé and being reunited with her best friend didn't deserve a splurge on her caloric intake, she didn't know what did.

"I'm thinking...tacos."

"Great. Katrina's it is. Say noon?"

"Sounds good. I'll see you then."

And for a moment, it felt like the good old days.

It wasn't until then that Emma realized how much she missed her old life. The funny thing was back in those days, she was so certain her best life was yet to come. Now she was wondering if she'd had her best life and left it in search of a dream that was never going to come true.

CHAPTER FIVE

B UZZ-BUZZ.
Ding.

The next day Emma's phone kept going off, alternating between the buzzing of a phone call and the dinging of yet another text message. JT had called a number of times. She had no idea what he thought they had to talk about at this point. As far as she was concerned, the time for talking had long since passed.

She pulled the diamond ring from her pocket. She had no idea what to do with it. Part of her wanted to take it and throw it into the ocean, but the more responsible side of her said she should return it. Adulting was so hard at times like this.

Maybe she'd deal with the ring later. She stuffed it into a dresser drawer. It was the least of her worries.

Between the whirlwind romance with JT and the concert tour her manager had managed to add her to, she was exhausted. Her words and lyrics had dried up. For the concert, she'd been reduced to singing her two hits from Songbird and doing cover titles. But she longed to be more authentic—more original.

If she could write more songs—songs similar to those that had turned her into a reality star—she was certain that one of the record labels would show an interest in her career. She just had to stop all of the voices in her head from the sensationalized headlines to the nasty comments on social media. And she knew where to go to find the peace she craved.

With a few hours to go until she would meet Summer for lunch, Emma grabbed her guitar, backpack, and a notebook. She went downstairs, heading toward the back door. In the kitchen, she saw her mother. "Mom."

Her mother turned from the kitchen counter with a big warm smile. "There's my girl. How are you?"

Emma shrugged. "Okay." Not really but she didn't want her mother to fret over her. "I just needed to come home and sort some things out in my mind."

"Bluestar is a good place for that." Her mother placed some muffins in a plastic to-go container. "I have to run out now, but can we talk later? That is, unless you need me now, and I'll just call and cancel."

"No, Mom. Don't let me stop you. Do what you need to do, and we'll talk this evening."

"You promise?" Her mother's eyes shone with concern.

"I do."

"Come here." Her mother held her arms out to her.

Emma walked over and wrapped her arms around her mother. She closed her eyes and breathed in her mother's gentle floral perfume—the same scent she'd been wearing all of Emma's life. At last, she felt truly at home.

A wave of emotions washed over Emma, from embarrassment for disappointing her family to her anger for believing JT had been genuine with her. As her emotions rose to the surface, Emma knew she couldn't fall apart now and ruin her mother's plans.

She blinked repeatedly as she pulled away. "I'm going out for a while."

"Okay, sweetie. I'm so happy to have you home. I just wish it was under better circumstances." Her mother closed the case of muffins and then turned to her. "Emma, it's all going to be okay. This is on JT. Not you."

"I shouldn't have trusted him. And that's on me. It won't happen again."

"Don't let him close off your heart."

Emma nodded, even if that was exactly what she planned to do. "I'm going to head out to the pier for a while. Are there any water bottles around?"

Her mother got her some ice-cold water, which Emma placed in her backpack. With a quick goodbye, she headed out the door. She had no intention of falling in love again—at least not any time soon.

She thought of walking to the northern tip of the island, but that would take some time, and she was anxious to get there and write some words. She always felt better when she was writing lyrics. She needed that feeling now.

On Bluestar Island, cars weren't permitted without a special temporary permit. The people either walked, rode a bike, or drove a golf cart. Luckily, it was a small island.

Her mother was known for keeping things long after people were done with them. Was it possible she'd hung onto her bicycle? Or one of her siblings' bikes?

She let herself in the side door of the garage. She was thankful for the little windows on each side of the garage, letting in a bit of sunshine. She couldn't remember the last time she was in there.

As she glanced around, she was a little surprised to see that it looked pretty much as it always had throughout her childhood. There were a couple of old mowers, a green wheelbarrow, and a bunch of her father's old tools. Her mother's new husband, Walter, must not have had a chance to make the place his own.

But for now, she was able to glance around and find so many memories of her father. There was his old red toolbox on the shelf under the workbench. There was not one, not two, but three snow blowers. Because the first two had broken, but he couldn't get rid of them because they might come in handy for spare parts. A sad smile lifted her lips. She missed her father so much. She had always been Daddy's little girl. If not for his constant encouragement, she didn't think she'd have had the courage to be on Songbird. And she certainly wouldn't have moved to Nashville.

If her father was there today, she wondered what he'd tell her. Probably it'd be something along the lines of Don't let that loser dull your shine because you're a star. Those were the sort of things he would tell her to bolster her courage. Standing up in front of a group of people to sing wasn't always easy for her, especially if she'd been previously heckled or booed.

You do you and don't let anyone stop you.

"Yes, Daddy. I hear you," she whispered, feeling his presence.

As she turned around, the sunlight streaming in through the window reflected off a bike. She moved closer to find it was her old purple bike. She had to move a gas can, some garden stakes, and a few other things, but she was finally able to get out her bike.

She found an old rag on the workbench and used it to wipe the bike off. And then in the exact spot it'd been in her whole life, she found the small silver oil can with the squeeze handle. She lubed up the chain and the wheels. Then she noticed the two flat tires. She hoped it was the passage of time that had allowed them deflate and there weren't actual holes. Otherwise, she just might be walking to the pier.

It took a bit to locate the tire pump that was hanging on the wall behind some other things. She set to work inflating the tires. And it worked. Both tires appeared to be holding air. She breathed out a sigh of relief.

She slung her backpack into the basket on the front, and with her guitar slung over her back, she climbed onto the bike. She found it was true about not forgetting how to ride a bike.

With the sunshine warming her face, she pedaled on the quiet lane to the northern tip of the island. When the lighthouse came into view, she knew she was almost there. Since this lighthouse was privately owned, it wasn't open for tours, and not many tourists bothered to meander this far from town. It was quiet and secluded, just like she wanted.

She made her way toward the beach. Leaving her bike in the rough, she crossed the rocky area and stepped onto the old wooden pier. She'd spent a lot of time there as a kid and literally nothing about it had changed.

With her guitar in one hand and her backpack in the other, she moved to the end of the pier. She placed her items on the sun-warmed wood and then settled down against a thick round piling. She leaned her head back. As the sun rained down upon her face, she closed her eyes. She drew in a deep breath, taking in the familiar scents of the sea. She let the familiarity calm and center her.

This is where she belonged. Bluestar was her roots. No matter how far she traveled in this world, Bluestar would always be home to her. Maybe this was where she should stay.

The thought appealed to her. It would be so much easier to stay there with her family and friends. And then she thought of something her father had told her—success isn't just a bit of luck but a lot of perseverance, especially in the face of setbacks.

She felt as though she was facing one setback after the other in all areas of her life. Okay, maybe not all areas. After all, she still had a warm relationship with her mother, brother, and sister. And then there was her sweet niece, Nikki. When she thought of them, she realized things didn't seem quite so dismal.

Ding.

Another message. She pulled out her phone to see that it was from her manager. She didn't want to read it now. She was certain it was more pressure about when she was going to return to Nashville and she didn't have an answer for him. Not yet.

She reached for her guitar. She'd been playing it since she was a kid. Her father played the guitar in a band when he was young. When she'd shown an interest in the guitar, he started to give her lessons. Who'd have thought that it would have led her to a reality show and then Nashville?

But if she didn't produce some new songs, she'd never have a chance of fulfilling her dreams. She withdrew her notebook from her backpack and read over the lyrics she'd written. It seemed like so long since she'd put pen to paper.

Her gaze moved down over the page, taking in the meaningful words so full of love. She remembered writing those words at the beginning of her relationship with JT. A frown pulled at her lips.

Words of love were far from her mind now. If she were to write any words today, they would not be of happiness and joy.

She knew that good songs—great songs—came from places of great emotion. She had a lot of strong emotions at the moment, but how did she translate them into a song?

Her thoughts were rambling. When she was in a mood like this, she found that just putting pen to paper was best. And so that was what she did.

At first, her pen hovered over the page without making a dot or a stroke. Her thoughts froze. She lifted her gaze to watch the gentle swells of the ocean. She drew in a deep breath and then blew it out. Relax. You can do this.

She had to write something, anything.

You lying cheat.

Not very good. Not very descriptive. Time to try again.

Your words were sweet as ice cream.

She recalled how their first date had included a trip to the creamery, where she'd gotten a vanilla cone with sprinkles. He had gotten double chocolate without sprinkles. Maybe that should have been her first clue that they were opposites, but then again ice cream can just be ice cream.

And your kisses made my heart pound.

We were living in a dream.

A dream that crashed into the ground.

She reread what she'd written and groaned. It was definitely not her best work. Not even close. What was wrong with her?

She was always able to write down her feelings before. Those poems were the basis for many of the songs she'd sold to other artists. Now that she needed songs for herself, the words were clunky.

Maybe she was pushing too hard, too fast. She set aside her notebook and then reached for her guitar.

Her fingers strummed the cords as she stared out at the swells in the ocean as the seagulls flew over the water and then settled onto the beach.

She started to play the first song that came to mind. It was about imploding dreams and rising from the ash. As she played, she wondered if she could be a phoenix. Could she return to Nashville and turn her singing career around? Did she want to?

CHAPTER SIX

MINUTES FELT LIKE HOURS. Noah had checked the time repeatedly that morning as he anxiously awaited his chance to see the beach house. Time moved so slowly he was starting to think his fitness watch was broken. Not only did the time feel off, but it wasn't adding much to his step count. His doctor had suggested 10K per day, and at this moment he wasn't close to that number.

Life was certainly different there on the island. Back when he lived in Chicago, time would go by in the blink of an eye. One moment he was filling his insulated cup with coffee for his commute to the office, and the next thing he knew, it was time to order dinner to eat at his desk.

But there on Bluestar Island many people closed up shop a little early on sunny afternoons so they could enjoy leisurely dinners and long walks along the beach. The pace was much slower. And he found himself drawn to the laid-back lifestyle.

People took their time to breath—except for Emma. She seemed like she was always in a rush. He wondered about her life story. After witnessing her giving the young girl an autograph, he was certain she was famous, but he failed at placing her.

"Noah?" The real estate agent's voice drew him from his thoughts.

"Hi, Madison." He sent her a smile as he stood on the sidewalk in front of 203 Surfside Drive.

Behind him stood a white craftsman house with robin's egg–blue shutters. The large covered porch looked welcoming. It had four bedrooms and one bathroom. He planned to add another bathroom eventually. And it had a detached, double-bay garage that Noah planned to convert into a woodshop.

Madison opened the white picket gate and held it for him before continuing down the walkway. "Now, I have to warn you that there are a lot of offers for the house."

"I understand." But he didn't really hear her as he took in the pitched roof and the windows of the second floor.

He stepped onto the porch with a swing at the end. The house represented a warm, cozy life he thought only existed in television dramas and books. But if his cardiologist could see him now, he'd give Noah a nod of approval.

As Madison took a moment to open the front door, he walked the length of the porch. There were a few boards that were rotted but for the most part, it was in good shape.

"Would you like to step inside?" Madison asked.

"I definitely would." Even though he'd viewed the interior photos of the house on the website, it wasn't the same thing as walking through the house himself.

The downstairs consisted of a living room that spanned the front of the house. It was huge with a fireplace at one end. In fact, it was so large there were two seating areas. He didn't need that much room.

The back part of the house was split between a kitchen with a pantry and small laundry closet and a large dining room. In his mind, he was already moving the dining room to the one end of the living room and switching the existing dining room into either a master bedroom or an office. He'd have to see the upstairs before he decided.

Upstairs, there were actually four bedrooms, each with built-in window seats. Three were exactly the same size. The fourth one was small as the bathroom took half of the space. On second thought, it was more suited to being a storage room.

The bathroom was older and could definitely use some updating, but it was sufficient for now. In fact, he wasn't seeing anything to keep him from buying the place.

When they returned downstairs, Madison showed him the most amazing part of the house the back deck. It was large enough for him to add a grill and small table. But it was the view of the Atlantic that captured and held his attention.

"And see that?" She pointed to a set of steps that led to the beach. "It has its own private beach access."

All of this and they hadn't even gotten to the garage yet. He was so impressed with everything he'd seen that he would have bought the place even if it didn't have a garage.

"Would you also like to view the garage?"

It was hard to drag himself away from the ocean view, but the garage was going to be important to his plans. "Yes, I would."

And then he planned to submit his offer. In fact, he was going to up his offer. He had a lot of competition, so he had to motivate the buyers to pick his offer.

——*ele*——

Was it possible to undo the past?

That was the question Emma had been asking herself on her way to lunch with Summer. She had a feeling they'd never be the close-knit friends they used to be. And that saddened her. Why hadn't she made the effort to keep in close contact?

Emma had a lot of regrets, not only her relationship with Summer but also with JT as well. She had to do better going forward.

For the beginning of the meal, the conversation was stilted and awkward. Emma did her best to steer the conversation back around to Summer's amazing yoga studio. It was a neutral topic that kept the attention away from her torpedoed romance and stalled career. But she knew she couldn't dodge the subject forever.

She wiped her mouth with the paper napkin before folding it and setting it aside. "It's good to be home." Her gaze met her friend's. "And it's good to spend time with you."

Summer glanced down as though there was something she wanted to say, but she wasn't sure if she should. This was it. This was when she'd tell Emma she was a jerk for moving away and letting their friendship fizzle out. And Emma couldn't blame her. She should have made more of an effort.

"Emma—"

"Summer—"

They both stopped and looked at each other.

"Go ahead," Emma said.

"Em, I just wanted to tell you how sorry I am."

She was confused. Why was Summer apologizing to her? "I don't understand. I'm the one that should apologize to you."

Summer shook her head. "I'm the one who got so busy by going back to school to get my business degree and then trying to get the financing in place for my yoga studio. I'm sorry I didn't stay in contact. I didn't stay in contact. I can't even imagine what you must think of me."

"I'm proud of you. You followed your dreams." Emma sent her a reassuring smile. "I'm the one who should be apologizing. In fact, that's what I came to dinner to do."

"You did? But you've been great. You've called and left messages. And you checked in when you were on the island. I'm the one that was always distracted."

Emma smiled and shook her head. "I'm the one who was distracted by my singing career."

"How is life in Nashville?"

Emma glanced around to make sure no one was sitting near them. Satisfied that no one was close enough to overhear their conversation, she said, "My career, if you want to call it that, is stalled out. I can't get the backing of a big label to move it forward. So I feel like I'm running in place."

"It doesn't seem like that to me. They play your song on the local radio all of the time."

"And I appreciate it. But the island's radio station isn't quite the same as those in LA or New York City." She sighed and leaned back in her chair. "I just don't know if I'm wasting my time in Nashville."

"Don't say that. You have a beautiful voice."

"The problem is that it takes more than a good voice. It takes the perfect song. The right timing. And a lot of luck. I just can't seem to get those things to line up for me."

Summer opened her mouth to say something but then pressed her lips together and reached for her cola.

"What?" Emma asked.

Summer shook her head. "Nothing."

"It was something. Come on, Summer. We've been friends most of our lives. Whatever it is, you can say it."

Summer hesitated. Then softly she said, "I'm just wondering if what happened with JT has you doubting yourself now."

"No." The answer was too quick. She sighed. "I don't know. Maybe. But I've felt like my career has been stuck for a while. But you don't need to hear any of this. Your dream has come true, and I'm so happy for you."

Summer looked at her with a serious expression. "I know you aren't ready to talk about JT and everything, but just know that when you need a friendly ear, I'll be around. I promise."

"Thank you. It means a lot."

From that point on, the awkwardness faded away, and the ease of conversation that they'd shared most of their lives returned. They talked some more about JT and how he wasn't the man he'd portrayed himself to be. They commiserated over their dating lives and laughed over episodes from their youth.

The time flew by too quickly. When Summer apologized because she had to get back to the studio to teach a class, Emma headed toward the beach. It'd been far too long since she'd felt the sand beneath her feet.

She headed toward Beachcomber Park, through the parking lot and then down the steps to the sand. The beach was crowded at that hour, but she didn't let it stop her. She moved to the water's edge. A couple was walking with their hands clasped. Another woman was walking her dog.

North? Or south?

She opted to go toward the southern tip of the island. She slipped off her sandals and enjoyed the feel of sand beneath her feet. She walked a little ways, enjoying the peace and serenity. Her phone was still turned off. She knew she couldn't keep it that way. The responsible side of her said that she might miss an important business call. The other part of her didn't care.

She needed time to clear her head—to figure out her next steps. And she had absolutely no idea what that might be. She just knew she couldn't go back to the way things had been in Nashville.

She liked her manager, but he just wasn't getting her where she needed to go. But the thought of firing Stan didn't sit well with her. He'd believed in her abilities since the beginning. In Nashville, he was her number one supporter. But if she didn't have a bulldog for a manager, how was she ever going to grow as an artist?

She stopped walking to pick up a small stone. It was cool to the touch. Her thumb moved over the smooth surface. She turned to stare out at the great big ocean. What was she going to do?

CHAPTER SEVEN

DOWNWARD FACING DOG.

The following morning at Beach Love Yoga, Emma struggled not to giggle at the name. She certainly didn't feel like a dog in this position. She felt awkward and knew she would feel this later. She'd obviously not been stretching enough. Most of her exercise had been in the form of cardio, from running on the treadmill to using the stationary bike and sometimes she used the elliptical.

"Heels down, ladies," Summer instructed.

Emma had to admit that yoga was a lot harder when you attempted to get the position just right. She chanced a glance at Hannah, who seemed to have perfected the pose. Why was Emma not surprised?

And to her other side was Aster, who was engaged to their brother, Sam. Even though they had yet to set a wedding date, she suspected it wouldn't be too long until Aster became an official part of the family.

It seemed that love was in the air, although it wouldn't sway her. She was firm in her decision to take a break from dating. She'd thought JT was a nice guy and yet he'd turned out to be a lying, cheating jerk. Until she could trust her judgment where men were concerned, she was keeping her distance from them.

When the class was over, Aster said, "I've got to be going."

"Aren't you even going to hang around for coffee?" Hannah asked.

Aster shook her head. She didn't smile. In fact, she hadn't smiled at all during their class. And she'd barely said a word to anyone. Emma hadn't gotten to know her future sister-in-law as well as she'd like, but even she could sense something was wrong.

The three of them exited the building together. Out on the sidewalk, Aster turned to them. "I'll be seeing you."

"Aster, what's wrong?" Hannah asked.

Aster shrugged. "Nothing for you guys to worry about." Her gaze moved to Emma. "How are you?"

It was Emma's turn to shrug her shoulders. "Okay. Or I will be."

"I was sorry to hear what happened."

Emma didn't want to talk about her disastrous engagement. She was more concerned about the shadows under Aster's eyes. Had something happened between her and Sam? Emma hoped not. They made such a great couple.

"Thank you," Emma said. "What's going on with you?"

Aster glanced around as people walked past them. "Not here."

"Why don't we grab something to drink?" Hannah suggested, as though she'd noticed the same worrisome signs that Emma had picked up on.

"I really shouldn't," Aster said.

"It won't take long." Emma looped her arm through her friend's. With her other hand, she waved to Summer, who was speaking to a couple of women from the class. Then Emma turned her attention back to Aster. "It's been too long since I last saw you at Christmastime."

They moved toward the closest restaurant, which happened to be Katrina's Kantina. It was the middle of the afternoon, so it shouldn't be busy. They started walking toward Main Street. Emma was on one side of Aster with Hannah on the other side. Behind Aster, the sisters sent each other questioning looks. It appeared they were both in the dark about what was going on with Aster.

When they reached the Kantina, Emma pulled open the large red door with oval glass inserts. The coolness of the air-conditioning rushed forward to greet them and draw them farther into the restaurant with its bright, colorful décor.

The sign near the door that usually read: Please wait to be seated, now read: Seat yourself. It was what they did during the quiet time at the restaurant.

As they made their way to a corner booth, Emma glanced around for a table away from the other patrons. This was a small-town where it was difficult, if not impossible, to keep a secret.

As soon as they were seated in the corner booth, a server headed toward them with a basket of warm tortilla chips fresh from the deep fryer and a bowl of fragrant pico de gallo. Emma's mouth watered as soon as the food was placed on the table. Up until that point she hadn't eaten much, unless you counted a large coffee and a muffin. But suddenly her appetite was coming back to her.

She glanced over at her sister, whose full attention was on Aster. The worry lines between her brows and her pale complexion were concerning. The chips would have to wait.

"What's going on?" Emma asked. "Are you and Sam fighting?"

"You know wedding planning can be stressful," Hannah added.

Emma's gaze shifted to her sister. Was this something she'd experienced with Ethan? Was that why they still hadn't set a date?

The questions rushed to the back of her throat, but she swallowed them down. Now wasn't the time for getting distracted.

Aster's eyes widened as she shook her head. "It's not Sam. He's been great."

Then Emma had an even more alarming thought. "Is it Nikki? Did she change her mind about you two getting married?"

Aster shook her head again. Anguish reflected in her eyes. "It's not about the wedding."

"Then what is it?" Hannah's voice was soft and comforting.

"What can we do to help?" Emma's problems shrank to the back of her mind.

"You both are so sweet." Tears welled in the corners of her eyes. She paused, as though she were figuring out her next words. "I... I don't want to bother you with this. You both already have so much going on in your own lives."

"You aren't bothering us." Hannah's tone was firm but soft.

"We want to help. After all, you're family," Emma said.

"Not quite." Aster fingered her diamond engagement ring.

"Close enough," Hannah said. "Now tell us what is going on so we can help."

Aster hesitated. When she finally spoke, her voice was so soft that Emma had to strain to hear her. "I've been summoned to testify against Oz."

There was a collective gasp. Aster's abusive ex-boyfriend had come close to killing her in California. If the police hadn't stopped him, well, Emma didn't want to think about it.

"But I thought he'd already had a plea deal over that," Emma said.

"He did. This is about him breaking house arrest, killing a cop, and coming across the country to uh...to kill me." Tears spilled onto Aster's cheeks. She swiped them away.

Emma wasn't sure what to say. Hadn't that monster done enough to Aster? They should just throw him in a jail and toss the key.

Emma was at a total loss for words. She glanced at her sister, who also appeared to be struggling to find the right thing to say.

"They want me to be a character witness or some such thing for the prosecution." Aster once more swiped at her cheeks. "I thought this was behind me. I thought at last I could move on. And now the district attorney wants me to relive the whole experience in front of a jury and the press."

Hannah slid over and wrapped her arm over Aster's shoulders and gave a squeeze. "Whatever you need, we are here."

"Yes, we are." Emma nodded. "When is it?"

"The trial is next week. They want me to arrive early to go over my testimony." She let out another sigh. "But I have a new job that I don't want to lose. And Sam insists he's coming with me, but there's Nikki to think about and the farm to take care of."

"Don't worry about Nikki," Hannah said without hesitation. "Ethan and I will look after her."

Emma wanted to help too. It wasn't like she had plans of returning to Nashville any time soon. "What can I do?"

Aster's lips parted as though she were about to say something, but then she pressed them back together.

"What is it?" Emma prodded.

Aster shook her head. "I couldn't ask you to do it."

"Yes, you can. Whatever it is, just ask." And then she had a worrisome thought. "Unless it's taking care of the farm. I've got a brown thumb. But if that's what you need, I guess I could give it a try."

Aster patted her arm. "Thanks but it's not that. Actually, what I need help with is more in your wheelhouse."

Emma sat up straighter, curious to know what Aster had on her mind. Hannah sent Emma an I-know-what-it-is-but-you-don't look. Emma inwardly groaned. She hated when her sister did that. It was never good. What exactly was she missing?

"Tell me." Emma eagerly waited, anxious to help her family—a family she missed when she was away in Nashville or out on the road touring in different cities.

"I'm organizing the Concert on the Beach, and I don't have anyone to take over. My budget is really small, so I don't have an assistant to hand it off to."

"I'll do it." Emma had no idea what she was getting herself involved in, but how hard could it be? After all, she was a part of the music industry. She had a clue how concerts worked. And this was just one big concert, right?

"I couldn't ask you to do that," Aster said. "It's a lot of work, and you must be busy with you being a big star."

"Not at all. I'm taking a break. So until I figure out my next move, I have time on my hands. Just tell me what needs done."

Aster's mouth gaped. It took her a moment before she pressed her lips together. "Are you sure? I mean I'm sure you didn't expect to come home for a visit and be put to work. I'd totally understand if this is too big of a project."

Emma shook her head. "Don't worry. I've got this."

Tears flooded onto Aster's cheeks. "How did I get so lucky to have you two as friends?"

"And sisters," Emma said.

"Yes," Hannah said, "you're a Bell now."

"Not yet." Aster toyed with her engagement ring.

"Soon," Emma said.

"Yes, soon." Hannah nodded in agreement.

Aster gave up swiping away her tears. "Thank you both. I'm not sure how long we'll be gone. They need me there early, and then I have to stay until the end of the trial, in case they want to recall me."

"We understand," Hannah said. "Have you heard from that monster?"

Aster shook her head. "It would seem he has bigger things to worry about than harassing me."

"Good." Emma was so relieved that Aster didn't have to deal with him tormenting her any longer. "They're going to lock him up for good this time. He'll never be able to get near you again."

"I hope so. I just keep thinking, what if he gets off on a technicality?"

"It won't happen," Emma said. It just couldn't. The man was the worst of the worst.

"Emma's right," Hannah said. "Everything is going to work out."

"Let's hope you're both right. I can't wait to close the chapter on this part of my life." Aster's voice held a weary tone.

Just then, the server approached them. After a brief conversation, it was decided they'd have a late lunch. None of them had taken time to eat one that day.

While they waited for their taco salads to arrive, Aster said to Emma, "I'll get you all of my notes. And don't worry. Everything has been planned out."

Aster seemed to relax when she talked about the festival, so Emma kept the conversation going. "And this is to take place on the beach in front of Beachcomber Park?"

"Yes. I've already hired someone to build the stage."

"And scaffolding for the lighting?"

"Yes." Aster smiled. "I can see I'm leaving this project in capable hands. And you'll like Noah. He's a really nice guy."

"Oh, yes, he is," Hannah said. "Since Noah moved to the island, he's made friends with Ethan and Greg Hoover. He's laid-back and easy to get along with. You'll like him."

Emma swallowed hard. "We've met."

Both Hannah's and Aster's brows rose. Emma chose not to expand upon her run-ins with Noah. She didn't want Aster to think her working with him would be an issue. One way or the other, they'd find a way to work together.

For the rest of their meal, both Emma and Hannah worked to keep the conversation away from the trial and focused on the concert. There was so much going on in Aster's life that it was easy to keep the conversation going without any chance of talking about the monster lurking in California.

It seemed like the right time to bring up the news Emma had learned the night before while talking with her mother. "Did you guys know that Walter retired from the fire department?"

Aster shook her head. "I hadn't heard."

Hannah nodded. "He asked Ethan to step in as the next fire chief."

"That's great!" When Hannah didn't immediately smile, she asked, "Isn't it?"

"Oh, yes." Hannah smiled but it didn't go all the way to her eyes.

"What's wrong?" Emma always knew when something was eating at her sister.

"Nothing. I'm very happy for him."

Emma wasn't so sure she believed her sister's response, but she would wait until they were alone before she pushed farther. "And now Mom and Walter are leaving on a trip to Cancun to celebrate."

"Mom called last night to let me know," Hannah said. "She must have phoned just after she spoke to you. I'm so happy for them. After Dad... Well, I wasn't sure Mom would be able to move on."

"Walter had a lot to do with it," Emma said. "He's impossible not to like. He's just the kindest guy around."

"I think they make the cutest couple." Aster smiled when she spoke of them. "Walter is always fussing over your mother, and her whole face lights up when she looks at him."

"I can't remember the last time Mom was on a vacation." Hannah reached for her iced tea.

"Well, she will be tomorrow." Emma reached for another tortilla chip and then dunked it in the homemade salsa that had some heat to it. Just the way she liked it.

Emma was glad she'd come home exactly when she did. She was able to see her mother and Walter before they left for two weeks. And she was there to help Aster. Sometimes life worked out in the most unusual way.

When they were ready to leave the Kantina, Aster turned to Emma. "I'll let Noah know that he can coordinate with you about the stage."

"Sounds good." Emma struggled not to let on that the thought of working with Noah bothered her.

And then they all parted, going in different directions. Other than working with Noah, she welcomed the job of coordinating the concert. It would keep her mind busy. And give her a legitimate excuse to stay on the island for a while.

In light of what Aster was dealing with, Emma's problems paled in comparison. She just needed some time to sort through a few things.

Knowing she'd been putting off this call long enough, she reached for her phone. There were dozens of missed calls. When she scanned down through the numbers, she realized the bulk of them were from her manager, Stan, and the others were from JT.

She understood why Stan would be reaching out to her. They were supposed to have a meeting today to discuss her next move now that the tour had ended. She'd been hoping to convince him to put her in front of a label head and give her a chance to convince them to take a risk on her.

What she didn't understand were the repeated calls from JT. He didn't phone her that much during the good times in their relationship. Now she wondered if they'd ever really had good times or if it all had been an act on his part. Had he ever cared about her? Or was she some sort of PR stunt?

She didn't want to be anyone's puppet. A frown pulled at her lips. And worse she blamed herself for falling for him, when all of the signs were there that he was a playboy. How was she ever going to trust her judgement again?

She was in no mood to deal with JT at the moment. She had more important matters on her mind than letting him have his say.

She drew in a deep breath and let it out. She did it again. Then she selected her manager's phone number. The line started to ring.

"Emma, how are you? Where are you?"

"Hi, Stan. I'm...well, it doesn't matter where I am." She didn't know why she wasn't ready to share her whereabouts. It just wasn't something she was willing to do. "I called to let you know that I'm taking some time off."

"Time off?" Surprise rang out in his voice. "But you can't. We have those morning show interviews."

"They'll have to wait." She definitely wasn't in the mood to talk about JT cheating on her.

"You don't understand. Something like this isn't going to happen again. We have to strike while you're big news."

How did he not get that what had happened was not business but personal—painful personal business. "I don't care. I'm not doing it."

"The Baxter Group phoned, and they want you for a commercial. And you've been invited to perform at the Carlson's anniversary party. Their parties are some of the biggest around. It's an invitation list of who's-who in Nashville."

It would be her very first commercial. That could provide some desperately needed funds. Stan certainly knew how to dig away at her resolve.

These were big events—events that she'd have been over-the-moon to do a month or so ago. There would be label heads at the party—people who could put her career on the fast track. But now that she was on the island, the urgency and hubbub of Nashville seemed so far away.

Besides, Aster was counting on her. There was no way she was going to let her down. Even if it meant sacrificing these prime opportunities.

"I can't, Stan. I already have a prior engagement. I've got to go."

She ended the call. One phone call down. One to go.

As she went to pull up JT's number, she hesitated. Now wasn't the time to talk to him. Let him sweat it out. But if he thought they were going to kiss and make up, he had another thing coming.

CHAPTER EIGHT

PLANS HAD CHANGED.

He was now supposed to coordinate about the stage with someone new.

Wednesday morning, Noah stood on the beach, sipping his coffee. When he'd signed on to build the stage for the concert, he thought he'd be working with Aster. He'd gotten to know her a little and knew she was pretty easy to work with. Plus, she'd promised to give him pretty much free reign over the construction. He worried this new person would want to take control of everything.

Aster had been in such a rush on the phone that she'd failed to mention her replacement's name, but they were set to meet that morning. Maybe he was worried about nothing.

After all, things were looking up. By this evening, he hoped to have his offer for the beach house accepted. In his mind, he was already planning the changes he wanted to make to the place. A smile pulled at the corners of his lips as he pictured it.

As he stood on the beach near the lifeguard shack, he surveyed the area. He turned toward the closest set of steps that led from the parking area. Each time a young woman came down the steps, he wondered if it was his new contact.

And then familiar brown hair with golden highlights caught his attention. He focused on the woman's face. It was Emma. The woman who'd stole his taxi and then his coffee.

She approached him. What did she want?

When her gaze landed upon him, her beautiful blue eyes didn't seem to be the least bit surprised to see him. "Good morning."

"Morning." He was no longer certain it was a good one.

He looked around for someone who appeared to be searching for him. There were mothers with small children. There were teenagers. But there was no one looking as if they were in search of someone.

Emma continued to linger. He should just walk away. That was the best thing to do. Their track record so far had been iffy at best.

She clasped her hands together. "I think there's a possibility that you're here to meet me."

"No." He shook his head. "I don't think so."

"I think if you check with Aster, you'll see that I'm right."

His gaze narrowed as an ominous feeling came over him. This couldn't be right. Of all the people on the island, why did Aster have to hand this job off to Emma?

"Noah!" The familiar female voice came from behind him.

He turned and his gaze immediately landed on Aster. She was smiling at him, but he noticed her smile didn't quite reach her eyes. Something was bothering her. He presumed that was the reason she'd pawned this job off on someone else.

"Hi." He returned her smile.

"Noah, I see you met my friend, uh, my future sister-in-law, Emma Bell."

His gaze moved to the right. When it connected with Emma's, there was a funny sensation in his chest. The woman was equal parts alluring and irritating. And he was most certainly in trouble.

"We've met," he said.

"Yeah," Emma said. "We met at the airport and then again at the Lighthouse."

That was one way of putting their run-ins. He didn't bother to fill in the details. It wasn't anything Aster needed to know.

Aster turned to him. "So then you know that Emma is Bluestar's celebrity."

"Celebrity?" His questioning gaze moved between Aster and Emma.

"Oh, yes," Aster said. "Our Emma won the Songbird competition." When he still had no idea what she was talking about, Aster continued, "It's a reality show with singers. Aster is a country super star."

"Not really a star." Color bloomed in Emma's cheeks. "And certainly not a super star."

"And with such modesty." Aster momentarily smiled. "We're so proud of her."

By now Emma's cheeks were full-on red. She lowered her gaze.

"Sorry," Noah said. "I don't listen to country music."

"You should check out Emma's songs. You'll be a convert."

"I'll do that." He didn't have any plans of doing it. He was just being polite like his mother had taught him.

Aster went on to briefly explain that she was going out of town, and Emma had volunteered to fill in for her. "I appreciate what you're both doing. I can relax, knowing this concert is in capable hands."

"You have nothing to worry about. We've got this. Right, Noah?"

"Uh, right." The words were automatically spoken. What was he saying? And why was Emma so anxious to have Aster believe they could work together when nothing could be farther from the truth?

"Great." Aster smiled, but it didn't light up her face like normal.

He noticed her eyes were a bit dull with shadows below them. He suddenly worried that Aster was sick. If that was the case, he understood why Emma was acting like they were good buddies. He didn't know Aster well, but she'd been the first person on the island to give him a job when she had hired him to build new goat houses on her fiancé's farm.

And not only that but Aster had talked up his work to everyone in town. He didn't have a problem getting his furniture business off the ground. Building the stage for the festival was a little out of his wheelhouse but with no other contractor available on short notice, he was willing to take on the project.

"I don't know how to thank you both." Aster drew him from his thoughts.

Emma smiled. "You don't have to thank us. Just do what you have to do, and don't worry about things here. We'll have them under control." And then Emma glanced at him. "Isn't that right, Noah?"

"Um, yes. We've got this."

"Oh. Okay." Aster hesitantly glanced at both of them. "I feel bad dumping this all on you two."

"Well, technically you haven't asked me to do anything extra." Noah noticed Emma frown at him. He had no idea what he'd said wrong. "But I'm still up for building the stage. The wood should be delivered soon."

Aster's expression looked a bit strained. "I was hoping you'd be able to help Emma. She might need some help with the plans and stuff."

"He doesn't have to help me," Emma said too quickly. "I can handle this."

"I know," Aster said. "It's just a lot. Especially for someone jumping in at the last minute."

Behind Aster's back, Emma gestured at him. What was she trying to tell him? Her eyes widened as she nodded toward Aster. Did she want him to agree to help her? Or not? As far as he could tell, Emma went after what she wanted, whether it was taxis or coffees? She wouldn't need his help.

"I've got this," Emma said. "And I'm sure Noah will be too busy to help me, right, Noah?"

Wait. Was she saying he wasn't capable of doing his work and helping her? Because that wasn't the case. With a pricked ego, he said, "I'll be here if Emma gets in over her head."

"In over my head?" Emma planted her hands on her hips. "Listen here, I can handle this concert on my own."

"I'm sure you can. But you might need help from each other from time to time." Aster's gaze moved between the two of them. "Maybe this isn't such a good idea."

When Emma frowned at him, he cleared his throat. "I'll help her." He wasn't sure why he was agreeing to help Emma when she clearly didn't want his assistance, but it was done now. "You don't have to worry."

Relief shone in Aster's eyes. "Thank you. You don't know how much this means."

He shifted his weight from one foot to the other. "It's no problem."

Aster smiled. "You two are the best. Do either of you have any questions for me?"

They both shook their heads.

Aster turned to give Emma a big hug. And then she turned to him. A flustered look came over her as though she were trying to decide if she should hug him or not. He held his hand out to her. Relief shone in her eyes.

"Thank you again." She gave his hand a quick shake. "You probably think I'm awful for just taking off in the middle of everything."

"I don't. Not at all." He knew if it wasn't something vitally important, she wouldn't be leaving.

"It's just that..." She hesitated. "Well, um, Emma can tell you. Now you both have my cell number. Call if you need anything."

"Don't worry about us," Emma said. "You've got other things to tend to. We'll be fine. Now go."

"Uh, yes. I have to pack. Our flight is first thing in the morning. We're spending the night in Boston so there's less running around in the morning."

"Sounds like a good plan. Say hey to my brother."

"I will. Thank you."

"Go." Emma pointed toward the steps that led up to the parking area.

"Okay." Aster looked hesitant. "If you're sure?"

"We are," Noah said. Whatever was going on was serious, and he didn't want Aster worrying about him or whether he and Emma would be able to work together. They were adults. They'd find a way to make it work.

"Okay. Bye." Aster walked away. Her shoulders were a bit drooped, as though she had a heavy load weighing on her.

Noah turned to Emma. "Is she going to be okay?"

"Yes. It's going to be a tough time, but she's one of the strongest people I know. And she'll have my brother to lean on."

He nodded in understanding. He noticed Emma was light on the details, but that was fine by him. He was good with minding his own business.

Buzz-buzz.

Emma held up her phone. "I need to get this."

"No problem. I have to be somewhere."

She frowned. "You aren't starting on the stage now?"

He glanced around. "With what?"

When she scanned the area, she realized there was no lumber in sight. "This isn't good."

"Relax. It's all taken care of."

She looked hesitant and then nodded. "Aster gave me your number, so I'll be in contact. You can fill me in on your timeline later."

She hadn't said it in so many words, but she'd just let him know she was the boss. He wasn't sure how he felt about answering to her. He stood on the beach and watched her walk away. He was as certain as the sun coming up tomorrow that this situation was going to be very complicated.

CHAPTER NINE

HER MOTHER NEEDED HER.
Emma couldn't remember the last time her mother had phoned her and asked her to come home right away. Her feet moved rapidly over the sidewalk. The large crowd of tourists were slowing her pace. It wasn't until she moved beyond Main Street that she was able to pick up her pace.

As she walked, she replayed her meeting with Noah. He certainly didn't appear happy to be working with her. In truth, she wasn't much happier. The man seemed to be everywhere she turned. So long as Noah did his job, she didn't see where they'd have to deal much with each other.

Emma was breathless by the time she reached the house where she'd grown up. She rushed up to the back stairs and hurried inside. "Mom!" Her mother wasn't in the kitchen. "Mom, is something wrong?"

As she moved through the rooms of the downstairs, her gaze strayed across some luggage by the front door.

Emma called up the stairs. "Mom, I'm here."

There was the sound of footsteps and the squeak of a loose nail in the landing. Then her mother rushed down the steps. "Thanks for coming home. Did I call you away from something important?"

Emma briefly thought of Noah and the irritating way he got to her. It annoyed her that he was so good-looking—the kind of good-looking that stuck in her memory. "Nothing important at all. What's going on?"

A smile bloomed on her mother's face. "Absolutely nothing, except that I feel so guilty about leaving. I know you have a lot on your mind. I was talking to Walter, and we could reschedule our trip."

"Don't you dare." Emma was touched that her mother and Walter would do that for her, but it wasn't necessary.

Concern shone in her mother's eyes. "I know how hard you must be taking your break-up with JT, and I want to be here for you."

"Don't stay for my sake. I'm fine." Not really but having something to focus on besides her own problems was a step in the right direction. "Besides, I'm not going to be around much."

"You're going back to Nashville so soon?"

Emma shook her head. "I'm staying on the island and coordinating the concert on the beach."

Her mother's penciled brows scrunched together. "But I thought Aster was in charge of that."

"She is, or was. She's been called out of town. So, I'm stepping in while she's away."

"I didn't realize the trial is so soon. I'm worried about her. When your brother told me, I had no idea it was happening right away." Concern reflected in her mother's eyes. "Maybe I shouldn't go. Now just doesn't seem like the right time."

"Of course it is. Us kids are all grown up. We can take care of things. You go have an amazing time with Walter."

"But what about Nikki? Someone needs to take care of her while your brother and Aster are out of town."

Emma nodded. "Hannah and Ethan are going to look after Nikki. And I'm going to keep the concert on track." Her thoughts momentarily returned to Noah. "I'll make sure there aren't any problems with it."

"Are you sure you can do that? I mean you have your own work back in Nashville. Can you afford to take that much time away?"

Hoping to divert the conversation, Emma asked, "Mom, are you trying to get rid of me?"

"What?" A horrified look came over her mother's face. "Of course not. You know I love to see you. I'm just sad that I'm leaving right after you got home. This seems like an awful time to be leaving the island."

"Mom, just go. How often do you have a chance to visit Cancun?"

Her mother paused as though to give her answer some serious consideration. She sighed. "Are you sure about this?"

"I'm positive. You raised three capable kids. We'll keep it all together while you're gone."

"Will you be here when we get back?"

"I'll be here until the concert." She stopped there because she hadn't made any decisions beyond the concert.

Just then Walter came down the steps with yet another suitcase. That was going to cost them a lot when they got to the airport, but she kept quiet. Her mother didn't need another excuse not to get on that plane. A smile lit up his face when his gaze landed on her. "Emma, you're just in time to wish us goodbye."

"I'm so excited for you both. I hope you have an amazing time in Cancun. And don't forget to send pictures. Lots and lots of pictures."

They hugged and said goodbye. And then Emma closed the door, feeling strange to have her childhood home all to herself. She glanced at the living room with its two large blue couches flanking the outer corner. They were old, but her mother took fine care of them. And there were two upholstered white armchairs with shades of mauve and blue flowers. The only piece of furniture missing was her father's old recliner, where he'd inevitably take a nap each evening after dinner.

So many memories were made in that room. She recalled the big Christmas tree her mother would insist on getting each year. And how her father would complain it wouldn't fit in the room, but still he brought it home. And after rearranging all of the furniture, he'd have to cut a couple of feet from the bottom.

Emma's idea for how to start her singing career had taken place in this room. When she'd been a teenager watching Songbird with her parents, she'd realized that was her ticket to bigger things. In the end, she'd been partly right.

Her father had believed in her singing abilities and her Nashville dreams, while her mother wanted to keep her safe. But none of them were ever truly safe. One barn fire that got out control had taken her firefighter father's life. It was a tragedy that had rocked the island. And it had left Emma more determined than ever to follow her dreams.

Sadness and grief filled her heart. Life had changed so much for all of her family since their father died. And now her mother had remarried. Emma never thought it would happen, but then one night she'd gotten a call from her sister that their mother was getting super friendly with Walter. Of course, Emma hadn't believed it, not until she'd seen it with her own two eyes. It took some getting used to, but she was happy for her mother and Walter. Time stood still for no one.

Her phone dinged with a new message. She hesitated to check it, but upon realizing it could very well have to do with the concert, she withdrew it from her pocket and checked the message. It was from JT.

Em, I'm sorry. Can we talk?

Sorry? For what? That he'd cheated on her? Or that he'd been caught on camera?

It didn't matter. That part of her life was over. But did that also include her time in Nashville? Was she ready to give up on her singing career too?

She didn't have an answer for that last question. She needed time to think, and that was why when her phone rang with her manager at the other end, she declined the call. She'd think about her career another time. At this moment, she had a concert to organize.

Ding.

Em, please.

Her fingers moved rapidly over the screen as she typed. Stop messaging me.

Not until we talk.

She didn't want to speak to him, but she couldn't have him continuing to blow up her phone with message after message. She supposed she could block his number, but there was a part of her that wanted resolution—wanted to know if she'd ever meant anything to him.

Before she could change her mind, she dialed his number. It barely rang before JT picked up. It was as though he'd expected her to give in to his demands. The thought made her even more angry with him.

"Hey, Em, I'm glad you called." His voice was casual, like he hadn't broken her heart in the most public way.

"Why did you do it?"

He hesitated as though surprised by her straight forwardness. "You know how it is out on the road night after night. It gets lonely. Don't tell me you weren't ever tempted."

If there was the slimmest chance she would have given him a second chance, it was totally gone now. He expected her to understand why he'd cheated, and he didn't even bother to acknowledge the pain he'd caused her.

"No." She gripped the phone tighter. "I take my commitments seriously."

"Em, come on. You know how much you mean to me."

This time his smooth words weren't going to get him what he wanted. "I mean so much that you were kissing someone else."

"She didn't mean anything."

Somehow that just made it worse. Their relationship meant so little to him that he threw it all away for someone who meant nothing to him. "That's too bad because now you're all alone."

"Em, where are you?"

"It doesn't matter where I am."

"Em, calm down. You're making too much of this. We just need to talk...in person."

Was he serious? From his tone, she'd have to assume he believed his own words. "JT, don't call. Don't message. I don't want to talk to you ever again."

"Just tell me where you are. I'll even come to you."

The arrogance of the man thinking that him coming to her instead of the other way around was a big consolation. How had she not noticed his giant ego before now?

"No, JT." She disconnected the call.

She groaned in frustration. Suddenly, she was grateful for that photo. It had saved her from making the biggest mistake of her life.

elle

With the house offer submitted, there was nothing to do but wait.

Noah had a good feeling about his offer. Everything was finally going to work out.

At noon Friday, he made his way along the sidewalk, smiling and greeting people. Some he knew, and some he didn't. It didn't matter today. At last things were going his way.

He glanced at the time and realized it was lunchtime. He'd better get something to eat before heading back to the beach where his lumber order was supposed to be delivered that afternoon. They had his number and were supposed to call before they arrived.

He approached The Lighthouse Café. He liked how the restaurant was shaped like an actual lighthouse. It was much smaller than the real thing, but it had a working light at the top of the white-and-black-striped tower.

He stepped inside the café and headed for the counter in the back. The place was crowded, but he was fortunate to get one of the two available stools at the counter. The waitress behind the counter wore a nametag that read, Lucy.

Her straight dark-brown hair was pulled up in a high ponytail. She held a pen and pad of paper. "Welcome. What can I get you?"

"You seem really busy. Will it be long to get a sandwich?"

"Uh." She glanced over her shoulder through the window into the kitchen area. "It could be ten to fifteen minutes."

That wasn't so bad. "I would like an Italian sub with the dressing on the side and some fries." Then, he thought of his doctor's warning about salt and fat. "On second thought, nix that order. Can I get a turkey sandwich on whole wheat and no sides?"

"Uh, sure. Would you like something to drink?"

His gaze moved toward the little fridge behind the counter. "Can I get a diet cola to go? In fact, I'll take the whole order to go."

"Got it." She turned and moved farther down the counter to put in his order.

He pulled out his phone and checked his messages. There was no word from the lumber company. They had a special driving permit for the island that was only good for that day. If they didn't show up today, they'd have to wait to get another permit approved. Noah had learned the hard way that they took those permits seriously. When he'd first moved there, he'd driven his rental car onto the island and was immediately pulled over by the sheriff.

"Something wrong?"

Noah glanced up to find Greg Hoover standing there. Concern reflected in his brown eyes. They'd met his first week on the island right there at the café. They'd hit it off from that first meet and soon found they lived near each other—well, they would until Noah's offer for the beach house was accepted. And when Noah had asked if Greg could use some extra work, his new friend had jumped at the offer.

Noah sent him a friendly smile. "Everything is great."

Greg's warm brown face lit up with a smile. He took a seat on the empty stool next to Noah. "That's great, man. So what has you smiling? It wouldn't happen to be working with Emma Bell, would it?"

The smile slipped from Noah's face. "No. Why would you say that?"

Greg continued to smile as he shrugged his shoulders. "Just thought you might enjoy working with the island's celebrity. I know a lot of men that would like to work with her."

"They can gladly take my spot." He thought of the way she'd rubbed him the wrong way with the taxi and then the coffee. He didn't think this working relationship would go any better.

Greg's dark brows rose high on his forehead. "What happened between you two?"

Noah told him about his first meeting with Emma. "So working together is going to be challenging."

"Actually, I don't see that. I think you two just got off to a bad start, and it had nothing to do with your personalities clashing or anything serious. Why don't you give her another chance?"

"I take it you're friends with her."

Greg shrugged. "Em is a really cool person. She can be sweet and kind. And I think she's a lot of fun."

Just then Lucy arrived with Noah's sandwich in a foil wrap and his bottle of cola. He placed some cash on the counter and told her to keep the change.

Then Noah turned to Greg. "I have to get going. I'm waiting for a lumber order. I'll be seeing you later at the beach, right?"

"Yeah. I'll see you after work. And think about giving Em another chance. You won't regret it."

Now that he knew Emma was a big Nashville star, he could imagine her wanting everything done her way. He remembered some of the celebrities he worked with at his previous job. They'd want to micromanage him, and that wasn't how he'd worked back then. And it wasn't how he worked now.

He came to Bluestar to get away from the pressure and the rush-rush of city life. Now Emma was going to be breathing down his neck.

CHAPTER TEN

FIFTEEN DAYS UNTIL SHOW time.

Emma was nervous that everything wouldn't be set to go by then. And that was why by two o'clock Friday afternoon, she'd spoken to all of the performing acts. Friday was a lineup of eighties cover bands, and Saturday's lineup consisted of country music artists. She was a little hurt that Aster hadn't asked her to perform, but she pushed those feelings aside.

With all of the acts confirmed, she needed to make sure they had a place to perform. When she reached the seawall of Beachcomber beach where the stage was supposed to be erected, she saw nothing. No workers within the roped-off worksite. No lumber. Absolutely nothing but sand.

This was unacceptable. The sooner the stage was built, the sooner the city works department could begin work on running the electricity to the stage and the spotlights could be installed. There was a lot more to the stage than just the woodwork.

Where was Noah?

She reached for her phone and dialed the number Aster had given her for him. It rang and rang, then switched to his voicemail.

"Good morning, Emma."

She'd know that sweet voice anywhere. She turned to her left with a smile on her face. "Good morning, Ms. Birdie."

"I'd heard you were back on the island, but we kept missing each other until now. I'm so glad Peaches insisted on an afternoon stroll. Isn't that right, Peaches?" When the little orange and white dog barked her agreement, Birdie petted her before turning back to Emma. "What are you up to today?"

"I came to see the progress on the stage for the concert series." Emma gestured to the large empty space. "But as you can see, the construction hasn't begun."

Birdie glanced toward the cordoned-off area. "I suppose I'm to blame for that."

"You? But how? I don't think you're planning to help Noah build the stage, are you?" She'd known Birdie all of her life, and the woman was known to surprise people, but Emma just didn't see Birdie slinging around two-by-fours.

Birdie let out a laugh. "If I was just a little younger, I'd definitely be down there doing my part. But I think my days of hard physical labor are behind me."

"Then why would you think you have something to do with the delay in getting the stage built?"

"Well, I'd hired Noah to build me some new chairs for out on my deck. The old ones were Adirondack style chairs and much lower than these old bones can easily get into these days, especially since my accident last year. But Noah said he could make high chairs that were easier for me to get in and out of."

"That was nice of him. We don't want you getting hurt again." Last spring Birdie had taken a tumble and worried the entire town. The island just wasn't the same without her presence. "How are you doing now?"

"Good as new." Birdie sent her a reassuring smile. "Peaches makes sure I get up and moving every day. And I even ditched the walker. I just have to keep moving. At my age, you can't stop, or you'll never get moving again."

"You have more energy than a lot of people I know."

"Thank you, dear. I was blessed with a lot of energy. There are just so many things I want to do." Then worry clouded her eyes. "I'm sorry about taking up Noah's time. I'm sure he'll get to the stage soon."

"Is he working at your place? The reason I ask is that I've tried phoning him, but he's not picking up. And I just wanted to touch base with him about the completion schedule. And to see if he needs more help." As her gaze strayed back to the beach, she worried this job was too big for Noah to complete in a timely manner.

"Oh, no. He's not working at my place. He has a little shop not far from The Elegant Bakery." Birdie gave her the directions. "Well, I should be going. Peaches is ready for her nap."

"And I need to track down Noah."

"Please tell him that I'm sorry for getting him in trouble with the stage and all. Tell him that he can put my chairs on hold until after the concert."

Emma was touched by the woman's generosity. "I'll do that."

"Goodbye, dear." Birdie turned, but Emma noticed her movements were a bit stiff and awkward.

Emma worried that Birdie wasn't doing as well as she wanted to let on to everyone. Worry pitted in her stomach. This island just wouldn't be the same without Birdie.

With a sigh, Emma turned with her digital notebook in hand. She'd transferred all of Aster's handwritten notes to digital format. For her, it just simplified things. And when she needed to send something to someone involved in the concert, all she had to do was make a couple of swipes. At this late stage in the planning process, time was a precious commodity.

She headed in the direction of Noah's woodworking shop with determined steps. She'd paused a couple of times to sign autographs when tourists recognized her. The fact the public still recognized her from her time on Songbird was impressive because the show was a few years in the past. She had only been on television once since then to present the next season's winner with their Songbird trophy.

And she realized it was her relationship with JT that had put her back on people's radar. It bothered her that her popularity hinged on her ex and not on her own talents.

She felt as though once she'd stepped off the Songbird stage that she'd lost all of her forward momentum. And she had been giving that a lot of thought. What had changed after she'd won?

She knew one of the things that had helped her win the competition was that she'd written some of her songs. In fact, those two songs were what she'd gone on to record and could still be heard on the radio.

But since then she hadn't written any songs. She'd been too exhausted with her busy schedule. But now that she was taking a break, she needed to work on new material to present to the big labels. She did not want to be a one-hit-wonder.

Maybe the truth of the matter was that she wasn't meant to be a recording artist. Maybe her path was something different. She just didn't know what that other path might be. The only thing she did know was that she wanted it to involve music, whether it was as a songwriter or a choir director. She just needed music to be a part of her life. It filled up her heart and made her feel complete.

She stopped and glanced around. She realized she'd been so deep in thought that she'd walked right past Noah's woodworking shop. Feeling a little foolish, she turned around.

Two doors down the walk, she moved past an old white two-story colonial house toward the backyard, where there was a large two-bay garage. As she approached the garage, she noticed one of the doors was open, and the sounds of a saw could be heard.

So Noah was hard at work, just not on the project he was supposed to be working on. She wondered if Aster had hired the right man. She should have hired Ethan. Her future brother-in-law was a full-time contractor and part-time firefighter, but then she remembered her sister mentioning that he'd picked up a big job on the mainland that had him pretty busy. Still, she wasn't so sure Noah was up to the task of building the stage.

Still, this was Aster's project, so Emma had to abide by her wishes. And Aster's wish was for them to work together. So Emma would do her best to make that happen.

She stepped up to the opening of the garage to find Noah sawing a piece of wood. His back was to her, so she waited. When the saw stopped, and he lifted his safety glasses, she rapped her knuckles on the garage door frame.

Noah turned. "Oh. Hey. Come on in."

She stepped into the garage that was more workshop than a place you would park your car. "Looks like you're busy."

He shrugged. "Yeah. I promised Ms. Birdie that I'd get her some new chairs as soon as possible."

Emma decided to get straight to the point. "Is that why nothing is being done on the beach? You know we have fifteen days until the concert series, and we need to have the stage built days ahead of time."

"Whoa! Take it easy." He waved his arms to get her attention. When she stopped talking, he said, "I know exactly what I have to do and when it must be completed."

She frowned at him. "We can't mess this up. Aster has enough on her mind."

"I don't know what's going on with her, but I don't want to add to her worries. I promised to have it done, and I will."

She glanced at the chairs that were in various stages of being built. "I'm not sure you're going to have time to work on two projects at the same time. The stage must be your priority."

"I don't think you understand the importance of me finishing these chairs for Birdie. As it happens, the chair on her deck rotted and gave way with her in it."

"It did?" She recalled Birdie walking with a slight limp.

He nodded. "When I heard she was going to start using her other chair, I went to check it, and it's not much better than the one that broke. I pleaded with her to let me make her a couple of new chairs—chairs that weren't so hard for her to get in and out of. And finally she agreed. I just want to make sure to get them over to her before she gets impatient and decides to use that other old chair."

Emma nodded in understanding. "I'm sorry. Uh. I didn't realize the urgency of the job."

"I'm also still waiting on the delivery of the wood. But don't worry. The stage will be done on time."

When he said it, he sounded confident and a bit laid-back. Did he know not only Aster but the town was counting on them to organize this concert? He sure didn't seem like it with his take it easy and relax statements. She was so far from relaxed.

She watched him as he resumed working. His muscular biceps flexed against the sleeves of his gray polo shirt as he lifted a stack of similarly cut wood from in front of the table saw and moved it to a work bench. When she caught herself staring, she averted her gaze. What was it about this man that intrigued her as much as irritated her?

She clutched her phone, willing it to ring so she had an excuse to leave, but the silly thing for once refused to make a sound. "Sounds good. I'll stop by the beach later. You know, just to find out if there's anything you need."

"Actually, there's something I need now."

"Oh." His words caught her off guard. "What would that be?"

"See those smaller pieces of wood on the floor?" When she nodded, he said, "Can you bring them over to the workbench?"

"Sure." The task certainly seemed simple enough. "Do you make a lot of furniture?"

He shrugged. "Since I've been on the island, I've made a few pieces. This is a new business, so I'm working on growing it. I was thinking of setting up a website."

"Oh." She started to worry that he was a novice with woodwork. She needed someone knowledgeable to build the stage. "If you don't mind me asking, what did you previously do for a living?"

"I was a hedge fund manager in Chicago."

"Oh." She certainly hadn't been expecting that answer. A financial background was a long way from working with a saw and hammer. "Um. So working with wood is all new to you?"

"What?" He turned to her with a puzzled look on his face. "Oh, you think I'm not qualified to do the job."

She shrugged. Yes, she did but she wasn't bold enough to blurt it out, not when she knew there was a reason Aster had hired him. Surely Aster couldn't have been desperate enough to hire just anyone. Or perhaps she'd felt sorry for him. Aster did have a big heart.

"Relax," he said. "I know what I'm doing."

"But how?" The question slipped past her lips before she could stop it.

"My father was a carpenter. A very good one. So growing up, he taught me everything he knew. I worked my way through college as a carpenter. And now that I'm no longer in finance, I've returned to what makes me happy—working with my hands." He paused to select some sandpaper. "What makes you happy?"

"Me?" No one had ever asked her that question.

He nodded. "Does your singing still bring you happiness?"

"Why would you ask that?" The defensiveness rang out in her voice.

"Because you're here on the island." When she didn't respond, he added, "And instead of performing in the concert series, you're organizing it."

"I still love to sing," she said quickly. "It's the other stuff that goes along with the singing that I'm not so crazy about."

Now what had she gone and told him that for? It wasn't something she'd admitted to anyone. But it was the truth. There was a lot more to being a performer than standing up on the stage and singing.

"But you're a big star," he said. "At least that's what I've been told."

The fact he hadn't known whom she was up until their meeting on the island was strangely comforting to her. There were so many people on the island who had watched her on Songbird and had high expectations of what her life should be like now. Noah didn't come with any preconceived notions about her.

"I'm pretty much a nobody in Nashville," she admitted.

He paused from sanding. "I don't believe that. I mean I don't know anything about country music, but I've heard the excitement in people's voices in the café when they were talking about you being on the island."

She shrugged. "I guess some people like the couple of songs that I have out." She studied him. "So you've never heard my songs?"

He shook his head. "I'm more into the Beach Boys."

"Oh. Okay."

"Here. Take this." He tossed her some sandpaper.

She caught it. "What am I supposed to do now?"

"Sand that piece of wood next to you."

She picked up the foot-long piece. She pressed the sandpaper to the surface, moving her hand back and forth. She had to admit that the smell of wood was nice.

"Not like that."

She stopped what she was doing to glance at him. "Not like what?"

"You need to move the paper with the grain of the wood."

She stared at the piece of wood. She turned the piece ninety degrees and began again. "Don't you have a machine to do this for you?"

"I do, but I like to do the final sanding by hand. I can use my fingers to figure out where each piece needs more work." He paused to blow the sawdust from his piece. "So, if you don't like all of the stuff involved with singing, what are you going to do?"

"I have no idea. That's what I'm here to figure out."

"And what about that thing with your boyfriend?"

She gasped. "You looked me up?"

A corner of his mouth lifted as he shrugged. "I had to admit that I was curious. Sorry to hear what happened with your boyfriend."

"He's not my boyfriend! He's... He's nothing to me." She'd said the words a little too fast to sound believable.

What was it with this guy that he could get her to admit things she wouldn't tell anyone else? She didn't want to talk about Noah with him or anyone. Among other things, it was embarrassing to have her fiancé cheat on her.

She put down the wood and sandpaper. "I have to be going."

He stopped working and turned to her. "Hey, I'm sorry. I shouldn't have mentioned it."

She waved off his apology. "It doesn't matter. My life is out there for the whole world to read about."

She rushed out of the garage, forcing herself to maintain a quick walk and not a run. She didn't run away from anything—not even a handsome guy probing into her messed-up romantic life.

Chapter Eleven

H E COULDN'T STOP THINKING of her.

Saturday morning, Noah used the nail gun to secure another two-by-four. As he worked on erecting the stage, he didn't notice the lull of the water, the heat of the sun, or the cacophony of sun-seekers just down the beach. He was distracted with thoughts of the brunette with the unforgettable blue eyes, who kept crossing his path.

He didn't want to like Emma. He didn't want to feel anything toward her. Yet he found with each run-in that he grew more curious about her. And the fact that she was now single wasn't helping matters.

He grabbed a two-by-four and moved it into position.

Sure Emma could be trying at times—like when she swiped his taxi. But she could also be fun to talk to. And when she smiled, well, it was like the clouds had parted, and the sun had come out.

He blew out a frustrated sigh as he reached for the nail gun. He was only going to get himself in trouble with those sorts of thoughts. He didn't want to be her rebound man.

"Noah?"

He paused what he was doing to turn to Greg. "What do you need?"

"I was just wondering how many nails you were planning to put in that two-by-four." Greg smiled and shook his head. "Something, or should I say someone, has you distracted."

Noah turned back to the board and noticed that he'd put in six nails—four more that it had needed. He sighed. "I need some caffeine."

Greg's eyes twinkled with merriment. "Uh-huh. Should I assume that things between you and Emma are getting better?"

"You shouldn't assume anything." He wasn't going to admit to Greg that he had been thinking about Emma. He'd never hear the end of it. And it wasn't like there was anything between them. And there never would be. "How's your section coming?"

"Good. Ethan said he had time to stop by later to help out."

"That's great. We can take all the help we can get because Emma is anxious to have this stage completed as soon as possible."

"This concert series is going to be great for the island. There aren't any vacancies left anywhere on the island. I haven't seen the islanders so excited about anything in a long time. Aster has been a great addition to the mayor's office."

"I don't know her well, but she seems like a ball of energy."

Greg nodded. "She's always on the go. It's just a shame she had to leave just when all of her planning was coming together."

Noah wanted to ask what had been so urgent to call her away, but it wasn't any of his business. He also noticed that no one on the island was talking about what was going on with Aster, and since this island had a healthy gossip vine, it told him that this thing with Aster was serious. He hoped everything worked out all right for her.

"There you are," said a familiar female voice.

Both men turned to find Emma approaching them. She smiled at Greg, a great big bright smile, but when her gaze turned to Noah, the radiance dimmed and went out.

He stifled a sigh. He wanted to apologize to her but not in front of Greg. He didn't want to make matters worse between him and her by publicizing their falling out.

"Hi, Emma," Greg said. "How's it going?"

"Good." The smile came back to her face. "I see you've been hard at work."

Greg glanced over at the framing they'd done so far. "It's a start."

"Well, I just stopped by because I had a complaint from city hall that there wasn't a permit displayed at the site. So they gave me another one with a warning to have it up today or we'd get fined." She held out the red, laminated paper.

Greg nodded and took it from her. "I'll take care of it. Do you care where I put it?"

As they talked about the best location to display the permit, Noah, for the first time in his life, felt invisible. And he didn't like it. Not one little bit.

While Greg stapled the permit in place, Noah said, "Emma, can we speak?"

She barely glanced in his direction as she started to walk away. "Now's really not a good time. I have a meeting with the mayor to go over some final logistics for the event."

"This won't take long." He didn't want this thing between them to drag out. The longer it did, the harder it'd be to fix it in the end. He took long, quick strides to catch up with her.

"Noah, there's nothing left to say. You know everything there is to know about me now that you read about me online." Her words dripped with sarcasm.

"Emma." He reached out, touching her upper arm. "I'm sorry. What can I say? I was curious."

She paused, but she still didn't turn to him. "You know they just make up that stuff, right?"

"I do. So does this mean you still have a boyfriend?"

Her head turned, and then her gaze met his. Pain emanated from her blue eyes. "No, I don't. That part they got right."

"I'm sorry." When she looked as though she were going to roll her eyes, he said, "No, seriously. I'm sorry we keep getting off on the wrong foot."

Her eyes shone with disbelief. And for a moment, he didn't think she was going to accept his apology, but eventually she said, "Apology accepted."

That wasn't enough. He knew she was going to continue to avoid him as much as possible. "I mean it, Emma." Why was he pushing this peace between them? He didn't have the answer. He just knew he wouldn't rest until he smoothed things out between them. "We've gotten off to a bad start, more than once, and I'd like to see if we can start over one last time and be friends."

She arched a brow. "Maybe we should stick with being co-workers."

It wasn't what he wanted, but it was better than them being at odds with each other at every turn. "You know I'm betting by the end of this project, we'll be friends."

Suspicion shone in her eyes. "Why are you pushing this?"

He shrugged. "I'm new on the island. I'm trying to make friends."

"But I don't live here. So why me?"

"Why not you?"

She sighed and shook her head. "Has anyone ever accused you of being stubborn?"

"I prefer determined."

She let out a laugh.

The melodious sound of her laughter brought a smile to his face. "Progress."

"What progress?" She glanced over her shoulder at the framework for the stage. "Surely you don't mean those few boards that you managed to nail."

"No. I meant making you smile. If you keep that up, we'll be friends in no time."

"Not going to happen. Now I have to go. I'll check in later."

As she walked away, his gaze followed her. "You know now that you've made this a challenge, I don't like to lose."

She shook her head as she kept walking. He chuckled to himself. There was something about her that kept drawing him back—kept him wanting to fix things between them.

Greg stepped up beside him. "What's between you and Emma?"

"Nothing."

Greg arched a dark brow. "Uh-huh. You just keep telling yourself that."

He walked away before Noah could argue with him. It really wasn't like that. Emma was different. She brought a spark to his life—something he didn't know he was missing. But life sure wasn't boring when she was around.

A smile tugged at the corners of her lips.

Emma kept walking all the while thinking about Noah and his parting words. She wouldn't admit it to him, but she liked the idea of them being friends.

There on the island she felt more like herself than she had in a long time. And there weren't photographers or people following her around to see if she was going to meet JT. And best of all, JT wasn't there.

Buzz-buzz.

Hopefully, her thoughts hadn't conjured up a phone call from her ex. She removed her phone from her pocket to check the caller ID. It was her agent, Stan. She'd dodged a lot of his calls lately. She couldn't avoid him forever.

She pressed the phone to her ear. "Hey, Stan, I don't have much time."

"We need to talk. I'm worried about you. Please tell me where you are."

She didn't want him to worry, and he had been good to her. "Don't tell anyone but I'm on the island."

"Bluestar?" Disbelief rang out in his voice.

"Yes."

"What are you doing there?"

That was a loaded question. "The tour was over and I need to recharge."

"This has to do with that photo that's all over the internet, doesn't it?" He didn't wait for her to respond. "JT phoned me. He's looking for you. He wants to explain."

"There's nothing to explain. He can't explain away a photo that the whole world has seen by now."

"Em, just give him a chance."

"What?" She couldn't believe what she'd heard. "You're siding with him?"

"No." His answer was firm. "But if there is any way past this incident, well, I'm just saying that you two together was like magic for publicity. The cameras loved you guys."

"Stan!"

Not everything was about publicity or making a headline on the gossip sites. She knew the saying that no headline was a bad headline, but she still had a hard time dealing with the fake news. You can take the woman out of the small town, but you couldn't take the small town out of her.

Stan sighed. "I'm sorry. I just know if we keep putting your name out there that big things are going to happen for you."

"You've been saying that since I won Songbird. And I still don't have my first album."

"I'm working on it. That's why you need to come back to Nashville."

"No."

"You don't understand. I have a meeting with Cades Records."

Her heart pounded. Was this it? Was this the big moment she'd been waiting for most of her life? Excitement coursed through her body.

She struggled to speak calmly. "What's the meeting about?"

He went on to tell her that the meeting pertained to another band and her heart plummeted. "But when I'm in there, I plan to mention you."

She came to a stop outside of the yoga studio. "It sounds like you don't need me for anything."

"Em, that's not true. When are you coming back?"

"I don't know." It was the truth. She had no plans to return any time soon. "At least not for a couple of weeks, maybe more."

"Em—"

"Sorry, Stan. Got to go. Talk later." And then she disconnected the call.

She knew she couldn't put off her return to Nashville forever, not unless she wanted to give up on her singing career for good. Was she fooling herself to think her big break was ever going to happen? She wasn't sure. She'd thought Songbird had been it, but that obviously wasn't the case.

ele

He didn't like exercise.

Noah pulled on his running shoes with their blue no-tie laces. It was early Monday morning, and it was time for his two-mile run. He'd promised his doctor he'd exercise at least five days a week.

As his mind rewound in time, his fingers moved to his chest. He recalled how one moment he'd been in his office, trying to explain to his client why their portfolio had taken a significant hit and promising that with a little more time, it would rebound. The next moment he'd been on the floor, clutching his chest. The rest of it was a blur as he'd been rushed to the hospital.

That was the day he knew he couldn't keep abusing his body. No more high-stress work days. No more skipping meals or worse eating greasy, carb-loaded food. No more skipping exercise to sit behind his desk and work from early morning until late at night.

Noah began to stretch out. He was more cautious these days than before his brush with death—more inclined to listen to the suggestions of the doctors. Even if he didn't like everything they had to say.

All warmed up, he set off down the sidewalk and then moved onto the road. As he set off at a slow jog, he realized he needed new goals. These would be more personal than his achievements as a hedge fund manager. And his first goal should be to run Bluestar's 5K that autumn.

Eventually, he'd like to be able to run from one end of the island to the other. When he turned his exercise into a challenge, it was more appealing to him. He didn't like to fail at anything.

Sometimes he timed himself, pushing to get a lower time for a mile. Other times he was happy to be able to jog for fifteen minutes straight. At this point, he wasn't a consistent runner, but he was slowly getting there. All of those years behind a desk had done a number on his stamina. He wasn't the athlete he had been in high school.

Sometimes he'd wake up in the morning and wonder how his life had taken this significant detour. But as he was told time and time again that this second chance of his was a miracle—that he should have died when his heart stopped in his office—he started to come to grips with the gravity of the situation. The fact they'd gotten his heart restarted was a miracle. He wasn't going to waste this second chance at life.

He picked up his pace with renewed determination. His gaze strayed across a familiar face. It was Emma. She was jogging through the intersection just ahead of him. Her moves were smooth and done with ease. She obviously had been running for quite a while.

If he was to pick up his pace and change his usual path, maybe he could work some more on them being friends. It was another of his goals. His steps came quicker. A smile pulled at his lips.

He was gaining on her. This would definitely make his morning run much more interesting. He pushed himself to go faster.

When he neared her, he was breathing heavily. Between breaths, he said, "Hey."

She didn't respond as she kept going. Was she ignoring him? He wasn't giving in that easily.

He raised his voice. "Good morning."

And still she didn't say anything. He reached out and tapped her upper arm. She came to a sudden stop. She turned to him with a startled look.

"Sorry," he said. "I didn't mean to scare you."

She removed earbuds. "I couldn't hear you."

He felt better, knowing she wasn't intentionally ignoring. "I was just saying good morning."

She gave him a quick once-over. "You run?"

He shrugged. "Yeah. Every morning."

Something flashed in her eyes. "Let's run together."

He'd already pushed himself to catch up to her. He wasn't sure he could keep up with her fast pace.

"Come on." She smiled as she lightly elbowed him. "Don't tell me you're worried about keeping up with me, are you?" A challenge glinted in her eyes.

His pride overrode his common sense. "Let's go." He took off. "To the beach," he called over his shoulder.

She caught up to him. "Don't worry. I'll take it easy on you."

He pretended he didn't hear her. He pushed himself even harder. His muscles groaned, but it didn't stop him. He knew he would pay for this later, but he kept going.

He chanced a glance over at her. She moved so easily. She didn't appear to be exerting herself in any way. He definitely had to work harder at this running stuff if he didn't want to embarrass himself come the 5K. At least he had a few months to practice.

The sun beat down on him, making him hot. His muscles strained as he forced himself to go faster than he normally would. He didn't want her to think he was a novice—even if it was the truth. His lungs strained to pull in more and more oxygen.

He stared straight ahead, wondering if he was going to be able to maintain this pace the whole way to the beach. Couldn't he have picked something closer? Like Main Street? Or The Lighthouse Café? He'd have groaned, but it took too much effort.

Yet, he kept putting one foot in front of the other. He wouldn't stop. He could do this.

Emma's hand reached out and touched his arms. He glanced over to find her stopped next to Ms. Birdie. A smile bloomed on his face, and he struggled to maintain his breathing. He'd never been so happy to see anyone.

"Good morning, you two." Birdie beamed at them as Peaches sat next to her. "I didn't mean to interrupt your morning run."

"No problem," Emma said. "Besides, I think Noah could use a breather."

He wanted to argue the point, but as he drew in rapid breaths, he decided words were overrated. One of these weeks, um...months, hopefully he'd be in shape.

"The reason I stopped you," Birdie said, "was that I wondered how my new chairs are coming along."

When they turned expectant gazes his way, he drew in a couple of deep breaths. "I'm...working on them...in between working...on stuff for the concert."

Birdie smiled. "I knew I could count on you."

"Yes, ma'am. I'll have them to you as soon as possible."

"You know I was at my friend Betty Simon's house, and her chairs aren't so great either. I'm afraid they're going to break like mine did. I was wondering if it'd be possible to get a couple more chairs. They'll be her birthday gift."

"I, uh..." He wasn't expecting his business to take off so suddenly. It was getting to the point where he had more business than he had time. "Well, the thing is I've got work to do for the concert—"

"But he'll make time to do the extra chairs," Emma said.

"Oh, wonderful." Birdie clasped her hands together and beamed at him. "Thank you. And I know Emma won't mind helping you with those chairs. She always was so good with her hands." Before Birdie moved on, she said, "I'll need those in two weeks. That's when Betty's birthday is. She'll be so excited."

As Birdie sauntered off with Peaches next to her, he frowned at Emma. "Why did you tell her I would be able to do those additional chairs?"

"Why not? You said you were trying to grow your business. Birdie knows everyone on the island. An endorsement from her is all the advertising you'll need."

"But I can't do all of that in two weeks." And then he had a thought. "At least not by myself."

"What's that supposed to mean?"

He arched a brow. "You heard Birdie. She thinks you'll make me a good assistant."

Emma emphatically shook her head. "No way."

"Why not?"

"You saw me. I don't even know how to sand correctly."

"That's true. But once I explained it, you had it. I'm sure I could find some other stuff for you to do."

She frowned at him. "This isn't going to work."

"Why not?"

"Because... Because I have the concert to coordinate."

"And I have the stage to build. Seems as if we're both busy." He wasn't going to let her off the hook. "And if I recall correctly, you were the one to volunteer my services."

She opened her mouth as though to mount an argument and then promptly pressed it closed again.

He subdued a smile of victory. "How about we walk the rest of the way to the beach?"

Buzz-buzz.

He should have left his phone at home. Now was not the time for a chat. But after his heart attack, he was unwilling to be parted from his phone.

He unzipped his shorts pocket and pulled out the phone. It was a call from his real estate agent, Madison. The moment that he'd been waiting for. Excitement pumped through his veins.

He held up a finger to Emma. "I need to get this."

"No problem. Do you want me to wait?"

"Yes." The answer popped out of his mouth. The thought of having someone to share his big news with sounded appealing. And it was even more appealing that it was Emma.

She nodded. "I'm just going to step over there and do a little window shopping."

When she'd stepped away, he pressed the phone to his ear. "Hello." He didn't wait for Madison to speak before he continued. "Did you hear something about the offer?"

"I'm afraid I have some bad news."

No. No. He couldn't have heard her correctly. "What did you say?"

She repeated her words. "I'm really sorry. They'd had a lot of offers on the table when yours came in. Your bid and another were the highest. And they went with the offer that came in first. It was a timing thing."

Disappointment gutted him as he disconnected the call. He was so sure that at long last this house was the one meant for him. He'd already envisioned himself spending the rest of his life there. And with it checking off all of his boxes, he was willing to invest the extra money.

A timing thing—meaning if he hadn't been delayed when he'd first arrived back on the island, then his offer would have been there first. If Emma hadn't crossed his path, he would be buying the home of his dreams.

Emma approached him. "Ready to hit the beach."

His interest in running fled him. He shook his head. "I don't think so."

"Are you sure?"

He nodded. "I have a lot of work to get done today. I need to get started."

She sent him a puzzled look. "Oh. Okay. I'll see you later."

He didn't say anything before he turned and started jogging his way back to his apartment. It looked like he would be reupping his lease for another year because trying to find the perfect home for him on this small island, where the inventory was quite limited, was going to take a long time.

Or should he expand his search to the Massachusetts coastline or even farther to Maine? Maybe his options wouldn't be so limited. It wasn't like there was anything holding him on Bluestar Island.

His thoughts turned to Emma. And just as quickly, he dismissed the thought. It wasn't like there was anything between them. After all, she was the one who'd cost him the house and now doubled his work at the shop while he was supposed to be working on the concert preparations. So much for his slower pace of life and the less stress that he'd promised his doctor.

CHAPTER TWELVE

WHAT HAD HAPPENED?

It was the question Emma had been asking herself for the last four days, ever since Noah had taken the phone call, and then his whole demeanor had changed. Although he hadn't said so, she got the feeling he was agitated with her. But why?

Since their run, he'd been distant as he made progress on the stage. He answered her questions, but he never went out of his way to make small talk. Maybe she was just over-analyzing things. But still she worried they were once more at odds with each other. And this time she had no idea why.

Both Hannah and her fiancé, Ethan, were working, so Emma had volunteered to spend the day with Nikki. With Emma now living in Nashville, she got so little time to spend with her niece, who was growing up quickly. In fact, each visit home, Emma found Nikki had noticeably grown.

Nikki was becoming a beautiful and energetic young lady. And she'd been so good for Emma that morning. While Emma had been on the phone, talking to the various artists about details related to the concert, Nikki had spent time with her goats.

Emma had no doubt that Nikki was going to be a farmer when she grew up. The way she loved the animals was evident in her facial expressions.

And then there was Dash, a little black pygmy goat. He was born on the farm a little more than a year ago. He was a bit smaller than the other goats, but what he lacked in size, he made up for in personality. He was bold and brave to the point where her brother worried that someday the little goat might get himself into big trouble. Emma seriously hoped that day never came.

Emma checked off the last thing on her list for that morning. Aster and Sam were counting on her to keep things running smoothly. When she'd talked to them last night, she'd informed them that everything was under control. They seemed to take some comfort in that knowledge. She wouldn't let them down.

Nikki, her seven-year-old niece, ran up the back steps to where she was sitting on the porch. "Auntie Em, can we go to the beach? Pleeease."

"Weren't you just at the beach the other day with Aunt Hannah and Ethan?"

"But that was so long ago. Pleeease."

"It was just this past weekend." Emma smiled and shook her head.

"But it's already Friday."

"I don't know. I should be heading to city hall to check on a couple of things."

"It's okay. I understand." Nikki's voice held a sad tone. "When are Dad and Aster coming home?"

"I don't know, sweetie. They still have some stuff to do in California."

"You can say it. I know. They told me about the court case and that Aster has to go put a bad guy in jail."

"Oh. Okay." Emma was surprised that Sam and Aster had revealed that much to Nikki. But she was a smart girl, who grew up much too quickly after her mother died. "You know that they'll come home just as soon as they can. They miss you."

"I miss them too. I can't wait for them to get married. Then I can call Aster, Mommy."

Emma's heart melted. She reached out and pulled Nikki close for a hug. She was sad and happy for her. And if she was feeling all of those emotions, she couldn't even imagine what Nikki was feeling. She hugged her niece even tighter.

With her priorities realigned, Emma said, "Let's go to the beach."

Nikki pulled back. "Really?"

"Yes, really." Emma smiled at her niece. Her priority now was making her niece as happy as she could be while her parents were away.

Emma paused after her last thought. She'd never thought of anyone besides Sam's late wife, Beth, as Nikki's mother. Now Aster was about to fill that role. Emma couldn't think of anyone more loving or caring than her. So official or not, Aster was, for all intents and purposes, Nikki's mother.

"But it's almost lunchtime. We should eat and then we can go." When the smile slid off Nikki's face, Emma asked, "What's wrong? Aren't you hungry?"

Nikki shrugged. "Can we go now and have a picnic lunch?"

"I don't see why not." Emma wasn't sure what was in the fridge. With Sam and Aster out of town, she figured there wouldn't be much, if anything. They'd have to stop by The Lighthouse Café and place a to-go order. "Run inside and put on your swimsuit under your clothes, and we'll head to the beach for a couple of hours. Is your swimsuit here or at Aunt Hannah's?"

"My new one is at Aunt Hannah's, but my old one is here."

"Okay. Put on the old one, and we'll get going."

They'd have to stop by her mother's house to grab hers. It wasn't on the way to the beach, but she didn't think Nikki would mind the detour as long as their final destination was the sand and ocean. She had to admit that a visit to the beach sounded inviting. She wouldn't mind wiggling her toes in the sun-warmed sand and cooling off in the water.

When Nikki didn't immediately return, Emma went inside. "Nikki, what's taking so long?"

"I can't find my swimsuit." Her voice echoed down the steps.

"When was the last time you wore it?"

Nikki appeared at the top of the steps and shrugged her slim shoulders. "I don't know."

"Did you check all of the drawers in your dresser?" When Nikki nodded, she said, "Check again." And then she had a thought. "What color is it?"

"Pink and blue."

While Nikki went to check her room again, Emma headed for the laundry room. There was a basket of folded clothes on top of the dryer. She carefully searched through the two stacks of clothes. The swimsuit was nowhere to be found.

And then she checked inside the dryer. It was empty. Where was it? Could both swimsuits be at her sister's place? Emma turned around and leaned back against the washer. She reached for her phone. In the process, her gaze caught something pink. She moved her gaze back until she zeroed in on the clothes hanging on a drying rack. And there was the missing swimsuit. Problem solved.

With the swimsuit in hand, Emma headed back to the kitchen. "Nikki, I found it."

There was a loud stomping of feet on the steps. Nikki appeared in the kitchen with a hopeful look on her face. "You did?"

"I did. Let's go. We have to swing by Gram's house to get my swimsuit. When I came over this morning, I had no idea we'd be spending the afternoon at the beach."

"It's gonna be so much fun." Nikki grabbed her swimsuit and ran back up the steps.

"Slow down. We don't need you getting hurt."

"I won't!"

Emma glanced around the house. She noticed the little differences, from the couple of houseplants in the living room window to the colorful throw pillows on the couch. They were small touches, but they were Aster's touches. Little by little she was turning this house back into a home for Sam and Nikki. That was good. Very good.

While Emma was away in Nashville, she'd have one less thing to worry about back on the island. That was if she went back to Nashville. But she didn't want to think about that now. Today was all about fun in the sun.

When Nikki barreled back down the steps all ready to go, she had a towel, a beach bag, and sunglasses. She looked adorable.

"One more thing," Emma said.

Nikki's smile drooped. "What?"

"Your hair. We need to put it up in a braid. It'll be easier to deal with when you're swimming and less messy to brush out later."

"Do we have to?" Nikki's big blue eyes, so much like her daddy's, begged her not to take the time.

"I'm afraid so."

A few minutes later, they were out the door. Emma had just turned the key in the deadbolt when her phone buzzed. When she grabbed it, she was surprised the caller ID showed it was Noah. What did he want?

For a moment, she considered letting the call go to voicemail. She didn't want anything to ruin this idyllic afternoon with her niece. These moments were few and far between. But she realized if he was taking time to call her, it had to be important.

"Hold on, Nikki. I have to get this."

"Okay, I'll go tell Dash goodbye." She started down the steps. "And Billy. And Rufus..."

Emma smiled as her niece's voice trailed off. She was such an amazing young lady. As Emma's phone continued to buzz, she expelled a resigned sigh.

She pressed the phone to her ear. "Hey, Noah, I was just heading out with Nikki."

"Sorry to disturb you. I just wanted you to know that there's been a holdup with the next shipment of lumber."

"What?" This was certainly not the news she was expecting.

"They were supposed to make the delivery this morning, but when they didn't show up, I called. It's not good."

Her grip on the phone tightened. "When will they have it to you?"

"They don't know." His voice was calm and didn't hold a note of irritation. "There's a supply chain issue." He seemed too at ease with this complication.

"Did you tell them that this is unacceptable, and if they ever want to do business with the town again that they have to make this right?"

"No. I didn't think this situation necessitated threats."

"Why not? We don't have much time to get the stage built."

"Relax. It'll get done."

Her fingers tightened around the phone as frustration had her grinding her back teeth. Why was he being so laid-back?

She drew in a deep breath, hoping it would calm her. Doing her best to sound calm, she said, "How about another supplier?"

"That's why I was calling you, to see if it would be all right to shop around. If it's a widespread shortage, I might have to take lumber from a number of vendors."

Before Emma could respond, Nikki called out, "Auntie Em! Come quick."

She lowered the phone. "What's wrong?"

"It's Dash! He's gone again." Tears welled up in the little girl's eyes.

"Are you sure? The penned-in area is pretty big. Maybe he's hiding from you."

Nikki shook her head. "I looked in all of his hiding spots. He's not there."

Just great. As if Sam and Aster don't have enough on their minds. If they hear that Dash is missing, it'll just worry them more. The only solution was to keep this quiet and find that goat as fast as possible. Because if Hannah found out, she'd be sure to tell their mother. And their mother would tell their brother. This family was terrible with secrets.

"Close the gate so the others don't get out." Emma glanced down at the phone in her hand and then realized Noah was still on the other end. She lifted the phone to her ear. "I'm sorry, Noah but I've got to go. I trust your decision as far as the lumber."

And with that she disconnected the call. Her gaze searched the area for the little black goat. Where can he be? She'd heard about his escapades from Sam and Aster, but she never thought she'd be involved in one of Dash's escapes.

Nikki ran up to her. "What are we going to do?"

That was a good question. And at this moment, she didn't have an answer. "I thought your dad fixed the gate so Dash couldn't get out anymore."

Nikki's head lowered as she toed the ground.

"Nikki?"

Her niece let out a big dramatic sigh. And then she lifted her head so their gazes could meet. "He did. But the new lock is hard to work, and sometimes I don't get it fully latched."

"Oh. I see."

Nikki's gaze filled with tears. "Please don't tell Dad. He's always reminding me to close the gate. He'll be mad at me for letting Dash get out."

"How about we find the goat, and then there won't be anything for your father to get upset about?"

Nikki eagerly bobbed her head. "Where do we start?"

"Can you recheck the pen and the goat houses?" When Nikki bobbed her head again, Emma said, "I'll start looking around the yard. Maybe Dash got distracted with something near the house."

"Maybe he went into town. Again."

Emma hoped that wasn't the case. But she was certain she'd get a phone call, correction, lots of phone calls, if he showed up in the middle of town. And then there'd be no way to keep the incident from Sam and Aster.

"Okay. Go look for him," Emma said. "And I'll work my way around the house. Then we'll meet back here."

Nikki ran toward the pen.

"Don't leave the gate open!" Emma didn't need to track down any other goats.

And then she set off, searching for Dash. How hard could it be to find a black goat? He surely hadn't gotten very far.

"Dash! Dash, come here!" She walked around the house, searching behind the larger bushes. "Dash, please."

The more time that passed, the more concerned she became. What was she going to do if they didn't find Dash lingering around the house? Where would he have gone? Which direction?

When Emma circled the entire house without any sign of the little goat, she glanced toward the pen. It didn't appear Nikki was having any better luck with her search.

Then Emma got an idea. It wasn't the best idea, because it would guarantee that this little mishap was relayed to her brother. So long as it was after the trial and they were home, it wouldn't matter.

She pulled the phone from her pocket. She pulled up Charlie McQueen's number. He was one of Sam's neighbors, and he was keeping an eye on the farm for Sam. As the line rang, she pressed the phone to her ear. It rang and rang. Please let him answer.

"Hey, Emma. What's going on?"

"Charlie, it's Dash. It appears he pulled one of his disappearing acts. I was wondering if you had any idea where he likes to go."

"I thought his pen was fixed."

"It is, but the gate wasn't properly latched." She didn't mention any names. She let him assume it was her.

"Well, um, Dash has a way of wandering about. He could be anywhere."

He wasn't telling her anything she didn't already know. "What does he like?"

"To eat? Well...that little goat could eat all day if you let him. And he has a sweet tooth."

Food. Where would Dash find something to eat? And then the answer came to her. "Thanks, Charlie. You've given me an idea."

"Do you want me to come over and help you look?"

"Thanks. But we've got this. You're already doing enough by stepping up and helping out with the farm while my brother is out of town. I know how much my brother and Aster appreciate your help."

"I don't mind. Neighbors help neighbors here. You know that if you need any assistance to let me know."

"I will. Thanks again." Emma slipped the phone into her pocket. "Nikki, I think I might know where he went."

Nikki ran up to her. "Where?"

"Did you secure the gate?"

"Uh-huh. But there's something you should know."

Emma's heart sank. Surely there couldn't be another problem. She hadn't even solved this problem yet. What was it with this day? It had started off so well, and now it was going downhill quickly.

Emma swallowed hard, straightened her shoulders and then asked, "What is it?"

"It's Billy. He's gone too."

She took a moment to digest this information. "Are the rest of the goats there?"

"Yes."

"Are you positive?"

"Yes."

"Okay. So Charlie told me that Dash likes to eat. A lot." When Nikki nodded in agreement, Emma said, "Then I have an idea where we might find them."

She glanced down at Nikki's flip-flops. "You better go change into some socks and shoes. We have some walking ahead of us."

"Okay." Nikki ran to the house.

Buzz-buzz.

What was it now? It seemed like her phone rang more now that she was on the island than when she'd been in Nashville, both from her agent and from JT. As she lifted her phone, she saw that it was JT. Again.

Worried about the goat and upset that she'd let this happen on her watch, she wasn't in the best of moods. She pressed decline. They had absolutely nothing left to talk about.

Maybe she should have answered. Maybe it would have let him know he no longer mattered to her and that she had risen above it all. But she hadn't risen above it. She was still hurt and beyond disappointed in him, in herself, in romance in general. Maybe someday in the future she'd be able to treat him like a mere acquaintance—someone she'd once known—but that wasn't today.

"I'm ready," Nikki said.

"Let's go." They started walking.

"Where are we going?"

"To the orchard. I hear Dash has a sweet tooth. He's probably in the orchard gorging himself on the sun-ripened apples."

Nikki's eyes widened. "He does love apples. I bet you're right. You're the best, Auntie Em."

If she was the best, she would have paid closer attention, and the gate wouldn't have only been partially closed. And then Dash and his buddy Billy wouldn't be off on an adventure.

CHAPTER THIRTEEN

SOMETHING IS WRONG.

As Noah stood on the beach at the site of the stage, he lowered his phone and stared at it for a moment. He attempted to make sense of what he'd heard on the other end. Emma must be at her brother's farm. Noah had been there recently, building new houses for the goats. He wondered how much Emma knew about farms and goats. He had to admit he knew nothing. He was a city boy, born and bred. Living on the island was a big change for him, but it was still a long way from farm life.

Noah tried to tell himself that it wasn't any of his business. That the goat would show up and in the meantime, Emma could deal with it. Yet he'd heard the worry in her voice. And there was that thing with her brother and Aster that no one was talking about.

He wasn't the type to sit back while friends were in trouble—not when he could help. And Emma did have a lot to manage—things she was doing to help others. Someone should help her out.

So he collected his tools and headed for his golf cart. He'd invested in one as soon as he figured out what he wanted to do for a living on the island. There was no way he could transport his woodworks on a bicycle, and he wasn't carrying everything by foot, especially when there were too many things to carry at once.

With his tools stowed away in the back of the cart, he pulled out and headed south of the town where the Bell Farm resided. He was certain by the time he arrived that the goat would be located. But that didn't stop him from searching the sides of the road for the goat as he drove.

He recalled this past autumn when he'd been passing through town, and three of the Bell's goats had wandered into town. By the time he'd happened upon them, Aster and Sam's mother had the goats under control.

This time he knew Aster and Sam's mother weren't around to help. Word around town was that Helen and Walter had gone off on a vacation to celebrate Walter's retirement. And without Sam around that left Emma alone to sort out the mess.

He pressed harder on the accelerator. His irritation over her costing him the house of his dreams drifted to the back of his mind. At this moment, she was just someone in trouble, and he wanted to do what he could to help out.

The ride out of town was short. Soon he made a left-hand turn onto a stone driveway. The cart bounced over the stones. He parked next to the house. He scanned the area for Emma or Nikki. Neither of them were in sight.

He moved toward the back of the house, where the penned-in area was for the goats. His gaze scanned the area.

"Maaah. Maaah." The goat call was repeated over and over again.

They missed their companion. Sympathy welled up in Noah. He wanted to tell them that it'd be all right, but he doubted they would understand him.

He turned in a circle, taking in everything around him. When he spotted the back of Emma and Nikki as they made their way up a slight hill, he started after them.

"Emma!" He picked up his pace. "Emma, wait up!"

They paused and turned. Emma's eyes widened while Nikki looked relieved to see him. He quickened his steps.

When he reached them, Nikki asked, "Are you going to help us find Dash?"

"Yes, I am."

Emma's brows drew together. "We don't need any help. We've got this."

He knew why she was shutting him out. He'd shut her out first, during their run. "Emma, please. Let me stick around."

Nikki turned pleading eyes to her aunt. "Please, Auntie Em. We have to find them."

"Them?" he asked. "There's more than one goat missing?"

"Yeah," Nikki said. "Billy's gone too."

Emma didn't say a word. She just stood there, staring at him like she was mad at him. He couldn't exactly blame her. But if he could move past the fact that she'd delayed him in turning in his offer for the house, then she could shove aside her hurt feelings over him bailing on their run to the beach.

The only problem was she didn't know what had happened with his phone call from his real estate agent. And as his gaze moved to Nikki, he didn't feel that now was the time to get into it.

"Sounds like I'm just in time to help you hunt for them." His gaze met Emma's, and he could see the resistance reflected in her eyes. "From what I hear, Dash is fast and ornery."

Emma didn't say anything but Nikki did. "He is. You should see Daddy try to catch him. It's funny. I wish Daddy was here. He'd know how to find Dash and Billy." She glanced at her aunt. "Can we call him?"

Emma pursed her rosy lips as though she were giving thought to the appropriate answer. "How about we call him later? After we find Dash."

"Okay." Nikki huffed out a breath as her little shoulders lowered. "Will Daddy and Aster be home soon? I miss them."

Emma wrapped her arm around Nikki's shoulders and pulled her close. "They will be here as soon as they possibly can. They miss you too."

Nikki nodded as though she understood, but Noah wondered how much she really understood. Something told him the little girl didn't know much more about why her parents were away than he did. Poor kid. It must be rough.

"I see something moving!" Nikki took off running.

"Nikki, don't go too far!"

"I won't. Dash! Billy!" She ran up the hill.

Noah watched her little legs go. He had no idea what she'd seen move because all he saw were some green leaves fluttering in the breeze and a few birds flying overhead. Although, he did hope she saw the goats. While this was a small island in general, when two goats were off on an adventure, it was a rather large area to search.

They quietly followed Nikki as she blazed her way to the top of the grassy hill. It wasn't a peaceful silence. Tension radiated from Emma. He couldn't exactly blame her. He'd been rather uptight since losing the house. Maybe it was time they talked—well, after the goats were found.

"Maybe we should split up," he said. "We could cover more territory quickly."

Emma nodded. "Sounds like a good idea. Why don't you go that way?" She pointed southward. "I'm going to keep going eastward toward the cliffs."

"Shall we meet back here in say ten minutes?"

They both consulted the time on their phones. And then Emma nodded. "Sounds good." She hesitated. "And thank you."

"Neighbors help neighbors." He'd heard that a number of times since moving to the island.

"But we're not neighbors."

"Okay islanders help islanders. And don't say that you live in Nashville. You were born here. The island will always be a part of you."

She nodded. "See you soon." And then she picked up her pace. "Nikki! Let's go this way." She pointed toward the easterly side of the island.

As he turned southward, he wished he hadn't suggested that they split up. Even dealing with Emma's displeasure was better than being without her. As soon as the implications of the thought came to him, he dismissed it. At this point, he wasn't even sure they were friends.

___ele___

No sign of the goats.

Emma was really getting worried. Where could those little goats have gotten to? They'd searched through the trees, but there had been no sign of them. She'd thought for sure they'd have been there gorging themselves on the fallen apples.

Nikki's constant chatter had grown quiet. She was worried. And Emma had no way to comfort her. She wished her big brother was there. Sam would know exactly what to do. It was so tempting to call him, but she just couldn't worry him.

This was her responsibility. She just needed to keep searching. And with Noah there, they'd be able to cover twice as much ground. What had made Noah decide to show up?

His willingness to help out said a lot about him. Maybe if they'd met under different circumstances, things wouldn't be so complicated between them. Maybe they'd be good friends. The idea appealed to her.

"Auntie Em, what are we going to do?"

She glanced over at her niece, who looked totally wiped out from their hike. "We are going to have a late lunch."

"But we can't. We have to find Dash and Billy. What if they need us?"

"Those little goats are smart. I'm sure they're off enjoying their adventure. And when they get tired, they'll make their way home. I bet they're home now, eating all of the flowers around the house."

Nikki's face lit up. "I bet you're right. Aster gets so upset when they get into her flowers and ruin them. I'll go see."

"Nikki, wait." Emma watched as her energetic niece race toward the house.

Nikki didn't seem to hear her as she continued running. Emma wasn't that energetic. She just kept walking at a steady pace.

When she reached the spot where she'd agreed to meet up with Noah, she found him waiting for her with no goats in sight. "I take it your search wasn't any more productive than ours."

He shook his head. "Sorry. But they're probably back at the house, waiting for someone to feed them."

"I just told Nikki the same thing. Do you think we could be that lucky?"

He shrugged. "Let's go find out." They walked a short stretch before he said, "Listen, about the other day, I'm sorry."

She glanced at him. "Sorry for what?"

"Bailing on our run without explaining why. I'd just gotten some unexpected news."

"Bad news I take it."

He nodded. "I should have said something then."

"It's okay. I know something about getting bad news and not taking it well. After all, I'm here instead of in Nashville."

"I guess you do. How are you doing?"

She shrugged. "I've been too busy to think much about it. I was planning on spending the day at the beach with Nikki. I don't normally get to spend much time with her, and I thought this was the perfect time to make some memories with her, but the goat escape ruined our plans."

"And I bet they're having the time of their lives."

"You're probably right. I just hope we find them soon."

"I'll keep looking," he said. "Where do you suggest I search next?"

"Nowhere. We're going back to the house for lunch. Have you eaten?" When he shook his head, she said, "Then you'll join us, and we'll figure out our next steps."

He hesitated. "Agreed."

"I'm just not sure what we'll eat. The house doesn't have much in it since Sam and Aster are out of town."

"I can run into town and pick something up."

"Good idea. I'll phone in an order to the Lighthouse. It's where I was planning to pick up a picnic lunch for Nikki and me." She pulled her phone from her pocket. "Anything special you want?"

He shook his head. "What are you having?"

"An Italian sub and chips."

"You know who makes really good subs?"

She smiled. "Wait. Is the newbie about to tell me where to eat on the island? You do know I grew up here, right?"

He laughed. "Okay. So where was I going to suggest?"

"Hamming It Up Deli." Then she stuck her tongue out at him.

He laughed even more. The sound of his laughter and the happiness that shone in his eyes lifted her spirits.

"I'm glad I can amuse you." She rolled her eyes. "Now what would you like to eat?"

"I'll have an Italian sub too. And one of those dill pickles."

"They come with all of their sandwiches unless you tell them that you don't want one."

"Oh. Okay."

She placed the call as they neared the house. They found Nikki sitting on the steps with her elbows resting on her knees and her chin perched upon her palms. That definitely wasn't a happy face.

The other goats lined up at the fence, staring at them. "Maaah. Maaah."

The sound was sad and mournful. Emma's heart squeezed. If she didn't know better, she'd think the goats were begging her to bring Dash and Billy back to them. Sympathy welled up in her. They were confused and sad. And there wasn't anything she could do to soothe their worries—not until the other goats were found.

"I'll run and pick up lunch," he said softly. Then he nodded toward Nikki. "She looks like she could use a friend."

"They aren't here." Nikki's voice wavered as tears welled up in her eyes.

Emma was really starting to worry. How much trouble could those little goats get into? She honestly didn't want to think about it.

She walked over and sat down on the step next to her niece. She wrapped her arm around her and pulled her close. "I promise that we'll find them. After all, this island isn't that big. We'll search it from end to end if we have to."

"It's all my fault." Her voice wavered with emotion. "If I'd have double-checked the gate, they wouldn't be lost."

She hugged Nikki tighter. "Stop fretting. It's all going to be okay. They'll be back."

They sat there quietly for a bit. It wasn't the fun afternoon at the beach that she'd been envisioning, but she would find time to squeeze that in before she left the island...if she left Bluestar. Her future was still up in the air.

Chapter Fourteen

H E WAS GROWING CONCERNED.
And he wasn't normally a worrier.

Noah was used to high stress and not sweating the small stuff where finances were concerned. But his job had been all about computers and numbers, not sweet little girls with tears in their eyes and a beautiful woman with worry lines on her face.

His ex-wife, Gwen, had never needed him this way. She liked to have him around like an accessory she wore on her arm for social events. When the subject of having children came up, she initially evaded the subject. A couple of years into the marriage, she became candid with him. She didn't want to be distracted from her law career. She wanted to make partner in one of the country's biggest law firms. Having a baby would delay her ascent to the top.

Now that he'd been on the island for a while, and his life was totally different, he wondered if he'd missed out on something special by not having a family. Getting to know Nikki certainly had him rethinking what he wanted out of life.

As he drove into town, he pressed the accelerator to the floor. He grew frustrated with the slow speed of the cart versus that of a car. If this island allowed real automobiles, he'd be in town already.

Throughout his drive, he scanned the sides of the road. There was something about the goats at the Bell farm. They were more pets than anything else. And from what he'd witnessed, they all had unique personalities.

He parked down the block from the deli. Even though it was the middle of the afternoon, the town was hopping. The tourist trade was alive and well in Bluestar.

"Noah!"

He stopped and glanced around. When he spotted Ethan standing in front of The Elegant Bakery, he waved.

Ethan walked over to him. "I was just at the beach. I thought I'd catch up with you and see how the stage is coming along."

"I was working on it earlier, but then Emma needed some help."

"Help?" Ethan's brows rose with interest.

Noah nodded. "It seems Dash and Billy made a break for it. You haven't by chance seen any goats around town?"

Ethan smiled and shook his head. "Dash is the orneriest goat. I'm sure they haven't wandered far."

"We've been searching for them for the past hour or so, and there's no sign of them."

The smile slipped from Ethan's face. "They're really gone?"

Noah shrugged. "It appears so."

"Who is searching for them?"

"Emma, Nikki, and myself. Emma's worried that the news will get back to her brother, and she doesn't want to worry him. And Nikki is worked up."

"Does Hannah know?"

"I don't think so. But I've got to go. They're waiting on lunch, and then we're heading back out to search some more."

"Oh, okay. I'll see you later."

"See ya." Noah turned toward the deli.

He hoped the food would be waiting for him. He'd already been gone too long. He wouldn't put it past Emma and Nikki to head back out without eating.

He knew technically none of this was his problem, but he wouldn't think of doing anything else until he was certain the goats were safe and sound. And then he would say goodbye and head back to the beach to work. It was nothing more than a friend would do.

Lunch didn't have much taste.

Emma forced herself to sit at her brother's kitchen table and eat the food Noah had been nice enough to pick up for them. Any other time a sandwich from Hamming It Up would hit the spot but not today—not when she stared across the table at her niece, who'd barely touched her food.

"You have to eat more if you want to go back out searching."

Nikki picked up a chip and then dropped it again. "I'm not hungry." She glanced at Emma's plate. "You aren't eating either."

Her niece had a point. Emma picked up her sandwich. "Okay. I'll finish mine, and you do the same. Then we can get going."

As she took another bite, she glanced over at Noah, who was almost finished eating. At least one of them had an appetite. He'd been working hard on the stage, until she'd distracted him with her problems. She felt guilty for drawing him away from his work.

She swallowed. "Noah, you don't have to stay. I know you have other obligations."

He shook his head. "It'll all wait."

Knock-knock.

"I'll get it." Nikki dropped her sandwich on her plate, pushed her chair back, and then headed for the back door. "It's Uncle Ethan."

"Well, invite him in," Emma said.

"He's not alone."

"Invite them both in." Emma stood.

"They won't all fit."

"What?" She headed to the door with Noah just steps behind her.

When she looked through the screen door, she immediately saw Ethan and Hannah. She smiled. It'd be good to have them there to help with the search.

"Hi," Emma said. "I'm so glad you're here."

"You still haven't found the goats?" Hannah asked.

Emma shook her head.

"Well, we're here to help." Then Hannah and Ethan stepped off to the side. "We're all here to help."

Emma was confused until her gaze moved past her sister and down to the backyard, where Birdie and Betty Simon stood as well as twenty-five or so other Bluestar residents. Emma gasped. She pressed a hand to her open mouth. She didn't know what to say.

She turned to glance at Noah. "Did you do this?"

Before he could answer, Hannah said, "Don't get upset with him. He didn't have anything to do with everyone showing up. He asked Ethan if he'd seen the goats in town. Ethan told me, and I told Ms. Birdie. And she knew of some people that would help in the search. There would be more people, but they're still working. They'll be here later if the goats aren't located by then."

Emma couldn't believe everyone had dropped what they'd been doing to go there and help her. Perhaps she'd been in Nashville far too long. She'd forgotten how the people of Bluestar were always willing to lend a helping hand.

Emma pushed open the screen door and stepped out onto the porch. "Thank you all for coming. You're so amazing. I'm hoping to find the goats before my brother and Aster call this evening. As you all know, they have enough on their minds. They don't need to worry about the farm too."

"We'll find them," called out Mr. Evans, the owner of Spot Clean dry cleaners.

"Yeah!" a chorus of voices followed.

"Let's get started," Pam, the mail carrier, said.

"We'll have them found before Sam and Aster find out," Josie Turner, manager of The Brass Anchor Inn, said.

Emma smiled. She had missed the strong bonds of Bluestar. When one of its residents was in need, the others pitched in—even if it meant closing the shop early or dropping a project.

Tears of gratitude filled her eyes. "Thank you all. We need to split up so we can cover more ground."

"I've got that covered," Birdie said as she held up a map. She glanced around for a place to spread out the map and then spotted the old picnic table beneath the oak tree in the backyard. She gingerly made her way down the steps. "This way, everyone. I'll give you a map with your designated area marked out on it."

Emma stood at the doorway and marveled at how Birdie took charge of the situation. She was blessed to have all of these people in her life.

"Noah, can you give me a hand?" Betty Simon asked. "I have supplies in both Birdie's and my cart. On this hot day, people are going to need water. And I brought dinner supplies if this search runs long."

"Excuse me." Noah rushed past Emma and was out the door.

"Auntie Em, let's go see where we get to search." Nikki pulled on her arm.

"First, did you eat enough?" She glanced inside the house and noticed Nikki's half-eaten sandwich.

Nikki vigorously nodded her head. "I'm full."

Emma wasn't so sure she believed her, but she supposed Nikki had eaten enough for now. Come dinnertime, she'd insist Nikki clean off her plate.

"Go to the bathroom while I clear the table. Then we'll head out."

Nikki smiled for the first time that afternoon. "We'll definitely find the goats with all of these people helping."

"I think you're right." At least that was what she wanted to believe for all of their sakes.

"Do you think I can call Kelly and see if she can come over?"

"I don't see why not."

"I'll be back." Nikki ran off.

Thwack-thwack.

The screen door swung shut. Emma glanced over, expecting to find Noah with his arms full of supplies but instead it was her sister.

"Hey. How are you?" Hannah asked.

With her sister, she could be honest. "Worried."

"Why didn't you call me as soon as the goats escaped?"

Emma sighed, feeling inadequate. "Because I thought I could handle it without bothering anyone.

I should have known with Dash involved that he wouldn't make this easy on me."

"That little goat is always up to something."

"And now if we don't find them, Sam and Aster will find out. Nikki already asked to call them but I put her off. They have so much on their minds. If only I had paid more attention. I should have been there with Nikki when she went to see the goats. If I had, I would have made sure the gate was closed securely."

"Emma, stop. This isn't your fault. It's no one's fault. It was an accident." Hannah's gaze searched hers. "You believe me, don't you?"

Emma shrugged. "It's just such bad timing."

"Sam and Aster don't need to know about any of this until they get home."

"But Nikki—"

"Nikki, will understand when we ask her to save this story for when her parents get home." Hannah paused. "Isn't it strange saying Nikki's parents?"

"I was thinking the same thing. Even though they aren't quite married, it feels as though they are an official family. And here I was beginning to think Sam would never let himself fall in love again."

"Just goes to prove that miracles do exist."

"I guess so."

She could use one or two in her life. And as soon as she thought that, she regretted it. There were people with a lot larger problems than her own that could use a miracle. She just had to sort out what she was going to do next with her life.

CHAPTER FIFTEEN

THEY JUST HAD TO find them.

Noah couldn't imagine where two little goats could have gotten off to that they hadn't found them yet. He wanted to fix this for both Emma and her sweet niece. He could not believe the goats were that good at hiding. But then again, he knew nothing about goats, other than they were cute and definitely had minds of their own.

As he'd unloaded the food and drinks from the two golf carts, more people showed up to help. He'd never lived in a place quite like Bluestar. His ex would have hated this place. She liked her fancy restaurants and country club. He wasn't sure there was any place on the island that required a tie for admittance—if there was he hadn't found it yet.

With the food placed on the kitchen table, Betty thanked him. He made his way back outside. He moved the coolers Birdie had brought and placed them in the yard near the picnic table. When he opened them, he found they already had bags of ice. He added water bottles to one cooler and soda pop to the other cooler. He was impressed with the thoroughness of the ladies' planning.

All the search sectors were handed out by the time Noah, Emma, and Nikki made it to the front of the line at the picnic table. Ms. Birdie frowned as she gazed down at her map. "There's just one place left to check. It's the farthest from the farm."

"Where's that?" Emma asked.

"We don't mind the distance," Noah added.

"It's out along the bluffs," Birdie said.

"We could take Sam's pickup," Emma said. "It'll save time."

"Okay." Noah reached for the map. "Let's go."

"But Kelly isn't here yet." Nikki's gaze moved toward the side of the house. "I promised I'd wait for her."

"Actually," Birdie said, "I was going to ask if you would stay with me and be my assistant. I figure those two unruly goats are bound to be bored about now and make their way home for some good food. And if they show up, and I'm here by myself, I'm not sure I'm fast enough to catch them. So what do you say? Will you help me out?"

Nikki was quiet for a moment. Her head tilted to the side as she considered the idea. "I can do that."

"Thank you so much." Birdie sent her a great big smile.

Then Nikki turned to Emma and Noah with a worried look. "I'm sorry, guys. I'm needed here." Then with the sincerest expression, Nikki asked, "Are you sure you'll be okay without me?"

Noah struggled to keep a straight face. Nikki was just so cute. And acted like she was six going on sixteen.

While he struggled to keep his amusement to himself, Emma said calmly, "I think we can manage, but thank you for staying here. If those goats do return home, it's important that someone they know and trust is here to help lead them back to their pen."

Nikki nodded. "And I'll make sure to double-check the latch."

Emma gave her niece a hug. Noah could so easily imagine her as a mother, hugging her own daughter. She would be a great one. She was patient, kind, and understanding. Someone would eventually be lucky to have her as a partner in life.

If he were to consider marrying again, he wanted to build a life with someone whose values aligned with his—someone different from his ex. He wondered if Emma was considering a different future—perhaps a quieter life on the island.

He gave himself a mental shake. Whatever Emma decided to do was none of his business. He needed to focus on finding the goats and then get back to work. Spending too much time with Emma in such a domestic role was playing tricks on his mind.

"We better get going," he said.

"Let me just grab the keys to the pickup." Emma hurried toward the house.

"I'll meet you at the truck."

"You don't have to hurry or anything. We've got things under control here. And I picked the most remote and beautiful spot for you and Emma." Birdie winked at him.

He couldn't believe his own ears. Birdie was playing matchmaker with him and Emma. He needed to straighten things out with her.

Just as he was about to clarify things with Birdie, Emma returned to the porch and shouted, "I found the keys. Let's go."

Birdie smiled and gestured for him to get going.

"It's not like you think," he said.

"Just enjoy the afternoon," Birdie said softly so only he could hear her. "Don't overthink things."

"Noah, are you coming?" Emma sent him a frustrated look.

There was no time to set Birdie straight about his relationship with Emma. Besides, he had this feeling she'd only hear what she wanted. But in time, Birdie would see that she was wrong about them. They were friends. That was all. At least he considered them friends. He wasn't so sure if Emma felt the same way.

Emma was in the driver's seat of the old robin's egg–blue pickup when he reached it. He pivoted for the passenger's seat. Once he was seated, she took off. He hadn't even had the door closed the whole way.

"I thought vehicles were restricted on the island," he said in an attempt to make casual conversation.

"There are exceptions. Could you imagine trying to tend to a farm this size with a golf cart?"

As the pickup moved over the uneven ground, he was jostled in his seat. His fingertips dug into the armrest as he struggled to stay in his seat. "I can't imagine a cart would make it over this bumpy terrain."

"But if Sam wants to drive his pickup into town to drop off produce and such, he has to get a morning pass. The town tries to get vehicles off the roads by nine a.m., before the tourists are out in full force, but as with everything, there are always exceptions."

"I already learned what happens if you don't have a permit."

"Ah. You got fined?"

He nodded. "I did. And I got a stern warning not to do it again."

"You aren't alone. Will Campbell was caught at Christmastime in this very truck going across town towing a sleigh. Even though he knows the sheriff personally, he got ticketed."

Noah searched his memory for someone by that name, but he couldn't place it. "Who's this Will you mentioned?"

"If you haven't met Will yet, you will soon. He's my stepbrother. He and Darla Evans are engaged. Her father is here helping with the search."

"There's a lot of that going around the island."

"What? Engagements?" She glanced his way as he nodded. "So I'm not the only one that's noticed the love bug has struck the island."

"It won't get to me. I'm immune." He crossed his arms.

She let out a laugh. "You say that like it's a virus."

"Might as well be a virus. It starts with your mind and then invades your heart. And then without warning, you are left disillusioned and your heart left in tatters. Been there. Done that." He wasn't going back for more.

"Wow! I thought I was jaded."

Feeling like he was on a roll, he kept going. "Actually love is worse than a virus. At least with germs, you get over them rather quickly. The love bug can linger for years and then end abruptly, sometimes without any warning."

Emma cast him a sideways glance. "You sound like you have experience with this."

He shrugged. "Divorced."

"That explains it. Sorry to hear it."

"It's for the best." It had taken him almost a year to be able to say that but now he was able to see that they'd never wanted the same things in life. He didn't want to talk about his past. It was time to change the subject. "And all I want to do is find these two goats. A lot of people showed up to help."

"Yes, they did. They too want to find the goats before my brother and Aster find out."

He still didn't have a clue what was going on with them. "I'm sure if your brother and Aster find out about the missing goats that they won't be upset with you."

"It's not me I'm worried about. It's Aster." Then she paused and glanced at him. "You still don't know, do you?"

"Know what?"

"Why they aren't here on the island."

"Nah. I figured it was none of my business. I'm just happy to be able to help out."

"Aster said I could tell you. I...well, anyway she flew to California with my brother to be a witness in a murder trial."

"Murder?" He had to admit he hadn't seen that coming. Bluestar seemed so far removed from the underbelly of society that he hadn't been expecting something so serious. "Was she the target?"

"In a way." Emma went on to tell him the sad story. "And that's why we're all trying to do our part to support them. This can't be easy on either of them."

"I understand." He felt good that Emma had trusted him enough to confide in him.

Then he glanced over at her as she navigated the pickup over the uneven ground. His gaze took in her hair pulled back in a ponytail. And how her tanned face only had the slightest amount of makeup. Not that she needed any—she was a natural beauty.

And then his gaze paused on her lips. He wondered what it'd be like to kiss her. As soon as he realized the direction his thoughts had drifted in, he halted them.

They'd barely figured out this friend thing; he was quite certain any advance on his part would be totally and utterly rebuffed. Too bad. Again, he stopped his thoughts. It wasn't like he wanted to start a relationship or anything.

The pickup hit a hole in the ground and jostled Noah. His shoulder hit against the door. He resisted the urge to rub his arm. The tires continued to hit rocks and uneven ground.

"Sorry about that." She slowed the pickup down to a crawl. "The closer we get to the bluffs, the rougher the ground."

He needed some fresh air to clear his mind. "Why don't we park and walk from here?"

"You don't mind?"

"No. The doc says I'm supposed to get in a lot more activity." Now what had he gone and said that for. He hadn't talked about his health problems with anyone.

She was quiet for a moment, as though considering his words. Then she slowed the truck to a stop and put it in park. "Sounds like a good idea."

They exited the vehicle and headed closer to the bluffs. They were both quiet as they scanned the area for the goats. There wasn't any sign of them. And even though he didn't know anything about goats, he just couldn't see them wandering all of the way out there.

The only thing they might eat was tall grass that swayed in the breeze and some weeds. They could get all of that closer to home, so why would they venture this far?

"Maybe I should call Hannah and see if the goats have been spotted." Emma pulled out her phone and stared at it. "Or maybe not."

"No signal?"

She shook her head. "Not one single bar." With a sigh, she shoved her phone back into her pocket. "We just have to find those goats. They are so much more than farm animals to Sam and Nikki."

"Don't worry. This island isn't that big. We'll search it from end to end if we have to."

"Knowing Dash, we just might have to do that."

And so they made their way to the bluffs' edge. It was a remarkable view with the waves crashing against the rocks down below. No one could survive such a steep fall, but from everything he'd learned about Dash and his buddy, they weren't stupid. They'd want to go somewhere with food and things to amuse them. This wide-open space with its rocky terrain didn't fit the bill.

Still, they were there, so they continued to search, and then they could officially mark it off their list. The time had been spent in silence as each of them were lost in their thoughts. When he glanced her way, he saw the worry lines etched upon her beautiful face. He had this urge to smooth them away. But the only way that would happen was to find those goats and then complete the preparations for the concert. For any of that to be accomplished, they needed to search a more likely spot for the goats.

He came to a stop. "I think we should head back. There's nothing out here to suggest they came this way."

She turned to him and then nodded. "You're right. I just don't understand why we can't find them."

"Maybe you should ask your brother where they might be." Sam knew more about the goats and their habits than anyone on the island.

"No. This isn't his problem. They escaped on my watch. I have to fix this." Determination glinted in her eyes.

"He'll understand. After all, it's happened to him before."

"But this is different. He's not here and he's dealing with so much already." Her voice wobbled with emotion. "Why does it feel like everything I touch ends up being a disaster?"

He stepped closer to her. "That's not true."

"Really? Because I got engaged, and that blew up for all of the world to see. Then there's the concert to prepare for, and there's a problem getting the supplies we need. Then I was going to take Nikki to the beach to have some fun and make some good memories, but the goats escaped. If I was a betting person, I'd say the odds were against me making anything work out." Her eyes shimmered with unshed tears. She blinked them away.

He didn't know what to say, so he said nothing. Instead he stepped up to her and wrapped his arms around her, drawing her close. At first, she was hesitant, but then she gave in. Her head rested against his shoulder as her arms wrapped around his waist. She felt good in his arms, as though they were two pieces of the same puzzle.

As the waves crashed against the rocks below, they stood in each other's arms. And for that precious moment, he finally felt as if he were home. It wasn't about having the right house in the right location. It was all about having the right person in his life.

When Emma pulled back ever so slightly to gaze up at him, the urge to kiss her grew within him. His gaze dipped to her rosy lips. The breath hitched in his lungs.

A quick kiss and then he'd have it out of his system. He would know that the real thing just wasn't as good as what he'd been imagining. One kiss and then he could move on.

But what would she think? His gaze rose to meet hers. Unspoken questions shone in her eyes. Was she wondering what it'd be like if they were to kiss?

As though she sensed the direction of his thoughts, she pulled away. With a sigh, he realized her answer. She wasn't curious about him the way he was about her. Disappointment grounded him once more.

"We should get back to the house." She turned and started back toward the pickup. "Maybe there's news."

On the walk back to the pickup, Noah felt like he'd just made a fool of himself. She'd needed comfort because she was worried about her family, and he'd let his thoughts spiral in a totally wrong direction. What was wrong with him?

He had to do better. He would do better.

Still, there was a part of him that regretted that she'd pulled away before he'd been able to kiss her. The other part of him was relieved he hadn't complicated their relationship, because he liked having Emma for a friend.

She wasn't some spoiled star that had to have designer water and was too caught up in her own life that she didn't have time to worry about the people around her. Emma was a genuinely warm and caring person—someone he wanted to get to know better. Much better.

CHAPTER SIXTEEN

H AD HE ALMOST KISSED her?
On the ride back to the farmhouse, Emma's mind replayed the scene by the bluffs over and over again. She tried to convince herself that she'd imagined the way he'd looked at her—the interest that flared in his eyes. But she couldn't fool herself. She knew when a guy was interested in her. Noah was definitely interested. Her heart skipped a beat.

But she wasn't ready to get involved with anyone. She still had that diamond ring stuffed in the back of the drawer at her mother's house. Even though she'd told JT they were over, the ring was still a link between them. She didn't want any strings that led back to him. She didn't want anything to do with him.

She needed to get rid of the ring. The sooner, the better. She thought of mailing it back to JT, but she didn't know his mailing address. And then a thought came to her. She could mail it to her agent and have him messenger it over to JT. She didn't care how it got back to JT. She just wanted it gone.

And she didn't feel bad about putting her manager in the middle of this mess, because the whole relationship had been the brainchild of her manager and JT's manager. They thought if she went out with

JT a few times that it would produce good publicity for both of them.

The only problem was that Emma had forgotten they were merely putting on a show for the cameras. She'd let herself fall for JT's smooth lines and his sexy smile. Why had she been such a fool?

"It looks like others are back." Noah's voice drew her from her thoughts.

She slowed the pickup to a stop. There was a group of people near the picnic table that was now laden with food and drinks. People were lined up to fill their plates. And it was all thanks to Birdie and Betty. She didn't know how she'd ever thank them.

Then her gaze moved to the goat pen. She did a quick head count and found they were still short two goats. "It doesn't look like anyone found the goats."

"You never know. Maybe they put them in the barn." Noah opened his door.

Could she be that lucky? She doubted it. And with the sun sinking in the sky, she knew her brother would be checking in soon.

She climbed out of the truck and shut the door. She scanned the area for Hannah. She was nowhere in sight. Next she looked for Nikki. She found her niece sitting on the porch next to Kelly. Nikki wasn't eating. She was just sitting there with a sad look on her face.

Buzz-buzz.

Dread filled her chest as she withdrew her phone. Was Sam calling early today? She checked the caller ID and found it was indeed her brother. Her heart sank. She'd let him down. The last thing she ever wanted to do.

She considered sending the call to voicemail, but he would just call Hannah. And Emma wanted him to hear the news from her because losing the goats had happened on her watch.

"I need to take this," she said to Noah.

He nodded in understanding. "I'll go see if Nikki had anything to eat."

"Thanks." She stepped away from the people. Then she pressed the phone to her ear. "Hey, Sam. How are things going?"

"Slowly."

"Aster still hasn't testified?"

"No. They're keeping her testimony until the end. The prosecution wants to put all of the medical and expert witnesses on first, and then they want her to follow up, leaving the jury with a more personal, emotional view of the devastation the creep is capable of." A sense of worry threaded through Sam's voice.

"I'm so sorry, Sam. That sounds horrible. How are you holding up?"

"I'm doing okay. It's Aster I'm worried about. She doesn't eat or sleep much."

"I wish there was something I could do to make this easier for the two of you."

"You're already doing it. You're there for Nikki when we can't be there. How's she doing?"

Emma pivoted around so she could see the porch. Noah was crouched in front of Nikki. She looked like she was crying and Noah was comforting her. Every hour that passed with no sign of the goats, the tension was rising for everyone.

Emma didn't want to tell her brother what had happened, but he'd eventually find out, if not from her then from Hannah or Nikki. She had no choice but to tell him, and it made her feel awful.

"Um...Sam, there's something I need to tell you."

His voice took on an urgent tone. "What? Is it Nikki? Did something happen to her?"

"No. She's perfectly fine."

"Then what is it? I can hear it in your voice. Something is the matter."

"It's Dash. He got loose again."

Sam audibly sighed. "Is that all? You had me worried."

"Well, um...yeah." She was surprised by his nonchalant response. "I'm sorry this happened."

"Don't worry about it. Dash has a mind of his own. He'll turn up soon enough."

She worried her bottom lip. "It's more than just Dash. Billy took off with him."

"Doesn't surprise me. Those two are always up to something. You don't know how much I wish I was there chasing around goats. At least then I would feel like I was actually doing something productive. The only thing I can do here is pace and offer some encouraging words. And between you and me, I'm not sure I'm that encouraging."

Her heart went out to him. "Oh, Sam, I'm sure your presence is a huge comfort to her."

"I hope you're right. I just haven't felt this helpless in a long time."

"Just keep doing what you're doing, and I'll work on finding the goats."

"Did you check the apple orchard? Dash loves to eat the apples."

"They weren't there." Just then Aster's voice could be heard in the background. It wasn't the right time to tell him that a search party had been formed to hunt for the goats. "I should let you go." Her gaze moved to Nikki. "Nikki is just getting some dinner, but I can get her for you."

"No. Let her eat. I'll call her a little later."

"Okay. I'm really sorry about the goats."

"I'm sure they'll turn up by the time I call Nikki."

"I hope you're right." They said goodbye, and then Emma headed toward the house. She stopped next to Nikki. "Did you get something to eat?"

Nikki shook her head. "I wasn't hungry."

"You have to eat. Go get something."

"Do I have to?"

Emma nodded. "You do. And I just spoke to your father. He didn't want to interrupt your meal so he said he would call you later."

Her gaze sought out Emma's. "No one has seen the goats."

Emma wrapped an arm around Nikki's slim shoulders. "We'll find them."

"You promise?"

"I promise." After all, the island was only so big.

Emma's gaze rose to meet Noah's. He nodded his agreement. In his gaze she found reassurance.

She just had no idea where those goats could have gotten off to. And the longer they searched for them, the farther behind they fell on the preparations for the concert.

Buzz-buzz.

Worried it might be Sam again, she pulled her phone from her pocket. When she saw it was her agent, she sent the call to voicemail. Her phone was nearly full of messages. She should clean it, but it just wasn't a priority at the moment.

Noah held out a plate of pasta and a cold-cut sandwich. "Here. Take this and go eat."

"I can't take your food."

"I'll get another plate." When she hesitated, he said, "You need to eat something before you drop, and I promise I'll get something for myself."

"Thanks." She walked with Nikki and her friend back to the porch.

They climbed the steps and took a seat. She ate quietly. Nikki and Kelly made short work of the food on their plates. Emma was pleased to see Nikki eating something.

"Can Kelly and I go play on the tire swing?"

"I don't see why not. Just stay where I can see you."

"We will." The girls took off down the steps and across the yard to a big, old oak tree.

Emma's gaze naturally drifted back to Noah. She wondered what was taking him so long to join her. He was holding a plate of food while talking to Ethan. She wondered if they were discussing the goats or perhaps the problem of the missing lumber shipment.

It was too late this evening to try to straighten out the lumber order. Tomorrow she'd call first thing in the morning. She refused to give up. This just had to work out.

"I heard you need some help." The familiar female voice drew her attention.

Emma's gaze moved to the steps where Summer stood. "Hi."

Summer approached her. Emma scooted over on the porch swing. "Thanks for stopping by."

"Sorry I wasn't here earlier. I was on the mainland and just found out that Dash pulled one of his disappearing acts."

"We've been looking for him and another goat all day. I just can't figure out where they are or why they haven't meandered back home."

"What can I do?"

Emma's gaze moved toward the horizon. The sun was sinking low in the sky. It was getting too late to send out any other search parties. "You could go get some of that food before it goes to waste."

"I was hoping I could do more than that."

Emma shook her head. "Not today. It's getting too late."

"Are you sure?"

Emma nodded as her gaze returned to Noah as if by magnetic force. He was staring back at her. When their gazes collided, warmth swirled in her chest and rushed to her cheeks. She glanced away.

"What have I missed?" Summer asked.

"What do you mean?"

"I saw that look between you and Noah. There's something going on with you two."

"No, there's not." The heat in her cheeks intensified.

"Really? Because if something hasn't started, it's going to."

"Keep it down. I don't need people having something new to talk about."

"So I'm right. You and Noah are together."

"No." The denial was far too quick. She turned to Summer. "I'm not getting involved with anyone."

"Too late." Summer leaned closer and lowered her voice. "So what happened between you two? I saw the sparks flying."

Maybe she just needed to talk to someone about it. It would help her make sense of it all. "There was a moment when we were searching for the goats when I thought he was going to kiss me."

"No way!"

"Shh..." Emma glanced around to make sure no one overheard them.

Summer's face lit up. "That's great, right? I mean he is very good-looking."

"Summer, no. My romantic life is a dumpster fire right now."

"Oh, right. But what better way to get over a nasty break up than to get cozy with a hotty?"

Emma shook her head. Why did she think telling Summer was a good idea? "Never mind. I probably imagined the whole thing, anyway."

Summer arched a brow. "You mean you really don't know if he was going to kiss you? Every woman knows when a guy's into them, don't they?"

Emma sighed. She replayed the moment in her mind. It was one of those moments when time seemed to stand still, and then all of the sudden, it moved into fast forward once more.

"All right. He was thinking about kissing me." She glanced over, and when she didn't see Noah under the tree, her heart began to race. And then the hairs on the back of her neck stood on end, the way they do when you can feel someone staring at you. Afraid to turn around and embarrass herself farther, she asked, "He's behind me, isn't he?"

Summer broke out into a big smile as she nodded. "I...I think I'll go grab a bite of food and let you two talk."

Red-hot heat raced from her chest to her cheeks. Her whole face burned with embarrassment. It was one thing to know something, it was quite another to say it out loud. How was she supposed to walk those words back? It was impossible. Diversion was her only hope.

"You don't have to go." Emma's gaze implored her friend to stay. She was desperate for Summer to act as a buffer.

"Oh, but I do." And then Summer quickly walked away.

Emma inwardly groaned. Who abandoned their friend in a dire moment of need?

Noah made his way over to take Summer's vacated seat. Suddenly the porch swing shrank considerably. Emma was very aware of his thigh brushing up against her. The contact sent her heart thump-thumping.

"This is some mighty good pasta." He took another bite. Then he glanced at her plate. "Doesn't look like you ate anything. Were you too busy evaluating our almost-kiss?"

She gasped as flames of heat licked at her face. "I was not."

He arched a brow. "Sure sounded like it to me."

Amusement danced in his eyes as he continued to eat. That man was having fun at her expense. Why, oh why, had she said anything to Summer?

Emma set aside her plate of food. Her appetite was long gone. "It's not like you're thinking."

"And what was I thinking?"

She inwardly groaned again. He was not going to make this easy for her. "We aren't talking about this."

"We aren't? It seemed like you were the one that started the conversation. I just have one question?"

She wasn't going to inquire. Nope. Not going to do it.

He gently elbowed her. "Come on. I know you're curious."

"Would you stop?" She shifted away from him, but there wasn't much space to move.

"I will if you answer one question."

Inside there was an inner struggle—to ask or not to ask. No question could be worse than this intensely embarrassing conversation. "What's your question?"

He leaned closer to her. And then he said in a low voice, "Did you want me to kiss you?"

"Oh you." She jumped to her feet. She was so over this conversation. "I have people to thank for coming out here to help."

She could feel his gaze following her as she made her way down the steps. She resisted the urge to fan her heated face. Her heart continued to thump-thump faster than normal. She was tempted to glance back at him, but she didn't dare.

She kept walking, forcing herself to walk at a normal pace. There was absolutely no way she was going to answer his question. Because if she were to be honest, in that moment she had wanted to feel his lips pressed to hers. And that worried her.

Noah was content on the island. To let herself get involved with him, she'd be drawn back there—back to her old life.

Being with Noah would mean giving up on her musical career. And she wasn't ready to do that.

There was something special about standing up on the stage and sharing her voice with countless others. It felt good to see people smile and cheer her on.

But there was something extra special about Noah. His touch wasn't something she'd forget any time soon.

—ele—

The sun was setting.

Everyone had gone home.

And yet he still remained.

Things were rapidly shifting with Emma, but Noah wasn't ready to explore what that meant to either of them. Being friends was all he could offer her. It was the reason he wouldn't try to kiss her again—even if it was what they both wanted.

For now, he had to focus on finding two lost goats. He worried that they'd been gone too long. He might not have experience with farm animals, but it seemed to him that the animals would gravitate toward home for dinner.

But Dash was known for his adventurous spirit, so Noah didn't want to jump to the worst-case scenarios. He knew Emma and Nikki had the worrying part totally covered.

He carried the last serving dish from the picnic table into the kitchen, where Emma was washing and Nikki was drying. The three of them made a good team.

He placed the large platter next to the sink. "This is it."

"Thank goodness," Emma said. "I never thought we'd get all of the dishes cleaned up."

His gaze moved to the kitchen table, which was now stacked with clean dishes. Some belonged to Sam, others belonged to Birdle and Betty.

"What else can I do?" he asked.

Emma rinsed the soap suds from the platter and then placed it in the dish drainer for Nikki to dry. Then Emma turned to him. "Thank you for your help. It was greatly appreciated, but you can go now."

"Go?" He didn't have any plans to go anywhere. "I was thinking I'd give you and Nikki a ride into town."

Emma shook her head. "That won't be necessary."

"We're staying," Nikki announced.

"Staying?"

Emma nodded. "Nikki wants to sleep here tonight, and I want to be here when Dash and Billy find their way home."

He didn't say a word as he digested the news. It made for an interesting turn of events.

"What?" Emma asked. When he didn't immediately response, she said, "What are you thinking?"

"That I was already planning to stay the night."

Emma shook her head. "There's no need for both of us to stay."

He wasn't leaving. He was too invested now in the safety of those goats. And if something had happened to them and they needed help, he wanted to be there. The farm might not be that far from town, but it was still a bit isolated, especially at night.

He also noticed the determined glint in Emma's eyes. She wasn't going anywhere any time soon. So there had to be some sort of compromise—a reason for her to agree to him staying. His mind raced. And then it came to him.

"You can't stay up all night," he said. "And we don't want the goats to meander back only to take off again."

She planted her hands on the gentle curve of her hips. She pursed her lips together as though considering what he had just said. "What do you have in mind?"

"We can take turns watching for the goats."

The frown on her face smoothed. "So you'd sleep for a couple hours while I watch and then we'd swap?"

"And me." Nikki placed the now-dry platter on the table.

They both turned to Nikki, who had the same determined look on her face as her aunt. He wasn't saying a word. This was totally up to Emma to handle as she saw fit.

"Aren't you tired?" Emma asked her niece.

Nikki shook her head. "I miss Dash and Billy." A sorrowful tone filled her voice. "Do you think they're hurt?"

Noah knelt down in front of her. "I think they just wandered so far from home that they're having a little problem finding their way back. And I'm sure they miss you too. They probably wish they were home right now with their comfy beds and food."

Nikki nodded. "Dash loves to eat and eat. Dad says he's going to eat us out of house and home. When they get back, I'm going to make sure they have plenty to eat."

Noah sent her a reassuring smile. "I bet they'll love that."

"Okay," Emma said. "Noah and I are going to go sit on the porch now. Why don't you watch one of your shows in the living room. And I'll get you a little later."

Nikki seemed to think it over. "What if Dash and Billy come back while I'm watching a movie?"

"I'll come get you. We'll need help corralling them."

Nikki stood a little taller. "I can do that."

"Okay. Go watch your show. We'll let you know if anything happens."

Nikki hesitated. "Promise you'll let me know as soon as you see them."

"I promise." Emma used her finger to cross her heart.

"Okay." Nikki tossed down the drying towel on the kitchen counter and headed for the living room.

Noah had noticed the worry reflected in Emma's eyes. He wanted to make this better for both of them, but there wasn't much they could do in the dark, except hope that the goats made their way home.

Buzz-buzz.

Emma reached for her phone. "It's my mother. I better get this and fill her in on what's happening."

"While you do that, I'm going to head outside and check the yard for any sign of them."

She nodded. "Thank you. You know you don't have to stay."

"I want to." He nodded toward her phone. "You better get that."

As she pressed the phone to her ear, he stepped outside. Thankfully, Sam had installed some outdoor lights that lit up part of the yard and the goat pen. At the moment, everything seemed peaceful—except for him.

He couldn't sit down, not yet. He moved down the steps and into the yard. He had never felt more useless in his entire life. And now he had to wait eight hours until sunup before he could get back out there searching for the goats.

CHAPTER SEVENTEEN

H IS TALL SILHOUETTE SHONE in the moonlight.
The breath stilled in Emma's lungs as she watched Noah stroll across the backyard. She held the phone to her ear as her mother chatted on about her trip. She sounded so happy—happier than she'd been in a long time.

It appeared her siblings had put on a happy front and kept the stress of the trial and the disappearance of the goats from her. Emma would follow suit. She wasn't going to let anything ruin her mother's trip. Her mother deserved this vacation. And Emma needed to show her family that she was capable of keeping things together.

"What's wrong?" It was as though her mother could read her thoughts.

"Nothing. Why would anything be wrong?" She attempted to sound upbeat.

"Because I can hear it in your voice."

"Hear what?" She thought her voice sounded normal.

"Emma, don't try to fool me. I know when something is wrong. Is it Nikki? Is she sick?"

"Oh, no. It's nothing like that."

"So there is something going on. I knew it."

Emma sighed. All of her life her mother was able to drag the truth out of her. Some things don't change.

Choosing to focus on the goats and not the trial, she told her mother about Dash and Billy's escape. She left out the part about Bluestar's residents forming a search party. It would have her mother feeling guilty for not being there.

"I'm so sorry this happened. You know Dash can be so ornery. But it's strange they've been gone so long and no one has seen them. Do you think something could have happened to them?" Worry filled her mother's voice.

"No." Yes. She wasn't going to have her mother stressed when there was absolutely nothing she could do from Cancun. "We'll find them and everything will be all right."

"But you're there all by yourself."

"No, I'm not." She spoke before realizing she'd have to admit to Noah's presence.

"Is it Hannah? Can I talk to her?"

Emma inwardly groaned because she knew mentioning Noah would have her mother interpreting it incorrectly. Still, what other choice did she have? "It's Noah. He's taking turns with me tonight and keeping an eye out for the goats."

"Hmpf."

When her mother made that sound, it always meant her mother's mind was churning. And Emma worried about what her mother was thinking. If she didn't straighten this out, her mother would tell her sister there was something going on between her and Noah, when nothing could be farther from the truth.

"Mom, don't go reading anything into this. There's nothing between Noah and me."

"Maybe not yet but it isn't like you're leaving any time soon." After a slight pause, she asked, "Are you?"

"I don't know when I'm heading back to Nashville." Hopefully, it'd be after the news of her breakup with JT died down. "But it doesn't matter if I stay for a year, Noah and I will be nothing but friends."

"Friends is good. Did I tell you that your father and I were friends in school for years before we started dating?"

"Mom..."

"Okay. Okay. It's just that Noah is a nice guy."

"He is but he's not my guy." The memory of the almost-kiss flashed in her mind. "And he's not going to be."

"All right. Just don't give up on love. I know JT was a creep, but not all men are like him."

She just couldn't continue with this conversation. "I should be going, Mom. I need to check on things."

"Okay. Are you sure we shouldn't come home? Because we will."

"No. Stay there and have fun. Everything is okay, Mom."

But was it really?

Emma hoped her words carried a note of certainty because at the moment she wasn't feeling so confident. She couldn't shake the feeling that everything in her life was in turmoil. Okay, maybe not everything but enough things that she felt totally unsettled—even on her beloved island.

After Emma finished speaking with her mother, Hannah called to check in. And then Sam called. He was sorry this had happened to her. She told him she was the one who should feel bad, since she'd let him down when he had other important matters to focus on. She promised to keep him updated.

After touching base with her whole family, she tiptoed into the living room and found Nikki sound asleep on the couch, clutching her little black stuffed goat—the one that resembled Dash. On her pale cheeks were tear stains.

Emma pressed a hand to her chest as her emotions bubbled to the surface. That poor little girl was going through so much. As her vision blurred with unshed tears, Emma blinked repeatedly as she tried to contain her own emotions. Nikki had already lost so much in life, from her mother's accidental death to her grandfather's fiery death. How much was a little girl supposed to endure?

Emma wanted to reach out to her—to comfort her—but she didn't dare wake her. Nikki's cherub face was relaxed in a peaceful slumber. All of the excitement and worry must have worn her out.

Emma grabbed a blanket from the back of the couch. She settled it over her niece before she turned off the television. At least one of them would be getting some sleep tonight. She was pretty certain it wouldn't be her.

In the kitchen she glanced out the window, wishing she would spot the goats in the backyard, but there was no sign of them. And she didn't immediately spot Noah. Had he changed his mind and headed home?

It didn't seem like something he would do—at least not without saying something to her. As she squinted into the darkness, she spotted him leaning against one of the log posts holding up the fence around the goat pen. She wondered what he was thinking about—not that she'd ask him. But she might take him a cup of coffee.

She set to work brewing them some coffee. She wasn't sure how he took his, but she hoped he wouldn't mind a little milk and a touch of sugar. She stepped out onto the back porch with a mug in each hand.

When Noah stepped up onto the porch, she held out one of the mugs. "I hope it's the way you like it."

He took a sip. "It's perfect. Thank you."

They both sat on the porch swing. For a moment, they enjoyed their coffee in silence. It was a warm evening with barely a breeze.

"Any sign of the goats?" She knew the answer, but it didn't keep her from hoping he knew something she didn't.

"Afraid not."

She'd been bottling up her worries all day, and now under the blanket of darkness, she felt safe to air them out. "I'm worried."

"They're okay. They probably found someplace to hunker down for the night."

She took a drink of coffee. "You don't think it's strange that no one has seen them?"

He shrugged. "I honestly don't know much about goats. I'm just thinking positive."

"I can't afford that luxury, because I have a little girl in there that's counting on me to get this right. I need a plan and right now, I'm running out of ideas."

"Just relax. Sometimes when you don't work so hard to find an answer, it just comes to you."

"I don't know about that. Is that how you did things when you were a money guy?"

"You mean a hedge fund manager and no, I didn't. And that's what led me to Bluestar."

"I don't understand." But she wanted to—she wanted to learn more about him.

"I lived a different life in Chicago. I was married with an eight-to-five job that never ended at five. It consumed my life so much so that my wife filed for divorce. I didn't find out until I was served papers at the office because when I came home at night, she was either out with friends or asleep."

Sympathy welled up within her. She knew what it was like to be blindsided with the end of a relationship. She couldn't imagine the devastation he felt by the end of a marriage.

He grew quiet as he took a drink of coffee. She wondered if that was all he planned to share. The urge to ask him to continue grew within her, but she resisted the urge. It was none of her business. She was touched that he'd started to open up to her.

"After a contentious divorce, I worked even harder. It felt like that was all I had in life. The work I did will eat up your soul if you let it. The stakes were so high."

"I can't even imagine being in control of that much money. You must have been very good at it."

"I was one of the best—until I wasn't. One moment I was placing a buy order, and the next I was on the ground, clutching my chest."

A soft gasp passed her lips as she reached out her hand and placed it over his. Her body tensed as she waited to hear what had happened to him.

"I remember lying there on the floor, staring up at the ceiling, and it was as if time stood still. You know how they say that just before you die that your life passes before your eyes?" He didn't wait for the nod of her head before he continued. "It happened for me. I saw my failures and the things in life that I'd never had time to do." His thumb gently stroked her fingers as he spoke. "And I realized that if those were my last breaths that there was no one to miss me."

No one should ever feel that way. "But what about your family?"

"My parents have already passed on. I don't have any siblings. And my ex, well, let's just say we won't be exchanging Christmas cards in the future. And I had a dog, but she won custody of him in the divorce."

"I'm sorry. It sounds really lonely. Do you think you'll want another family?"

He shrugged. "It would depend on a lot of things."

"Such as?" The words slipped past her lips before she could stop them."

He leaned back and stared out at the starry night. "If I found someone that wanted the same things as me. A quiet island life with a view of the ocean and maybe a dog."

"And kids?"

"Yeah. If it worked out. One or two would be nice."

Eventually, she wanted a couple of babies too. She just didn't want them at this moment. Her career had her on the go too much. But maybe someday...

Trying to stop her mind from conjuring up the image of an adorable baby, she said, "You must miss all of your friends in Chicago."

He rubbed the back of his neck. "Not really. I'd just moved into a new condo, and I worked so much that I never had time to meet any of the neighbors."

"What about at the office?"

He shrugged. "There were people I exchanged greetings with and talked about sports but never much more than that. I didn't need more than that, because I had my work."

"I understand. I have friends in Nashville, but they are more acquaintances than friends. They aren't like Summer or Hannah or Aster. Those three I could talk about anything to." Except perhaps her relationship with him. The heat crept up her neck and settled in her cheeks. This thing between them was too new to examine it too closely.

He nodded. "Those are the kind of friends I've started to make on the island. Like Ethan and Greg Hoover. Anyway, I was a very different person when I was back in Chicago. I lost consciousness by the time the ambulance arrived. They took me to the hospital. When I came to, I didn't know what to expect, but I feared the worse. There was test after test. I was informed that I'd had a coronary event, and my life had to change drastically. They opened my eyes to my poor diet, my lack of exercise, and the stress. The doctor told me in no uncertain terms that if I didn't change my life, I wouldn't make it to get senior discounts."

"And so you quit your job and moved to Bluestar?"

"It didn't happen all at once. After I got out of the hospital, I turned in my notice. I knew there was no way to keep that job without the stress and the long hours. There was no compromise. And I'd already earned enough money to give me options."

"So how did you end up here on Bluestar?"

He drank some more coffee. "I'd been here as a kid with my parents for vacation. I remembered the island fondly. And so when I recovered, I decided to take a vacation. And that's all it took for me to know this is my future."

She nodded in understanding. "There's something special about the island. I know I'm biased because I grew up here, but I've been traveling a lot lately doing concert engagements, and I still think Bluestar is very special."

"Do you plan to move back here permanently?"

That was a question she'd been struggling with. It'd be so easy to step away from the notoriety of her life in Nashville and come home to this laid-back island, but was it truly what she wanted?

She still didn't know the answer. Because moving back would lead her to new problems. Like what would she do for a living? All she knew was how to be a singer and a songwriter. What was she supposed to do with that on the island?

"I don't know. I love what I do," she said honestly. "But my career is stalled. So I don't know what the future holds."

He moved his hand, capturing her fingers with his own. His fingers laced with hers, sending her heart tumbling. And then he turned his head so their gazes met. "Would it be wrong of me to hope that you don't find those answers any time soon?"

Definitely not. As she gazed into his eyes, she was thinking that she didn't want to go anywhere. The thump-thump of her heart echoed in her ears.

He didn't move but she couldn't help wishing he'd try to kiss her again. This time she wouldn't pull away. This time she'd lean into his arms.

Maybe instead of waiting around for him to kiss her again, she would take the lead. The idea taunted and teased her.

And yet there was another part of her that hesitated. It told her she was exhausted and not thinking straight. Otherwise, she would see the fallacy of such thinking.

But her desires were in the driver's seat now. And her curiosity to know what it'd be like to be kissed by him had her leaning toward him.

"Maah... Maah..."

They both jerked around to stare out into the backyard. Outside the pen stood a goat. She couldn't be certain which goat it was since it was standing in the shadows. However, where there was one goat, there would likely be the other goat.

"They're back!" Her heart leapt with joy.

"Shh…" Noah's voice was so soft. "We don't want to spook them away."

He was right. They needed to quietly approach them and get ahold of their collars so they could get them back in the pen. "So, how do you suggest we get them in the pen?"

"You said Dash likes to eat, right?" When she nodded, he asked, "Do you have something inside that they'll like to eat?"

"Let me look." She jumped up off the porch swing and the floor of the porch creaked.

She froze. When she glanced over her shoulder, she noticed the goat's head turned toward her. The breath caught in her lungs.

Please don't run. Please stay right there.

She didn't move. She didn't even breathe until the goat lowered his head and began munching on some weeds.

This time she moved carefully, trying to avoid any other sounds that would spook him. She carefully opened the screen door and tiptoed into the dimly lit kitchen. She headed straight for the fridge, knowing there were leftovers inside. She opened the door and stared at the contents. What would a goat eat?

She just started grabbing food. Surely there would be something between the bread and fruits that the goats would want. She rushed outside, and at the last minute remembered to catch the screen door so it wouldn't slam. They were so close to capturing them, and she didn't want to miss the opportunity.

Noah was standing there at the top of the steps, lounging against a post. He was staring out into the yard. The silhouette of his tall, lean physique made the breath catch in her throat.

What was it about this man that had her entertaining the thoughts of letting her guard down with him? It had to be the long day, the exhaustion from all of the walking, and the warm summer night. They were all playing games with her mind. Because there was no way she wanted to get involved with anyone anytime soon.

Forcing aside her troubling thoughts, she whispered, "I've got some food for them."

"I think we have a problem."

She inwardly groaned. "Please don't say that."

Problems were all she seemed to be facing lately, and she was so ready for some good news. "What is it?"

"I've been watching, and there's no sign of the other goat."

"But they're always together. They're like bonded or something."

"So I've heard but something happened to the other one."

Her heart plummeted down to her flip-flops. "Do you know which one is here?"

He shook his head. "It's just too dark. Let's take the food and see if we can catch this one. And maybe the other will come out of hiding."

Oh, she liked that idea. "Do you want to try and feed him or should I?"

"Do they know you?"

She shrugged. "Not really. They're Nikki's pets, but I don't want to wake her up. She was so tired."

"I agree. Let her sleep. Because if one of the goats is missing, it'll upset her again."

"Agreed," Emma said. "So I'll try to coax the goat to me with the food."

"And I'll come up on it and grab his collar."

"It's a plan."

And so they set off, moving slowly so as not to spook the goat. She walked very slowly, allowing Noah a chance to make a sweeping arc around the goat.

When her foot landed on a twig, the crack of the wood sounded so loud in her ears she froze. The breath hitched in her lungs.

Her gaze locked on the goat. It stopped munching. The goat's head lifted. It stared right at her.

Her heartbeat echoed in her ears. Please don't run. Please just stay right there.

For what seemed like forever, they were frozen in this position. Then, the goat must have decided she wasn't a threat and returned to eating. She just hoped what she had in her hands was better than what it was already eating.

She continued her approach. She had no idea where Noah was now. There were too many shadows beneath the trees.

At last she was within a few feet of the goat. It was Billy. She wanted to look around for Dash, but she didn't dare take her gaze off Billy. It would only take a second for him to make a run for it. But it didn't seem he had any interest in going anywhere. Perhaps the silly goat was relieved to be home.

In a soft voice she said, "Hey, Billy, I've got some treats for you."

He lifted his head. His nose started to move as though he were sniffing out the cookies.

"You know you want these, don't you? You were gone all day. You must be hungry."

With the goat distracted by the tempting treats, Noah was able to rush up behind him and grab Billy's collar. The goat didn't put up a fuss. Billy was indeed happy to be home. But where was Dash?

As they led Billy back to the pen, she asked, "Did you see any sign of Dash in the yard? Is he perhaps hiding behind a tree or a bush?"

Noah sighed and shook his head. "I don't think he's here."

"Why would they have separated? They are always in close vicinity to each other." Emma held the food in one arm while attempting to open the gate latch with the other. She struggled with one hand, but it wouldn't budge. "Now I see why Nikki has problems closing this latch. I can't even get it open."

"Here. Hold onto Billy and I'll get it."

She moved to the animal's side and took ahold of Billy's collar. Her fingers brushed over something caught in his collar. While Noah opened the gate, she examined the thing caught in Billy's collar. It was a twig with leaves.

Perhaps this was the clue of where the goats had been that day—where Dash might still be. She grabbed her phone from her pocket and selected the flashlight app. She wasn't an expert on tree leaves, but she had an idea.

"Hang onto him." She picked up each of his feet, searching for clues.

"What's the matter?"

"I think I know where Dash is." It wasn't so much what she saw on his feet, but what she smelled—rotten apples. "They were in the orchard."

"But we looked there."

"I think we should look again. Dash would be here if he wasn't in trouble." A sense of urgency came over her.

"Why don't I feed Billy some of his food, and you can call your sister. Maybe she can come stay with Nikki."

"Good idea."

When they found Dash, she was going to buy him a tracking device. This wasn't going to happen again. She knew that given the chance, Dash would make a run for it—again.

As she selected her sister's number on her phone, she glanced over at Noah, who was talking softly to Billy. For someone that hadn't grown up on a farm, he was doing a good job.

Her heart swelled with gratitude for all he'd done for her and her family that day. She didn't know many people who would go above and beyond for someone they'd only recently come to know. JT certainly wouldn't be out there in the dead of night helping her with a missing goat.

But Noah acted as though he had nowhere else to be and no greater priority. And she knew that wasn't the case. He had a lot of his own work to do—like the stage and the chairs for Birdie. And yet he was there, expecting nothing from her in return. How was she ever going to thank him?

CHAPTER EIGHTEEN

A MIDDLE-OF-THE-NIGHT HIKE.
It certainly hadn't been on Noah's bucket list. And yet he wouldn't be anywhere else but next to Emma. He wanted to ease the worry lines bracketing her beautiful face. The only way to do that was to find one wayward goat.

When Emma had called her sister, both Hannah and Ethan had showed up to help. Hannah stayed with Nikki while Ethan opted to help them search the orchard. Perhaps Dash's collar got hung up on some branches. Or maybe he got stuck in some overgrowth.

And so they searched and searched. Noah had no idea how much time had passed, but no one had spotted Dash, though they did spot a lot of partially chewed apples. The goats had definitely been there at one point, but there was no sign of Dash now.

They had split up in order to cover more ground. They'd agreed to check-in in an hour. Since they'd entered the orchard from the west, Emma agreed to do a more thorough search of this section while Ethan checked the north and Noah moved farther east toward the bluffs.

Noah walked softly, hoping to hear the little bell on Dash's red collar. Emma had told him about it and how Aster had bought it for Dash so it'd be easier to locate him. So every now and then he would stop, turn off his light, and listen. No matter how much he hoped to hear the tinkle of that bell, all he heard was the quietness of the night and the distant sounds of the ocean.

Eventually, his phone vibrated as the timer went off. It was time to meet up with Emma and Ethan. Trying to make it back to the middle of the orchard was harder to do in the dark than he'd first thought.

He walked in what he hoped was the general vicinity of where he'd last seen Emma and Ethan. When a flashlight shone in the distance, he picked up his pace. He hoped one of them had Dash on a lead rope.

But when he reached the meeting spot, they were both empty-handed. Disappointment assailed him. It was getting late, and though he didn't want to admit it, he was growing tired. And when he caught a glimpse of Emma's face in the light, he could see the long day and sleepless night was catching up with her too.

"I think we should call it a night," Noah said.

"I agree," Ethan said.

"You guys can head back, but I'm staying. We've check three directions, north, east, and west. I'm going to check the south part of the orchard."

He glanced at Ethan, who glanced at him. There was no way Noah was going to leave Emma out there in the middle of the night alone. He didn't care if he had to sleepwalk, he was staying.

"I'll go with you," Noah said.

"Me too," Ethan chimed in.

"I'm too tired to argue with you guys, so let's go." Emma didn't wait for a response as she turned and started walking.

They fanned out, but they were still close enough to each other to see the glow of their flashlights. Noah

yawned as he continued to put one foot in front of
the other. He wasn't going to be able to do this all
night—no matter how much he wanted to keep going.

At last they made it to the edge of the orchard. Thank
goodness. It was time to head back to the house. He
just hoped Emma would agree to call it quits, at least
until sunup.

He turned and started toward her. He noticed she
was still walking southward. Where was she going?
There weren't any more trees in that direction. In fact,
there was some dense vegetation not far off.

She stopped and shone her light on the ground. And
then she dropped to her knees. "Guys! Come quick."

The tone of her voice sent Noah's heart into his
throat. He took off in a run. He reached Emma at the
same time as Ethan. "What's wrong? Are you hurt?"

"It's not me. Look at this." She pointed her light on
some broken boards on the ground. "Do you think
Dash could be down there?"

"What is it?" Ethan asked.

"I think it's an old well," Emma said. "I remember
there being a couple on the property when I was a
kid. My grandfather would warn me to stay away from
them, even though they were boarded up. I think the
boards must have rotted by now and given way."

If Dash fell in a well, it didn't sound good. And as
Noah bent over the well and listened, he didn't hear
any signs of life. He moved closer to the wood planks.

"Be careful," Emma said.

"Yeah," Ethan said. "It's hard to tell how old those
planks are, and with the salt breeze I'm sure the nails
are completely rusted."

Ethan lowered himself to his hands and knees and
moved the last few inches. He turned his head to the
side and lowered it to the hole. Nothing.

Maybe they were worried about nothing. He hoped that was the case. He didn't think a goat would survive a fall down a well.

When he lifted his head, he saw Noah on the other side of the well where the wood was totally broken away. He flashed a light down the hole.

"I see something," Ethan said. "At least I think I do."

Noah carefully moved the wood from his side. He stuck his head over the edge of the hole. "I think I see something red."

"Dash's collar?" Emma shimmied up next to him. Dirt spilled over the edge and into the hole.

"Be careful." He hoped the ground wouldn't give way.

"Dash!" Emma called out. "Dash, is that you?"

"Maaah. Maaah."

"It's him!" Emma lifted her head to look at Noah with tears in her eyes.

He couldn't tell if they were tears of joy or tears of sorrow. He didn't know what to say. They might have found Dash, but that didn't mean he was out of the woods just yet.

"We have to get him out of there." She sat up and looked around. "What are we going to use to get him out?"

"I'm working on it," Ethan said with his ear pressed to his phone. He stepped away and started talking.

A couple of minutes later, Noah heard the faint sound of a whistle blowing. "Do you hear that?"

Emma paused to listen. "It's the fire whistle." Her gaze moved to Ethan, who was still talking on his phone. "It's Ethan. He's calling for help."

"I guess it helps to have friends in high places."

RISING STAR   191

"It does. Since my mother's husband retired, Ethan was asked to step up as the new fire chief. I just don't know if we're going to need all of the help."

"We're going to need it," Ethan said. "Dash is wedged in there pretty good. We have to make sure he doesn't slip farther down the well."

"Why don't you lower me down there?" Noah asked.

"Because you don't have the proper equipment," Ethan said. "We're going to have to be extra careful. The sides of the well aren't reinforced. So any contact with it is going to send more rocks and dirt down on Dash, which in turn is going to get him more worked up and increase the risk of him slipping farther down the well."

For Emma's sake, Noah wanted to argue with Ethan and tell him they didn't have to wait around, but the man was right. Ethan surveyed the area as the fire whistle continued to blow in the background. The one thing he'd learned about Bluestar was that the town pulled together in times of need—even in the middle of the night.

And from what he could tell, this little goat was beloved not only by Nikki but also by many in the town. When he glanced over at Emma, he saw the tears in her eyes.

Without a word, he moved to her. He pulled her into his arms, and to his surprise she let him hold her. "It's going to be okay."

"You don't know that. He's down there so deep."

"I believe he hung in there, knowing you would come find him. He's going to hang in there a little longer until we're able to safely extract him."

She hugged him tighter. "I sure hope you're right. Nikki will be devastated if anything happens to that little goat."

Noah didn't say it, but he was certain more people than just Nikki would be devastated. Him included.

When she pulled back, she glanced up at him. "Thank you."

He swiped a tear from her check. "My shoulder is yours any time you need it." And he meant it. "Now I better see what I can do to help."

Ethan had started clearing the rotted wood from around the hole. Noah joined him and in no time, they had the wood moved away from the well.

The entire fire department soon showed up with flood lights, ropes and rappelling gear. Noah helped set up framing over the hole to lower someone into the well.

The plan was for someone to go down into the hole, wrap a rescue harness around Dash, and carefully lift him out of the hole. The problem was the diameter of the hole was small and the sides were loose. And Noah was too big to get down the hole without loosening more of the dirt.

When he let out a frustrated sigh, he glanced around to find that the crowd of people wanting to help had grown. Some were dressed, others were in mismatched clothes, and others looked like they'd shown up in their pajamas. And no one cared what they looked like. All they cared about was doing their part to help a neighbor.

Together they worked until everything was set up. Then it was time to lower someone down the well. The firefighters were all too broad in the shoulders, including Noah.

"I'll do it," Emma said.

Noah shook his head. "No. We'll figure something out."

She straightened her shoulders and lifted her chin ever so slightly. "I wasn't asking your permission. I'm telling you and everyone else that I'm going down the well."

Ethan stepped up to her. "I think you'll fit. But are you sure you want to do this?"

"I'm certain."

"You realize you'll have to go down the hole upside down? There's no room for you to turn around once you're down there."

She nodded. "I'll do it." She looked pointedly at Noah. "I have to do this."

"The other thing to remember is touch the wall as little as possible. We don't want the ground coming lose," Ethan said.

Noah didn't say a word. She wouldn't like anything he had to say. Because he was not at all comfortable with this plan. There were too many variables like the loose sides to the well. What if the dirt and rock gave way? As soon as the thought came to him, he pushed it away. The thought of anything happening to her was just too much for him.

He followed her over to the opening to the well. She reached for the harness. He took it from her and helped her hook it all up. He double and tripled checked it. And then he moved aside so Ethan could a thorough check of her equipment.

Once Ethan finished, Noah stepped up to Emma. With his face mere inches from hers, he said, "If you're having doubts about doing this, just say the word. We'll figure something else out."

She shook her head. "I've got this."

He wanted to pull her into his arms. He wanted to claim her lips with his own. But instead his gaze caressed her face. When they could no longer just stand there, he said, "Be careful."

"I will."

And then he backed up so Ethan could give her instructions about Dash's harness. All the while Noah's heart pounded in his chest with anxiety. If anything were to happen to her, he wouldn't know what to do with himself.

CHAPTER NINETEEN

WHY HAD SHE AGREED to this?

It was the last thought Emma had as she stood at the edge of the well. Someone placed a safety helmet with a light on her head and clipped it under her chin. She was too nervous to look at them or make idle conversation.

She wouldn't admit it to any of the strong, brave people around her, but she was scared to get lowered into a deep, dark hole. But she wasn't going to let that stop her. Nikki needed her to do this. Her brother needed her to do this. And most of all, Dash needed her to do this. She wasn't about to let any of them down.

And suddenly, Noah was one of the men next to her. Before she could say anything, her feet were off the ground.

She was being held over the great big bottomless hole. At least it looked to her to have no end. But somewhere in that darkness was Dash. He just had to hold on until she reached him.

Her heart raced. Her pulse echoed in her ears, drowning out all of the encouraging words from Noah and Ethan. She was all right as long as they were holding her, but as the line started to lower her into the hole, they had to let go. And then suddenly she was on her own.

Her breath started to come in short gasps. She was going to hyperventilate if she wasn't careful. Think about the ocean. The soothing sound of the water lapping against the shore. Soon she'd be there, playing with Nikki in the surf while Dash was safe at home in his pen with his other goat friends.

"Emma, are you okay?" Noah's voice echoed down the well.

She imagined the sun warming her face as the surf washed over her toes. And then she imagined Noah next to her in his board shorts. His hand would reach for hers. His fingers would interlace with hers. The image helped slow her breathing. She just had to hold onto that image as she used her hands to center herself as she descended.

"Emma?"

"I'm good!" Maybe good was a stretch, but it was her goal.

The descent was much slower than she'd expected. And hanging by her feet was definitely not the most comfortable position with all of the blood rushing to her head. But it wouldn't be that long until she reached Dash. It was just a little farther.

The farther she descended into the earth, the colder it became. Goosebumps trailed down her limbs. She should have worn something warmer, but it was too late now.

However, if for any reason she needed to be extracted sooner, they'd attached a back-up line to her. She just had to give a couple of tugs on it, and they'd lift her back out.

It was so dark down there. Thankfully, there was a light attached to her helmet, or she wouldn't be able to see her hands in front of her face. But her light wasn't strong enough for her to see Dash.

Quietness surrounded her. The only thing she could hear now was the beat of her heart. Soon this would be over and Dash would be safe. She had to believe it.

Time seemed to slow down. Seconds felt like minutes. Minutes felt like hours. And deeper into the dark she plunged.

The line jerked to a halt. She swung to the side, hitting the wall with her shoulder. "Ompf!"

The air escaped her lungs and pain radiated from her shoulder. Dirt and stones tumbled down the well. Oh, Dash, I'm sorry.

When she didn't continue the descent, she called out, "What's wrong?"

"There's a problem with the wench! We'll have it fixed in a moment."

Just great. She was already getting a headache from hanging upside down. Why anyone would want to stand on their head was beyond her. She never wanted to do this again.

Her shoulder continued to throb. That was going to leave an ugly bruise. She'd deal with it later—after Dash was safe.

Her patience was wearing thin. "Hurry up!"

"Almost have it!"

The line lowered her downward a few inches before jerking her to a halt. Her injured shoulder smashed into the wall again. A sharp pain was followed by cold, wetness. Not far away she heard Dash call out softly. She didn't have time to worry about her shoulder. A flood of adrenaline helped her push past the pain and continue her mission.

"Emma?" Ethan called to her. "We're going to pull you up."

"No! I'm almost to him."

"We're having a problem with your line."

Her body tensed. She refused to let her mind conjure up all of the worst-case scenarios. "Can you fix it?"

There was a hesitation as though he was discussing their options with the others. "Yes, but it's going to be another few minutes. Are you okay?"

"Yes!"

She stared into the darkness searching for Dash's red collar. She couldn't make out any sign of him. He couldn't be that much farther. And then her stomach knotted as she wondered if he'd fallen farther down the narrow shaft?

"Emma, the problem is the wench. It stopped working, so we're going to lower you by hand. Don't worry. We've got all of the firefighters holding onto the line plus Noah."

"Let's do this."

She started the descent once more. It was faster but with jerkier motions. She had to use her hands on the wall to keep from bumping into it. The walls were damp. The chill in the air grew more intense. But she didn't have time to worry about any of that now.

She squinted into the darkness. Where was he?

And then she heard a sound. It was Dash moving. He shifted enough for her to see his red collar again. Hope swelled in her chest. "Dash, I'm almost there."

She wanted to yell to Noah and Ethan that she'd found Dash, but she didn't want to startle him. If Dash moved around too much, he was likely to slide farther down the shaft.

Dash was face up in the shaft. His eyes were open. When she got close, he started a high-pitched bleat as he tried to kick his feet.

"It's okay, little fella." She gave one firm yank on her supplemental line. Her descent stopped. "We're going to get you out of here."

She reached out her hand to pet him. Dash moved his head away from her. He was frightened, and she couldn't blame him. He didn't make any sounds. He was exhausted from trying to fight his way out of the hole. She suspected that all of his struggling had only succeeded in him dropping farther into the hole.

"It's okay, Dash. We're going to get you out of here." She kept her voice soft and calm.

As she spoke to him, she used her hands to help assess the situation because her light just wasn't bright enough. She found that his front hooves were dug into the sides of the well. And his back feet were resting on a rock sticking out from the side of the well. She was amazed that he hadn't fallen farther.

"It's okay, Dash. You're safe now. I'm going to wrap this harness around you so that you can be lifted out."

As she worked the red harness around his chest, he started to fight her. Rocks and dirt were loosened from the wall. Afraid he would cave-in part of the well, she grabbed him to her chest.

"It's okay, boy. I've got you." She continued speaking to him in a soft, semi-calm voice.

Eventually, he settled. But what was she going to do now? She couldn't let go of him because he'd fall. Luckily, he was on the small side but still he had to weigh about fifty pounds. She couldn't carry him to the surface, because the shaft was too narrow to get a good grip on him.

She'd already worked the harness around one leg before he'd gotten worked up. If she could just get the other leg through the harness, she'd be able to fasten it and have his weight on the line.

In order to do all of that, she was going to need both of her hands. She turned them slowly until Dash's back feet were once again on the rock sticking out from the wall.

She knew the stakes were the highest now. One wrong move and she could lose Dash. Her niece's face flashed in her mind. She could do this. There simply wasn't any other option.

"Listen to me, Dash. I need you to trust me and not throw a fit. Please." She struggled to keep the fright from her voice.

She ignored the cold seeping into her bones. She pushed past her now-pounding headache. And she didn't panic when she noticed Dash was trembling.

The only thing she focused on was holding the goat close to get the harness securely attached. Because it was the only way they were getting out of there any time soon.

Her own teeth began to chatter. As the cold continued to lower her core temperature, her fingers became stiff and clumsy. Emma clenched her teeth together. She could do this. They were so close to being out of there.

—ele—

What was taking so long?

Worry rippled through Noah as he stood at the opening of the well, holding the line with Emma at the other end. He shouldn't have agreed to let her go down there. It had been a bad idea. They should have worked to find another solution—he just didn't have a clue what that alternative idea might have been.

When the wench had broken with Emma already down in the well, he'd lunged for the line. He'd never been so scared in his life—even more so than when he'd had his heart attack. He didn't know that was possible. But in that moment, he would have done anything to change places with Emma.

All he knew was that he needed to see Emma come out of that hole in one piece. He couldn't remember ever being so worried about another person. If anything happened to her, he would blame himself for not putting up a firmer stance about her volunteering to go down in that deep, dark hole in the ground.

He halted his thoughts. What was wrong with him? He used to be calm and steady, even when he had a billion dollars on the line. When had he started worrying about this woman? She was what to him? His girlfriend? Definitely not. His friend? Yes, definitely his friend.

"We have two yanks," Greg Hoover called out.

"Let's get them out of there," Ethan said. "A slow, steady pull."

Noah didn't want to do it slowly. He wanted to yank her out as fast as he could so he could reassure himself that she was all right.

But Ethan was closest to the well. He set the pace. Noah was next to him, and then there were a half dozen or so guys farther down the line.

Hand over hand.

Pull after pull.

Slow and steady.

And then at last there were feet sticking up out of the hole...followed by legs. Other people rushed forward to help Emma and Dash. He wanted to be one of those people, but he didn't dare release his hold on the line. They had to hold their positions until both Emma and Dash were released from their lines.

It felt as though it was taking forever. His gaze followed her. He noticed how she was smudged from head to foot with mud. Her body trembled while her teeth chattered. Her shirt sleeve was torn exposing a gash in her shoulder.

As soon as her and Dash's feet touched the ground, he let go of the line and raced to Emma's side. She fell into him. He wrapped his arms securely around her.

"Don't worry. I've got you," he said gently.

For the first time since she'd gone down that well, he felt as though he could take a full breath. He didn't ever want to let her go again. He was so thankful she was safe.

"I think I need to sit down." Her voice wobbled.

With regret, he released her just enough to help her to the ground.

"Sorry," she said. "I'm...I'm a little dizzy." Her teeth chattered.

"Does anyone have a blanket?" he called out.

"I have some supplies in my truck," Ethan said.

Noah's gaze followed him to the fire chief's truck—one of the exempt vehicles on the island. Ethan hurried back with a blanket and a first aid kit. He handed Noah the blanket, which he wrapped around Emma's shoulders.

"How's Dash?" The chatter of her teeth became more pronounced.

Noah craned his neck. "I can't see him. There's a crowd of people around him."

"He...he wasn't so good down in the hole." Worry shone in her eyes.

"Don't worry. He's getting lots of attention." He helped her sit on the tail gate of Ethan's truck.

"I...I..." She pressed her lips together, trying to calm the chattering. "He needs to see a vet."

"Okay. But first let's get you taken care of." He glanced down to where Ethan was cleaning one of the gashes on her leg.

Noah straightened to get some pads to clean the wounds on her arms when she reached out, catching his forearm with her fingers. "Don't go."

He placed his hand over hers. "I'm not going anywhere. I was just going to get some supplies to help clean you up."

"Oh."

He set to work gently dabbing at the gash on her shoulder. It was deep and bleeding a lot. He applied a couple of large gauze pads. It dug at him that she was hurt by doing something he should have done, if he could have fit in the hole.

After a few moments, he lifted the blood-soaked gauze. The bleeding wasn't slowing down. He was starting to wonder if she was going to need a stitch or two as well as a tetanus shot. Maybe it was time for a trip to the doctor. He wasn't going to take any chances that her beautiful skin was scarred or worse that she had acquired an infection.

CHAPTER TWENTY

S HE DIDN'T THINK SHE'D ever get warm again.

Emma was now seated in the front of her brother's pickup. Ethan was at the wheel with Noah on the other side of her. They were headed back from town.

Noah had insisted she see the doctor. She was not happy that they'd wakened Doc Mullins in the middle of the night. She insisted she could wait until morning, but both Noah and Ethan argued that her shoulder wasn't going to stop bleeding without stitches. In the end, she'd had two serious cuts, one on her shoulder and the other on her leg, which needed stitches. She hadn't had those since she was a kid climbing on the rocks along the shore.

While she'd been getting stitches and some antibiotics, Dash had been taken to the vet's office. Nikki insisted on accompanying Dash to the vet's office. Hannah was overseeing things with Greg Hoover helping out.

And her sister had been thoughtful enough to grab some loose-fitting clothes from her place and brought them over to the doc's office so Emma would have something dry and warm to wear. Thankfully, they were about the same size. It felt so good to take off the muddy, blood-stained clothes.

With the sun hoovering on the horizon, sending pinks and purples cascading off the clouds, they were finally back at the farm. The only thing was that Dash wasn't with them. He was staying at the vets for a while to get IV fluids and some medicine. The vet had assured them that he didn't see any reason Dash wouldn't be home by the next evening. It appeared she'd taken the brunt of the injuries.

Noah and Ethan helped her up the steps of her brother's house and onto the couch. She wanted to spend the night there and make sure everything was situated before she returned to her mother's house. But right now, she just wanted to sit down for a few minutes.

"I'm good here," Emma said. "Thank you both for all you did."

"Would you like something to eat?" Ethan asked.

She shook her head. She was too tired to have an appetite. "I'm not hungry. But thank you."

Hannah and Nikki came in the door. Nikki ran up to Emma and gave her a hug. Emma pushed through the pain as Nikki touched upon some of her cuts and bruises.

Nikki pulled back. "I'm sorry you got hurt, Auntie Em."

"I'll be fine. Don't worry about me."

Sadness pulled at Nikki's face. "I hope Dash is okay."

This time Emma reached out with her good arm and hugged her niece. "Dash is going to be fine. He just needs a little rest and some medicine. But he should be home in time for dinner. Okay?"

Nikki nodded. "Can I call Daddy and tell him what happened?"

Hannah stepped up next to the couch. "Your dad is going to be asleep. We don't want to wake him. How about we try to call him in the morning?"

Nikki expelled a resigned sigh. "Okay."

Emma felt bad for her niece. It had been an eventful night, to say the least. "Why don't you run upstairs and crawl in bed?"

"I can take her home with me," Hannah said.

"Can I stay here, pleeease?" Nikki's gaze pleaded with both of them. "I want to be here when Dash gets home."

"Honey," Hannah said, "he won't be home until later tomorrow after the vet makes sure he's ready to go."

"I still wanna stay with Auntie Em. Please."

Emma was too tired to argue with her niece. Wherever she wanted to sleep was fine with her. Her adrenaline had worn off, and the painkillers were barely kicking in. And to top it off, she was exhausted. She knew she should get a shower, but she just needed to close her eyes. Just for a few minutes.

She would sit there for a little longer, and then she'd get up and do things. After all, she needed to have someone cover that giant hole in the ground. She didn't want anyone or anything to fall in that hole. The fact that Dash was alive was a true miracle.

Darkness called to her. Her eyelids grew heavy. Her thoughts scattered and then drifted away.

Lunchtime had come and gone.

The next day Noah was existing on three hours of sleep. Not that he could complain, as he wasn't the only one getting by without much rest.

He'd stretched out on a cushioned chair on the back porch at the Bell farm. He was close enough to hear if Emma needed anything. And yet he was far enough away that he didn't feel the need to watch over her every breath just to assure himself that she was all right.

He'd only planned to close his eyes momentarily. The next time he'd opened them, it was a few hours later, and Ethan as well as Greg had shown up with some lumber to cover the hole. He hadn't wanted to leave in case Emma or Nikki needed him, but Birdie and her dog, Peaches, had also stopped by the house to check on everyone. Birdie had insisted on sticking around while they worked on covering the hole.

The three men loaded up Sam's pickup and headed up the hill. With the three of them working, it didn't take too terribly long to frame in the hole and then cover it securely.

Noah pounded the last nail in the reinforced cover they'd made. "Thanks for the help."

"We do some pretty good work together," Ethan said.

"So how are things with you and Emma?" Greg picked up some of the wood scraps to put in the back of the pickup.

Noah knew what Greg was asking, but he chose to ignore the romantic implications to the question. "She's been sleeping peacefully since we got home. And Nikki was out immediately."

"That isn't what I meant." Greg arched a brow.

"When are you going to ask her out on a proper date?" Ethan asked.

And here he would have thought that Ethan would understand that they were friends—nothing more. "I'm not."

Even to his own ears that sounded like a lie. The idea of taking Emma out to dinner definitely appealed to him, but realistically it just wasn't going to work. He had to focus on finding a permanent place to live before his lease was up in a couple of months. And Emma, well, she still loved her fast-paced life in Nashville. And as soon as she figured out how to put her career on an upward trajectory, she'd be gone. She'd be happier with someone who was in the industry—not someone like him, who craved a quiet life.

Chapter Twenty-one

L IFE WAS SO MUCH better.

Sunday morning, Emma sipped at her coffee as she stared out at the sunny day. It was amazing what a good night's sleep could do for a person. Emma was back at her mother's house, and Nikki was back with Hannah. And Dash was now back at the farm, where he could continue to recuperate.

It was lunchtime by the time she got cleaned up without getting her stitches wet. Feeling like a new person and not someone that had been lowered upside down into the depths of the earth, she was ready to get back to work.

Buzz-buzz.

Emma picked her phone up from the kitchen table. When she saw the caller ID, she groaned. It was Mayor Tony Banks. He undoubtedly wanted to know about the progress on the summer concert. And she didn't want to tell him they were behind because of the mess-up with the lumber order.

She swallowed hard as she pressed the phone to her ear. "Hello, Mayor. What can I do for you?"

"I was just down at the beach to inspect the stage, and it's not complete. And no one is working on it. Maybe hiring Noah wasn't a good idea. Perhaps the project is too much for him."

What? Where was Noah? Why wasn't he down there? The questions raced through her mind with no answers.

"This isn't Noah's fault. It's mine." She wouldn't let Noah take the blame when he'd been nothing but generous with his time. He'd been gentle and caring when she'd been hurt. And he'd been so helpful in finding Dash and Billy. "I distracted him when two of my brother's goats ran off."

"I'd heard something about that. How are you?"

Her gaze strayed to the gauze wrap peeking out from under her shirt sleeve. "I'm good. As for the concert, it'll happen as scheduled. I promise."

"You do know if the concert is a failure, the city council will pull all of the funding from the special events department?"

Translated to mean Aster would be out of a job. Emma wasn't going to let that happen.

"Understood. I'm headed to the beach now. Everything will be ready for sound checks on Thursday and Friday."

"You're sure about this?" Doubt rang out in his voice.

"I am. Trust me." She wouldn't let Aster down.

When they disconnected the call, her appetite was long gone. She didn't care if she had to pound the nails into the boards herself. This stage would be completed on time.

She moved to the counter and filled up a to-go cup with coffee, then added some sweetener and milk. She winced when she moved her injured shoulder. With the cap screwed on tight, she grabbed her backpack with the notebook for the event as well as her laptop. Everything she would need for a mobile office.

She went outside and climbed onto her bike. It was a beautiful day to be out and about. There was only one puffy white cloud in the sky with a gentle sea breeze. And yet she wasn't smiling or enjoying the perfect weather. The pressure of completing the project weighed heavily on her shoulders.

Her lips were pressed into a firm line as she quickly pedaled her way to the beach. Along the way, she did the obligatory smile and nod, but she just wasn't feeling it. Her stomach was knotted up with worry. And her wounds were hurting more today.

But she just couldn't sit around again for another day. Sitting around gave her too much time to think—about the diamond ring that she'd been delayed in mailing—about her stalled-out singing career—about how Noah had been there for her throughout the Dash ordeal. She felt closer to Noah than she'd felt to anyone in a long time. It both scared and exhilarated her in equal portions.

She had one stop to make on the way to the beach. She pulled her bike to a stop in front of the post office. It was long past time she did this.

She hopped off and kicked the bike stand. With her backpack over her shoulder, she headed inside the post office. Lucky for her there was only one person at the window. She lowered her backpack and withdrew the padded envelope.

After a minute, she moved to the window. She placed the package on the counter with her manager's name on the front of it. "I'd like to send this the fastest way possible."

The clerk took the envelope and placed it on the scale. She named off a price for it to be in Nashville in two days and Emma paid her. That was it. Her engagement was officially finished, even though it'd ended the morning she'd seen a picture of Noah kissing another woman.

She felt as though a big weight had been lifted from her shoulders. When she passed by Birdie and Peaches, she shared a genuine smile. "Good morning."

Ms. Birdie waved her over. When Emma stopped, Birdie said, "I wanted to know how you're doing."

"Good. Thank you for all you did. It is so appreciated."

Birdie waved off Emma's words. "It was nothing. I love to help out where I'm needed."

"What would we do without you?"

"I'm sure you'd get by. It's Noah you should thank. He was the one who helped you find Dash. He's such a good guy."

"Agreed." There was no way Emma could deny Noah's wonderful qualities. It still didn't mean there was anything romantic between them. "I'm on my way to the beach to see him. He's finishing up the stage for the concert."

"I'm looking forward to the concert. I should let you go so you can see that young man of yours." Birdie gave a little wave.

By the time Emma lifted her sagging jaw at the reference to Noah being her man, Birdie had moved on. Part of Emma wanted to follow her and clarify matters, but the other part of her wondered what it would be like if Noah was her guy. Not that it would happen. She'd had her heart broken by the nation's beloved number one ranking country artist. She wasn't ready to put herself out there again.

As she pedaled away, she noticed that with the ring gone, she felt so much better. In fact, she was starting to wonder if JT had meant as much to her as she'd let herself believe. Perhaps she'd let herself get caught up in the splashy headlines of the pending nuptials and a storybook happily-ever-after. Maybe she hadn't truly loved him like she'd thought.

In that moment, she realized the bullet she'd dodged. What if she had married him only to realize later that it wasn't love? She inwardly groaned. She didn't want that to happen again. How was she ever supposed to trust her judgement again?

It was just after one o'clock when she reached the beach. She left her bike in the parking lot and made her way down the steps. She glanced at the stage and found no one working. This wasn't good. Not good at all. Why wasn't Noah there?

She reached for her phone in her pocket. She went to select his phone number, but she hesitated before dialing the number. Maybe this conversation would be better done in person.

With hurried steps, she made her way back to her bike. She thought of going to his apartment but then decided she probably had a better chance of finding him at his woodshop.

Her progress was hampered in this part of town by the large number of tourists. But eventually, she made her way along Main Street. She could hear a saw going inside the garage.

She paused in the doorway and watched him work. She noticed how his movements with the saw were smooth and quick. Piece by piece he cut sections and then stacked the cut wood off to the side.

When he turned off the saw, she stepped farther into the garage. "Looks like you're busy."

He spun around. "Oh, hey. I didn't hear you arrive."

"You had the saw going, and I didn't want to startle you."

He nodded in understanding. "I was out at the farm checking on Dash this morning, and you can't even tell that anything happened to him."

Guilt assailed her. She'd been so caught up in her own drama that she hadn't been out to the farm today. "I...I was going to head out there after I touched base with you. I stopped by the beach, but no one was there."

He nodded. "We were there this morning, and we did all we could until the lumber delivery is made."

"When will that be?"

"As you know, I had to get a special permit for the delivery, and since this is the height of tourist season, I was told it had to be before nine a.m. or after eight in the evening. So the delivery is scheduled for seven a.m. tomorrow morning."

"Oh." Her mind started going over all of the work left to do on the stage, and then she counted down the days until the first sound check. There was no way that everything was going to be done on time.

"I know we're behind. I'm sorry about that. I'll do everything I can to get us back on track."

She believed him. She just didn't know if his best intentions were enough to get them back on track. "We can't mess this up. The mayor called this morning. He let me know in no uncertain terms that if we aren't successful that Aster's job is on the line. So just let me know what I can do to help."

"You take care of yourself. I've got this."

There was no way she was going to let her future sister-in-law down. She didn't care if she had to build this stage herself or if she had to work side-by-side with Noah from now until the concert. It was going to be a success.

He would do whatever it took to meet the deadline.

And yet Emma stood there, looking at him with doubt reflected in her eyes. Noah wanted to reassure her that everything was going to work out.

He mentally inventoried everything left to do. "The stage and scaffolding will be done by Thursday."

Her eyes shone with relief. "Are you sure?"

He nodded. "It'll get done one way or another." His gaze moved to the gauze on her arm. "How are you doing?"

"Good. The painkillers have kicked in, and I'm feeling much better."

"Don't overdo it." He already felt terrible that she'd been injured.

"I won't. I promise. But I want to make myself useful." When he arched a brow at her, she said, "I mean it. I want to help with the stage."

"I'm not sure about helping with the stage, but I have another important task you could help me with." He nodded toward some chairs. "I just finished my order for Birdie and Betty. Would you mind helping me deliver them?"

"How can I help?"

He didn't really need the help, but he did want her company. "I was hoping you could drive while I keep the chairs from bouncing off the back of the cart."

"Oh. I can do that." She smiled as though happy to be needed.

And then he had another idea. "Have you eaten yet?"

She shook her head. "After the mayor phoned, I was in such a hurry to get out the door that I didn't bother."

"Then in payment for your assistance, I'm buying lunch."

"You don't have to."

"I want to. What are you hungry for?"

"I...I don't know."

He had the four chairs stacked together. Individually, they were rather light, but all together they were hefty. He ended up moving them two at a time to the back of his cart. He used bungee cords to help secure them.

And then they were off. His gaze moved to Emma. Something told him that he'd never tire of spending time with her—there was something very special about her.

Chapter Twenty-Two

THE SUN WAS SHINING.

The birds were singing.

And Emma was smiling—truly smiling. It was the kind of smile that started with a bubbly happiness deep within her and radiated its warmth outward.

As she sat in a booth at the Purple Guppy Pub for a quick lunch, she couldn't stop smiling. It was something about being around Noah. He made her happy—a happiness that she'd never felt before.

She didn't know if it was the way he listened to what she said or if it was the way he made sure the conversation wasn't all about him. The conversation flowed easily both ways. He wanted her input and her perspective. She felt valued in way she hadn't with JT.

They paused to place their order. While he'd opted for a salad with the dressing on the side, she'd gone with a fish sandwich and chips. And then they talked some more.

"Where did you grow up?" She longed to know more about him.

"In a little town in Illinois. It was the type of town that had one stop light and everyone knew your name."

"So it was a lot like Bluestar, except we don't have a stoplight."

He paused as though giving it some thought. "I guess so. But it definitely didn't have the amazing views."

She nodded in understanding. Bluestar's ocean views were spectacular. "Do you still have family there?"

He shook his head. "It was just my parents, and they've passed on now."

"I'm sorry. I know how rough that can be."

"It was a while ago. Although sometimes I do miss the amazing aromas of my mother in the kitchen. She was the best cook ever." A smile tugged at his lips as the memories came to him. "I was never a big cake fan, but for my birthday she would make me the lightest, fluffiest angel food cake with fresh berries and a scoop of vanilla bean ice cream. It was the best."

"She sounds like a wonderful mother."

"She was. My father was a good guy too. He's where I got my work ethic. I learned a lot from him."

"And you never thought of moving back there after you quit working in Chicago?"

He shrugged. "A lot of time has passed. I'm sure it's not the same place I remember."

After a sip of tea, she lounged back in the booth. "You're sure you want to make Bluestar your permanent home?"

He shrugged. "I thought that I did, but with things not working out with buying the house, I don't know."

"You wouldn't happen to mean the Merriweather house, would you?" When he nodded, she said, "I'm sorry it didn't work out." She paused for a moment as she recalled something. "Wait. Was that the call you got when we were jogging?"

He nodded. "Yes."

"What happened?"

"It's not important." When she looked at him expectantly, he said, "I didn't get my offer in on time, and I lost out to another bid."

"Why didn't you get your bid in on time?"

He raked his fingers through his hair. "You do realize that none of this matters now? It's over and done with."

It mattered. She could feel it in her bones. He was still upset that he'd lost the house, and she was starting to get the feeling she had something to do with it. She racked her mind, trying to figure out how she might be involved, but she came up with nothing.

"It matters," she said softly but firmly. "Tell me."

He didn't answer at first. In fact, the silence dragged on so long she didn't think he would answer at all. "You know you can be very bossy when you want to be."

"Only when it's important."

"And you feel this is important?"

"I do. Somehow I feel it's what keeps coming between us, and I can't fix it if I don't know what the problem is."

There was another pause. "When I returned from selling my condo in Chicago, I missed the ferry back to the island. And that caused me to miss my appointment with my real estate agent, Madison."

It was all starting to make sense now. "You missed the ferry because I took your taxi."

His toyed with the straw wrapper again as he shrugged.

She felt awful that she'd been so focused on herself and her problems that she'd messed up his plans. She reached out and placed her hand over his. "I'm sorry. I was in a really bad frame of mind that day. I don't normally act like that. Please forgive me."

His gaze once more met hers. "That's the reason I didn't want to bring this up. I'm already over it."

"Are you sure?" When he nodded, she asked, "Is there anything I can do?"

He shook his head. "I just need to figure out if I'm going to sign another lease on my apartment or move on."

Her eyes widened. "You mean like leave Bluestar?"

"Yeah."

"But where would you go?" And then Emma wondered if this was some sort of sign. "You could come to Nashville."

"Nashville? What would I do there?" And then his eyes widened as though he realized she'd be there.

This time she shrugged as she smiled. "I'm sure you could do your wood work there. And you would have a friend nearby."

A slow smile pulled at his lips, making her stomach dip. "I would, huh? And who might that be?"

"Me." And then realizing her hand was still touching his, she gave it a squeeze. And then ever so reluctantly, she withdrew her hand from his. "Just think about it."

"I will." But there was a sadness reflected in his eyes. "Does this mean you've made up your mind about resuming your singing career?"

"Not at all." She sighed as she thought of the big decision awaiting her. And then she realized if she expected Noah to open up to her, she needed to do the same. So she told him how amazing the Songbird competition had been and how she thought by winning the show that she'd finally made it in country music. She admitted how naive she'd been back then.

She appreciated how Noah listened without inserting his thoughts. He didn't push her. He let her tell him her tale the way she needed to do it.

"So now I don't know if I'm ready to go back to the rushed lifestyle." It was the most honest she'd been with anyone about her future.

"Do you feel better here on the island?"

She nodded. "I don't feel so burnt out."

"Then maybe you should stay longer. Like you said, there's nothing forcing you to go back." His voice lacked any judgement. It was more a matter of him laying out the facts.

"And if I stay, will you stay too?"

"You mean, will I extend the lease on my apartment?" When she nodded, he said, "It doesn't seem as if I have much choice if I want to remain a part of Bluestar." His gaze met and held hers. "And right now, there's no other place I'd rather be."

Her heart fluttered. "I knew coming home was exactly what I needed."

When lunch was over, was over and they returned to Noah's workshop, Noah made his apologies and headed back to the beach. As Emma rode her bike away, she still felt bad that her actions had cost him the Merriweather house. She wanted to fix this for him, but she didn't know how.

However, she knew his real estate agent. Maybe she'd give Madison a call and see if there were any upcoming beach-front properties he might be interested in. It wasn't much, but she just felt like she owed him to try to do something. Anything.

She pulled her bike off to the side of the road and stopped. She withdrew her phone from her pocket to look up his real estate agent's number. Madison was a few years older than her, so they weren't close, but they knew each other from around town.

She dialed the number and it started to ring. When Madison picked up, Emma said, "Hi. It's Emma Bell."

"Hi, Emma. What can I do for you?"

This is where it became difficult. Emma decided to give Madison the abbreviated version of what happened the first time she'd met Noah and why he hadn't made it to his meeting with her.

"So you see it's my fault he wasn't able to make it to his meeting with you and to submit his offer for the Merriweather house."

"I'm sorry all of that happened, but why are you telling me this?"

"Because I was wondering if there was anything I could say or do to get him another house similar to the Merriweather's. He loves that house."

"I'll tell you what I told him. It's a seller's market on the island. And there aren't any houses quite like the Merriweather place. One of the things that drew him to it was the double-bay garage."

Emma envisioned Noah running his saw with a contented look on his face. "Ah...yes, he would want it for a woodshop. Surely there has to be something for him to look at."

"Not that would fit his needs. Currently, the only available properties are bungalows. He wants something larger. I would suggest if he wants something immediately to look on the mainland."

"Oh. Okay." Disappointment flooded her body. "Well, thanks for talking to me."

"I'm sorry I couldn't be more helpful."

They said goodbye and disconnected the call. Emma felt awful that she hadn't been able to do anything to help Noah. And she was out of ideas.

But if Noah didn't find his forever home on Bluestar Island, was it possible he'd give Nashville a chance, and maybe then they could find out where things were headed for them? Hope swelled in her chest. She hoped their futures would intertwine. There was just something about him that made her want to spend more time with him—a lot more.

Chapter Twenty-Three

F AMILIES PULL TOGETHER.
  The Bells were no exception.

And that was why on Wednesday morning when Hannah had a last-minute change to a large wedding order for a destination wedding at the Brass Anchor Inn, and Ethan was on the mainland for work, Emma stepped up to spend the day with Nikki.

It definitely wasn't a hardship. Not in the least. She loved spending as much time as she could with her niece. And now that Noah had the stage almost finished, she had a little extra time.

She'd picked up Nikki from Hannah's place, and they'd taken her mother's cart to drive out to the farm. And there before them was Dash. He was isolated in a smaller pen until his injuries healed. He had a cone on his neck to keep him from ripping off his bandages, but other than that he looked good for having fallen down a well.

Nikki withdrew a baggie of cookies from her pocket. "I brought him a treat." She pulled out a sugar cookie. Then she hesitated and turned to Emma. "Would you like to feed it to him?"

She would but she knew how much Nikki loved to dote on Dash. "It's okay. Go ahead. I'll watch."

Nikki fed him all three cookies, which he munched down in record time. And then Nikki attempted to hug him, but it didn't go so well with Dash's cone.

Nikki promised him she'd be back real soon. And then she made her way out of the pen. She paused to double-check that the latch was secure. Then she turned to Emma. "Could we have a picnic at the beach?"

"I don't know. I have some phone calls to make for the concert." However, she had promised they'd go to the beach before she left the island—if she left the island.

"Do you have to do them now?" Nikki pleaded with her eyes.

"Well...maybe I could do them later this afternoon."

Nikki clasped her hands together. "Does this mean we can go? Pleeeease."

"Yes. But first we have to swing by the stage and check on things." She stopped there every day.

"Will Uncle Ethan be there?" Nikki fell in step with her as they made their way to the cart.

"Uncle Ethan, huh?"

"Well, he is going to be my uncle as soon as he marries Aunt Hannah."

It was true. Their family was suddenly expanding with their mother remarrying, and now both Sam and Hannah were engaged. She did notice that neither sibling had set a wedding date, but she was certain it wouldn't be a long engagement for either of them.

Her thumb rubbed against her bare ring finger. She was supposed to be planning her wedding too. She had come way too close to making the biggest mistake of her life with JT. If it weren't for that photo, she might actually be picking out a wedding dress right now. She shuddered at the idea.

And the thing was that she didn't even miss him. She missed the idea of what they were supposed to have shared, but she didn't miss the reality of what they'd become.

JT had always been wrapped up in himself, and she was always making excuses for him. She told herself that with more time he would change. Now she knew that was not going to happen. And that wasn't the way she wanted a relationship to be.

"Are you cold, Auntie Em?"

She glanced over at her niece. "What?"

"You just shivered. I thought you might be cold."

It definitely wasn't a cold morning. It was just her thoughts that had sent a cold chill down her spine. "I'm fine. It's going to be a beautiful day to spend at the beach."

"I can't wait."

Nikki continued to chit-chat about this and that on the ride into town. Emma only had to utter the appropriate response here and there for Nikki to continue talking. Emma couldn't help but smile. Nikki was a wonderful little girl.

They found a parking spot along the seawall and then made their way down the steps to the beach. Her heartbeat quickened with each step. She couldn't wait to see Noah again.

She knew she shouldn't let him get to her. She'd promised herself that she wouldn't move too fast again. But it wasn't like they were in a relationship. They were friends, nothing more. But it sure felt like more.

———— *ele* ————

It had been a warm morning.

With it being the latter part of June, most every day the temperature in the sun was somewhere between hot and steamy. Noah mopped his brow with a rag from his back pocket. Today was no exception.

When he gazed at Emma's beautiful face, her radiant smile made him all that much warmer. What was it about her that had him feeling so out of character?

Though her beauty was second to none, he'd never been caught up in the superficial. No, there was something more intrinsic that had caused his pulse to race whenever he was in her orbit and for his thoughts to become a bit scattered.

Am I falling for her?

"Noah, did you hear me?" Emma sent him a worried look.

"Um, what?" He wasn't about to admit he was thinking about her—about them—about any of it.

She frowned. "Have you been drinking enough water? It's really hot out today."

"Uh, yeah. I was just thinking about some stuff I need to get done before lunch."

She nodded in understanding. "Then we won't keep you. I just wanted to check in and see if you needed anything."

He glanced over at the stage, which was at last almost finished. He found it easier to think when he wasn't staring into her mesmerizing blue eyes. "Everything is back on track."

"Really?" Her eyes brightened with hope.

He arched a brow. "Do you doubt me?"

"Oh. No. That wasn't what I meant."

"Relax. I'm just giving you a hard time."

She visibly expelled a breath. "You had me worried for a moment there."

"Don't be. For the first time since we started this project, I can honestly say that we're in a good place."

Emma's smile broadened, making his heart thump-thump harder. "Thank you. This means so much not only to me but also to Sam and Aster. How can I thank you?"

"Invite him to our picnic," Nikki piped up.

"A picnic?" He couldn't remember the last time he'd been to a picnic. The idea definitely appealed to him.

Nikki smiled and nodded. "Auntie Em is taking me on a picnic at the beach. We were supposed to do it before but Dash escaped."

"I see." His gaze moved to Emma to see if it was all right with her.

Upon realizing that both he and Nikki were looking at her expectantly, Emma's eyes widened as her lips formed an O. She nodded. "Yes, please join us."

He honestly liked the idea of spending a bit of leisurely time with these two. "What time?"

"Well, um..." Emma checked the time on her phone. "I still have to get the food together."

"And dessert?" he asked.

"Oh, yes." Nikki clasped her hands together. "Dessert is a must."

Emma looked flustered. "And dessert. How about...uh, twelve-thirty?"

That would give him a few more hours to work on the stage. By then he'd be ready for a break. "Sounds perfect. And now since I have plans with two lovely ladies, I have to get back to work."

"We'll see you soon," Emma said.

"And we'll have dessert," Nikki said.

"Can't wait," he called out as they walked away.

He should get to work because honestly, he didn't have the time to spare for a leisurely lunch. But how was he supposed to turn down such a tempting offer?

For a moment longer, he watched as Emma and Nikki crossed the sand to the wooden steps that led up to the parking lot of Beachcomber Park. He was already getting hungry, but it wasn't the food he had on his mind. He was anxious for more of Emma's smiles and to hear her laughter. He just couldn't get enough of her.

—ele—

Why had she agreed to this?

Emma remembered the way Noah's eyes had lit up when Nikki had invited him. Emma never imagined he'd be interested in a picnic lunch. But why wouldn't he want some downtime? After all, she should be doing final check-ins with the performers to make sure there weren't any problems with their travel plans.

Emma suddenly felt the pressure build as she tried to figure out a picnic menu that would be suitable in this heat. Her mind raced for ideas the whole way back to her mother's house. Fried chicken? Did he like chicken? Potato salad? No. It was too hot out, and she didn't want to have to worry about keeping it cool enough.

"What are we going to eat?" Nikki's voice interrupted her thoughts.

"What would you like to eat?"

"I don't know, but Noah said we had to have dessert."

Emma had an idea about that. "How about we make an angel food cake?"

Nikki's nose scrunched up. "Why would we make that?"

"Because Noah likes it." She moved to the drawer in the kitchen where her mother kept her recipes.

Emma searched through the collection of notecards with handwritten recipes that had been passed down through the generations. Some were legible, and others were a bit of a head-scratcher.

For a moment, she considered going to the Elegant Bakery and picking up a dessert. It would undoubtedly be worth every single calorie, but she resisted the idea. She wanted to show Noah that she was good at baking. Hannah wasn't the only one that had learned from their grandmother. She just didn't have the occasion to use her skills very often.

In a sing-song voice, Nikki asked, "How do you know Noah likes angel food?"

"Um..." She paused her search. "He told me. It's something his mother used to make for him."

Nikki seemed to think this over. "Why doesn't she make it for him anymore?"

"Because his mother passed away."

"Oh. Like my mom."

Emma's heart ached for her niece. She'd lived through so much loss in her young life from her mother to her grandfather, who'd doted on her. "Not exactly the same." Not wanting Nikki to dwell on her loss, she said, "So how would you feel about helping me bake a cake?"

Nikki hesitated before bobbing her head. "Okay."

"Good. All I need to do now is to find the recipe." She didn't realize until this moment just how many family recipes her mother owned and just how disorganized they were. It sounded like a big organizational project that she just didn't have time to do if she were to return to Nashville after the concert. But maybe if she were to stay on the island, it would be something she could do in her spare time. And then there was the part about getting to know Noah a lot better.

It was getting easier to come up with reasons to stay on Bluestar Island. And it was becoming harder to find reasons for her to return to her life in Nashville. But she didn't want to think about any of that now. She had a cake to bake.

CHAPTER TWENTY-FOUR

LUNCH HAD NEVER BEEN so exciting.

Noah pounded one last nail into the board before he straightened. He swiped his forearm over his brow. He turned his head to the right and stared out at the tempting ocean. It looked cool and inviting. And it was the very reason he'd gone home briefly to switch into a pair of blue and white board shorts.

This northern part of the beach was roped off for the construction of the stage. Farther south of his spot, lots of tourists had their colorful umbrellas up. Some were in the shade, reading, while others were soaking up the sun's brilliant rays. And there were others playing in the surf.

The scene before him was idyllic and made him appreciate his decision to move to the island permanently. The only problem was he didn't have a home yet. Sure, he had an apartment but it wasn't the same as having his own house with a woodshop. But he wasn't giving up on his dream. Not yet.

"Are you ready for lunch?" The familiar female voice drew him from his thoughts.

He turned around to find Emma standing there with a large insulated cooler bag in one hand, a white backpack over her shoulder, and an umbrella in the other hand. His stomach rumbled in eagerness. "You don't have to ask me twice."

"Hi, Noah." Nikki held a red blanket.

"Hi, Nikki."

"We'll just go set up the blanket while you finish up," Emma said.

"I'll be right there." He moved with lightning speed to secure his tools and give the worksite a once-over to make sure everything was secure.

A quick stop to clean up and then he was on his way across the sand to the spot where Emma and Nikki had laid out the blanket and set up a rainbow-colored umbrella to give them some shade. They were both laughing about something, and they looked as if they didn't have a care in the world.

A smile pulled at the corners of his lips as he approached them. It'd been a long time since he'd walked around with a smile on his face for absolutely no reason at all. That wasn't true. There was a reason and her name was Emma.

He never would have thought after their first encounter at the airport that she'd turn out to be so nice and caring. As he continued to take in her smiling face, a warm, fuzzy feeling grew in his chest. He refused to evaluate what it meant.

"Looks like you two are having fun." He lowered himself to the blanket.

"Auntie Em is the best." Nikki sent him a smile that plumped up her cheeks. "We had the best time baking."

"Baking?" He couldn't wait to sample Emma's baking. "What did you bake?"

"You have to wait and see," Emma said quickly to cut off Nikki from spilling the information.

He turned pleading eyes to Nikki. "Won't you give me a hint?"

Nikki's eyes widened as she shrugged her shoulders and then turned to her aunt. Emma pursed her glossy lips and shook her head before handing out bottles of soda.

Nikki turned back to him. "Sorry. I can't."

He expelled a sigh. "I guess I'll just have to wait."

"Don't worry," Nikki said. "You'll like it."

"I will?" He couldn't imagine what it might be.

Nikki gave a dramatic nod of her head.

Emma unzipped the red insolated bag and withdrew wrapped sandwiches. She handed one to him. "I hope you like it."

He stared at the white paper and the piece of white tape. "You didn't make these."

This time Emma shook her head. "We were too busy."

"Baking," Nikki supplied.

"So we picked up sandwiches and chips at Hamming It Up." She proceeded to hand each of them a wrapped pickle spear and a small bag of chips. "Eat up."

He could certainly get used to this. Not just sitting on the beach and enjoying the sea breeze, though that was the utmost relaxing, but rather the company. He enjoyed being with Emma and Nikki. He started to wonder what it'd be like to have a family of his own.

He was only in his thirties, definitely not too late for him to have a family. But there was the problem of his heart. What if he had another heart attack? Did he want to start a family only to have something happen to him and leave them to get by on their own?

It was a heavy thought with major implications. It was too much for him to consider on such a beautiful day. It wasn't like he was planning to propose to anyone today. His gaze strayed to Emma as the tip of her tongue swiped at a dab of mustard on her lips. His thoughts spiraled back to their almost-kiss. It was a subject he planned to revisit soon.

"Can we go swimming?" Nikki asked.

"After lunch." Emma unwrapped more of her sandwich. "Maybe Noah will go with you."

He turned his attention to Nikki, who was rushing through her lunch. "I think the ocean is calling our names. But slow down, it'll be there when you finish."

Nikki swallowed and then in her familiar sing-song voice, she said, "Okay."

He turned his attention to Emma. "Aren't you going to join us?"

Emma shook her head. "I can't get these bandages wet. Besides I have a book to read."

"Read? At the beach? On a sunny day?"

"Yes. I started this thriller last night, and I have to see what happens next." She withdrew an e-reader from her backpack. "See. I came prepared."

He shrugged. "If that makes you happy."

She smiled. "It really will."

When his chips and sandwich were finished, he asked, "So what's for dessert?"

"I thought maybe we'd eat it later," Emma said.

"You're going to make me wait? I don't know." Sure he was having fun with her, but he was also anxious to see what she'd baked.

Dessert had never been a big draw for him but suddenly he was looking forward to a sweet treat. His gaze dipped to her berry red lips. That was one indulgence he would have to wait on.

"It'll be worth the wait," Emma said.

His gaze rose to meet hers. Had she read his mind? It sure felt like it. "I'm sure it will be."

Was it his imagination or was she blushing? Maybe she had read his thoughts after all.

—ele—

She read the same page three times now.

Emma rested the e-reader against her chest as she stared off in the distance to where Noah and Nikki were playing beach volleyball. They didn't have a net, and the ball was just an ordinary bouncy ball and not an official volleyball. But they didn't seem to mind. They were jumping and diving for the ball as if it were a regulation game.

Nikki giggled as Noah dove and landed in the sand. And then he hit the ball, but it went off in the direction of the ocean. Nikki chased after it before the tide could sweep it away.

Emma found watching them far more entertaining than her book. And that was saying something because she was up until the wee hours of the morning reading it last night. With her hectic life in Nashville, she'd gotten away from reading in the evening. And she missed it.

This trip home had shown her she needed to put some balance back in her life. Was that the answer to her problems? Had she been so focused on performing and attending meet-and-greets that she didn't have time for anything else—including her songwriting?

And where had all of that socializing with radio personalities and journalists gotten her? No closer to having a label sign her. Even though her agent was all for the schmoozing, she didn't think it was the right direction for her at this stage in her career.

She needed to turn the tide. Because it felt as though she were being drawn farther from her goal of cutting her own record and headlining her own tour. And in order to do all of that she needed more material.

When she'd been out on the road being the opening act for the opening act, she'd been too tired and too distracted to write songs. Now that she'd been back on the island for a couple of weeks, she felt rejuvenated. Maybe it was time to get back to songwriting.

She thought of the song she'd attempted to write when she'd first arrived on the island. It'd been full of disillusionment and anger. That wasn't the tone she wanted for one of her songs. It was time to start a new song.

She reached for her backpack. One thing that hadn't changed about her was that she never ventured out without having a pen and paper with her. Her pen started moving over the page. The words coming one after the other.

Then she paused and mentally sang the lyrics. Some words were scratched and replaced. Lines were dropped. New lines were written.

An excitement came over her as she found her creative energy wash over her. A smile pulled at her lips as she continued to work on the bouncy, sunny tune. Who knows? This might be the hit song she'd been searching for that was going to make her stand out to the label heads.

"Whatcha doing?" Noah settled on the blanket next to her.

She immediately pressed the notebook to her chest. She never liked to share her work-in-progress with anyone. It made her feel too open and vulnerable.

Deciding to change the subject, she said, "Who would have guessed you'd be good at beach volleyball?"

He sent her a tummy-tumbling grin. "Did you like my moves?"

She nodded. "I did, especially when you ate sand."

"I did not. Well, not really."

Her gaze moved to Nikki, who was close by building a sandcastle. "Thank you for this. Nikki needed it. I know she's missing her father and Aster a lot."

"Any idea when they'll be home?"

"Soon from what I understand. The prosecution rested their case so as soon as the defense closes their case, they can hop a plane homeward bound."

"I bet they're as anxious to get home as Nikki is to see them."

"I agree. Aster is so amazing with Nikki. They both love each other."

"Nikki loves you too. You should hear her singing your praises."

Emma's cheeks grew warm. She didn't know what to say to that, so she changed the subject. "Thank you for playing with her today. She had a lot of fun."

"I should thank both of you. I haven't had this nice of a lunch in a long time."

"And now we're keeping you from getting back to work."

He waved away her concern. "Don't worry about it. I was here early, and I'll be here late. Ethan has been helping here and there. And Greg has been a huge help." And then he mentioned a few other men in town who had lent a hand. "So you have nothing to worry about."

"Thank you for all you're doing. It is much appreciated."

"You don't have to thank me. Remember, I'm getting paid to do the work, unlike you who is volunteering her time."

She shrugged. "I don't mind. Aster would do the same for me. It's what family does for each other."

They were quiet for a moment as they watched Nikki finish her sandcastle. It was a peaceful silence. The kind you imagine having with someone you've been with for most of your life.

"So are you going to tell me what you were writing?" he asked.

She looked at him and then glanced down at her notebook. "It's a new song. The words suddenly came to me, and I had to write them down before I forgot them."

"Is that the way it always is for you?"

She shrugged. "Lately, I haven't been able to write. The words just wouldn't come to me. I was starting to worry that I wouldn't be able to write another song."

He smiled. "But the island's calming breeze and soothing sunshine worked its magic."

She smiled at him. "Maybe you have a bit of a songwriter in you."

He shook his head and waved away the idea. "Not even close. I just know what this island has done for me. It's a special place."

"Yes, it is."

Nikki came running up to them and plopped down on the blanket. "Can we have dessert now?"

Emma returned her notebook and pen to her backpack. "Yes, we can."

"Thank goodness," Noah said. "I worked up an appetite." He glanced toward Nikki. "She's a volleyball star in the making."

"Or a country singing star," Nikki said, "like Auntie Em."

The smile slipped from Emma's face. She didn't feel like a star. She felt more like a failure. She'd gone to Nashville to fulfill her dream and her father's last wishes. And now she was home, and she didn't feel as though she'd accomplished what she'd gone there to do.

But not wanting to ruin the moment for Nikki and Noah, she didn't say anything. Instead, she reached into the insulated bag and removed the cake holder.

She lifted the cover. "I hope you like it."

Noah stared at the cake for a moment. "You made angel food cake?"

Emma nodded.

"She said it was your favorite," Nikki said. When Noah didn't respond, she asked, "It is your favorite, isn't it?"

He cleared his throat. "Yes. Yes, it is."

"Are you sure?" Nikki studied him. "You don't look happy."

"It's just that no one has made it for me since I was a kid and... Well, it brings back memories."

Emma was touched by his words. She had no idea it would mean this much to him. "And I have some berries to put over it."

His gaze met hers. "You remembered."

"I did. I can't promise it's as good as your mother's. I used my grandmother's recipe."

"It'll be delicious. Thank you." He sent her a smile, but it was the look in his eyes that swept her breath away.

No one had ever looked at her like she was the only woman in the world—certainly not JT. Whereas her ex was always distracted with his phone, Noah truly paid attention to what she said. And when she did something special, Noah genuinely appreciated her efforts.

Noah was a really good guy. It was a shame they hadn't met at a different time, under different circumstances. He was looking for a quiet, relaxing life there in Bluestar, while there was still a part of her heart in Nashville. And even if she felt uncertain about what the future held, there was a part of her that couldn't give up on her lifelong dream.

CHAPTER TWENTY-FIVE

THE DAY AT THE beach had been perfect.

It had been better than perfect. Was there such a thing?

And now two days later, Emma's feet felt as though they still hadn't touched the ground. Noah had been sweet, thoughtful, and attentive. Nikki had a wonderful time and made Emma promise they'd do it again. Emma had readily agreed.

Not only had she spent time with two of her favorite people, but she'd actually written a new song. It was a fun, summery song about finding love when least expected. She couldn't wait to record it. If listeners enjoyed it half as much as she did, she'd have a hit on her hands.

All through her yoga session that morning, she couldn't stop thinking about their picnic at the beach. If she suspended reality for just moment, it was so easy to imagine them as one happy family. Noah would be an awesome father with his calm and caring manner. Not to mention, a wonderful husband.

She halted her thoughts. She'd just finished promising herself that she wasn't going to rush into another relationship, and yet she was already imagining having a family with Noah.

And now it was time for the final round of sound checks. The scaffolding was all in place, the sound equipment had been set up, and the sound checks were commencing. Aster had a sound engineer and crew hired to run this part of the concert. Emma just had to make sure the right groups showed up at their designated times.

Tomorrow kicked off the biggest concert series that Bluestar Island had ever seen. And instead of her being in front of the microphone, Emma was holding a clipboard, making sure everyone was where they needed to be. It was a strange sensation for her, but one she didn't mind.

Being away from the stage for a while had gotten her creative juices flowing once more—or maybe it was the crew's temporary stage hand. She watched as Noah climbed up to the spotlights and made a manual adjustment. Bluestar's budget was slim, and so there weren't any fancy lights that could be adjusted remotely. These were old lights. She didn't even want to know where they'd been dug up, only that they were safe to use.

Noah climbed the rigging as though he'd been doing it all of his life. She couldn't help but notice how his white T-shirt strained each time his tanned biceps flexed. She wondered if he'd found the gym in town.

"How's it going?"

Emma turned to find Summer standing there. "It's going well."

"I can't wait. I'm even closing the studio early tomorrow so I can spend my afternoon here listening to the music. And since we're always closed on Sunday, I have all day to hangout."

"That's great." Emma's gaze strayed back to Noah before returning to Summer. "I can save you a seat."

"You have a date." Summer paused and gazed at Noah. "Unless you already have another date."

"What? Me? No." Though the idea did appeal to her.

Her gaze strayed to him again as he was climbing down a ladder. Just then he turned his head and their gazes met. A smile lifted the corners of his mouth. Heat warmed her face as she smiled back at him. Then someone called out to him and the moment ended.

"Oh, you've got it bad for him," Summer said.

"I...I do not. We're friends. That's all."

"Uh-huh. You keep telling yourself that because you're the only that's going to believe it."

She turned to Summer. "Are you saying the whole town is talking about us?"

"Maybe not the whole town. There might be a couple of people that don't follow the gossip, but the rest are taking bets of whether you stay here and get married or not."

Her cheeks burned with embarrassment. "But why? We aren't even dating."

"Really? Because you two were spotted at the Purple Guppy having a cozy lunch. And then there was your lunch at the beach. Seems to me you've got it bad for him. And the way he looks at you, it's like you're the only woman in his universe."

"He doesn't look at me like that?" Her heart skipped a beat. Did he?

Summer smiled and nodded. "Oh, yes, he does."

She wasn't ready to admit she was romantically interested in him. What if he didn't feel the same way about her? There she'd go again, falling for a guy without taking her time—thinking it through and being cautious. Because she didn't want to make the same mistakes she'd made with JT. Definitely not.

The smile slipped from Summer's face as she gazed past Emma. "I should be going."

Emma turned to find out what or whom had her friend rushing off. At first she didn't spot anyone, then she noticed Greg Hoover. Was he the reason Summer was suddenly in a hurry?

"Summer, wait. What's going on?"

"Uh, nothing." Summer suddenly looked awkward. "I just don't want to be in your way."

"This isn't about me. Is there something going on with you and Greg?"

"What? No. Why would you think that?" Her gaze darted from Emma to the place over her shoulder where Greg stood in the distance.

"You two used to be such good friends." She remembered when they were younger how there would be a group of them that would hang out together. Greg was one of them. He and Summer hit it off, but for some reason they never dated. Emma never knew why they hadn't gotten together.

"That was then. This is now. I'll talk to you later." And then Summer was gone, leaving Emma with more questions than answers. But they would have to wait until later.

Emma yawned. She'd been on the go since her alarm went off at 6:00 a.m. that morning. She was going to need a caffeine boost soon. She glanced around for Noah, hoping to talk him into taking a coffee break with her. And then she spotted him standing off to the side of the stage, talking to a band member.

She missed spending one-on-one time with Noah, now that they were both rushing to deal with final adjustments for the concert. So when he'd asked her to have dinner this evening, she'd readily accepted. She just hoped there weren't any snafus with the concert that would have to force her to cancel. She was looking forward to relaxing at the end of a long day with him.

The Squawking Crows took the stage and started to play an eighties rock cover song. They had an amazing sound. Emma knew her mother would enjoy it. Her mother was supposed to be back on Saturday. Even Sam and Aster might make it back for the concert. At least that was the hope. When she'd last spoken to her brother, he wasn't sure if the closing arguments would start today or if they would carry over until Monday. Once the closing arguments started, Aster was free and clear to go home.

The band paused part way through the song to make some adjustments with the sound engineer. She didn't know how they could sound any better, but she would leave that up to them. Every artist knew what sound they wanted to project.

"Things must be going well."

The familiar male voice startled her. She couldn't believe she'd been so caught up in her thoughts that she hadn't noticed someone approaching her. She turned to find her agent, Stan, standing there.

He was in his fifties; at least that was what she'd surmised. He was only a couple of inches taller than her. He dyed his gray hair brown and had it cut short. On his left hand he wore a wide gold wedding band. He'd been married to the same woman for three decades. When Emma saw them together, she thought they still looked like kids that couldn't take their eyes off each other. If she ever married, she wanted a relationship that endured like theirs had done.

"Stan, um, what are you doing here?"

"Where else did you expect me to be? I've called and left you messages to the point that your voicemail is full."

"It is?" That wasn't good. She supposed she had been ignoring it more than she should.

He crossed his arms and nodded. His brows furrowed together. "What are you doing?"

"Orchestrating Bluestar's first ever concert on the sand." She wanted to smile over playing a part in this important event for the island, but Stan's disapproving stare subdued her excitement.

"Seems to me that you're hiding from your life."

"I'm not hiding from anything." Her answer was quick and sharp. "My family needed my help, and so I stayed."

"And what about your career?"

She sighed. "What do you want me to say? It's stalled out."

"Is that what you think?"

"Of course I do." She tried to hold in all of her mounting frustrations and disappointments. After all, she needed to act professional and take it all in stride. And where had that gotten her? Standing on the beach with a clipboard in her hand, making arrangements for other talents to have their moment in the spotlight. Suddenly, all of her pent-up emotions came rushing forth. "I still only have a couple of songs recorded. No label wants to take a chance on me. Maybe I need to stick with my song writing." And then without thinking of the consequences of her words, she blurted out, "In fact, I just wrote a new song."

A broad smile covered his face. "That's great. When can I hear it?"

Suddenly she realized her error. She wasn't ready to share this song with anyone. It was too personal—too close to her heart.

"It... It's not finished." It was the truth.

"Well, hurry up. You're going to need it."

"For what?"

"To play for Cades Records."

She wasn't going to get drawn in. She knew how her agent bent things to work to his best interests. "You mean that meeting you have with them for another artist?"

"No. I mean a meeting all about you." He smiled, looking rather pleased with himself.

"What?" Surely she hadn't heard him correctly.

His smile broadened. "We're having a meeting with Cades Records to discuss your future."

Her mouth opened, but no words came out. She was going to tell him she didn't even know if she was going back to Nashville, but in her heart, she'd always known she was going back. Singing was in her blood as was writing new songs. Even if she never made it big, it wouldn't stop her from doing what she loved.

"When is the meeting?"

"Wednesday morning. Will you be ready?"

"Yes." She uttered the word before she had a chance to talk herself out of putting herself back out there with the potential of being rejected...again.

"That's great. We should get back to Nashville right away."

"I can't."

His brows furrowed together. "Why not?"

"I'm organizing this concert series. It runs Saturday and Sunday."

He turned to the stage where the Squawking Crows were getting ready to play again. "Are they all cover bands?"

"No. Saturday is rock and Sunday is country."

"Interesting. Maybe I'll stick around and see if there are any potential clients."

"Are you serious?"

Stan nodded. "Of course. I'm always looking for the next big thing." Then he paused and looked at her. "But none will be bigger than you."

She shook her head. "I'm a nobody in Nashville."

"That's not true. You've been learning the ropes, but soon your name will be known in every household. Your songs will be at the top of the charts. Trust me. I've been at this more years than I'm willing to admit."

He'd been saying those words to her for a while now. She'd trusted Stan this far. Maybe she'd trust him one more time.

"I hope you're right," Emma said. "So we'll fly out on Monday."

"I'll make the reservations." He pulled out his phone. "Now don't mind me. I'm just going to mingle."

"Okay. I have to go grab some coffee. It's been a long day." She paused. "We'll talk later."

"Definitely."

And then she walked away. And the reality of what she'd agreed to sank in. She was going back to Nashville to face all of the questions about what happened to her engagement to JT. Well, not really that particular question. Everyone knew what had happened, but they'd want to know the details. Did she know the other woman? Were her and JT going to get back together?

The thought of dealing with all of that almost made her change her mind. But she felt her confidence coming back. She was ready to face off with the label heads and sell her abilities. And as for the questions, she'd deal with them too. She could do this.

Still, she had to tell Noah. She wondered how he'd take the news of her leaving. Would he want to continue whatever this was between them? She hoped so.

___ele___

He wanted to catch up to her.

Noah had been trying to have a word with Emma, but whenever he was free, she was busy dealing with someone. With the concert set to kick off at noon the next day, there was a lot to do. But he missed spending time with her.

With no other demands upon him, he scanned the area for Emma. She was alone at last, He set off after her. She was headed away from the beach. He wondered where she was going with this being their last chance to make any adjustments before the big show.

He was done after today. He was just a volunteer. When the show went live, the experienced stage hands would handle everything. He was thinking that perhaps he could watch the show with Emma. In fact, he was planning on it. These days it seemed like they were spending all of their free time together.

He took long rapid steps to catch up with her. Slowly, he gained on her. She was in the parking lot by the time he was close enough to call out her name.

She stopped and turned. When her gaze met his, a warm smile lit up her whole face. "I thought you were busy."

"I was. I'm just taking a break. I didn't have a chance to speak to you today. We keep missing each other."

"I know. I'm sorry. With the concert set to kick off tomorrow, there's just so much to do."

"I understand. I just wanted to check in with you. How are you doing?"

She shrugged. "A little tired. In fact I'm just walking over to The Lighthouse Café to grab a coffee and a quick bite to eat. Would you like to join me?"

"I'd love to, but I promised I'd be right back to help adjust some of the spotlights."

She nodded. "I understand. I won't keep you."

"Are we still on for tonight?"

"Definitely." She smiled at him again and that gave him a warm fuzzy feeling in his chest.

He gave her his apartment address. "I'll meet you there at what? Six?"

"We better make it seven. I have a feeling this sound check is going to run long."

"Okay. Seven it is. Do you like anything special on your pizza?"

"As long as there's no anchovies or pineapple, I'm good."

"Okay. I'll see you then."

"See you." She turned and continued to walk away.

For a moment he stood there, wishing he could go with her. He watched the gentle sway of her ponytail as she strolled across Beachcomber Park. He couldn't wait until their date tonight.

He paused as the thought came to him. Was it a date? He supposed it was. He smiled. They were dating, and he felt good about it. She made his life brighter.

CHAPTER TWENTY-SIX

IT HAD BEEN A wonderful evening.

Emma smiled every time she thought about sharing pizza on the couch with Noah while a movie played on his large screen television. Honestly she couldn't recall the name of the movie. They'd talked through at least half of it. But it had been an action-adventure movie. The title was Hunting something or other. At least she thought it was the title, but she wasn't certain. And honestly it didn't matter.

Noah had been attentive and engaging. He'd been everything she'd ever wanted in a partner. Her thoughts halted. Is that the way she truly saw him? As a partner?

The idea definitely appealed to her. And yet there was a part of her screaming out that she was moving too fast. What would happen when she returned to Nashville? He'd already said he wanted a quiet life. She didn't think that would include society parties and months of being on the road promoting an album.

She inwardly groaned. Why did she have to find the right guy at the wrong time?

And then she remembered how after their conversation had dwindled into a companionable silence, he'd slipped his hand next to hers. It had been all so easy, so natural. And then his long fingers had laced with hers. The gentle touch had sent a zing of electricity up her arm to her chest where her heart had pitter-pattered. It was how they'd remained until the end of the movie.

When the night had concluded much too soon, he'd insisted on walking her home. She told him she would be fine on her own. After all, this was Bluestar Island, where crime was virtually non-existent. But he wouldn't hear of it. Hand-in-hand they walked to her mother's house.

At the door, she'd turned to thank him when their gazes connected. When his gaze dipped to her lips, her heart had skipped a beat. She wondered if he was planning at long last to kiss her. With common sense long forgotten, she willed him to kiss her.

As though he were privy to her thoughts, he'd leaned in close and pressed his lips to hers. Her heart had launched into her throat as his mouth pressed to hers. It was as if her feet floated off the ground. A kiss had never felt like this with anyone else. Noah was special. If she'd had any doubts before, she no longer did.

Before she was ready, he pulled away. He wished her a goodnight, and then he turned away. With her lips still tingling from the most delicious kiss, she'd watched him walk away into the night.

The only part of the evening that was bothering her was the fact she hadn't told Noah about her decision to return to Nashville. She knew she should have told him already, but they were both tired, and it was so nice to relax together. It might have been selfish, but she didn't want to ruin their evening. He would understand, wouldn't he?

And now that it was Saturday morning, it was only a few hours until the concert series kicked off.

Emma rushed downstairs, anxious to get to the beach. Nothing could go wrong today. Everyone had worked too hard to make this event a success.

"We're home." Her mother entered the house through the side door with her carry-on bag in hand. "Did you miss us?"

"Of course I did." Emma rushed over and hugged her mother. When she pulled back, she asked, "Did you have a good vacation?"

"It was pretty good." Her mother placed her bag near the steps.

Emma arched a brow. "Just pretty good?"

"Well, I was worried about you and your brother. You both have so much going on in your lives. I felt guilty for just up and leaving."

"Oh, Mom, you shouldn't have. You do realize that Sam and I are all grown up. We can deal with our own stuff."

"I know." She sighed as she pulled out a chair at the kitchen table. "But to me you'll always be my babies, and when something upsets you, it upsets me. I don't think that's ever going to change. Speaking of which, how are you doing?"

Walter entered the door with two large suitcases. "Hi, Emma."

"Welcome home." She sent her stepfather a warm smile.

His gaze moved from her to the serious look on her mother's face and then back to her. "I think I'll just take these suitcases upstairs now."

He quickly made his exit. It appeared Walter was quick to learn the signals from her mother—like the one when she wanted to have a heart-to-heart with one of her children.

When Walter's footsteps faded away, Emma said, "Mom, I don't want to discuss this."

"Sit."

"Mom." She didn't want to have a deep conversation. Not today. Not now.

Her mother arched a brow the same way she'd been doing since Emma was a little girl. And then because it was easier, Emma took a seat across the table from her mother.

Her mother leaned her elbows on the table and laced her fingers together. "I know your heart was bruised by JT. I'd say it was broken, but I don't think he meant as much to you as you originally thought. I've gotten to know Noah since he moved to the island. He's a good guy. He's been hurt in the past, but I think with the right person he can move past it."

She stifled a sigh at her mother's blatant matchmaking. "And you think I'm the right person?"

"I think you could be, if it's what you wanted." Her mother's gaze searched hers. "Do you know what you want?"

"I do." She hadn't planned to say anything to anyone until she'd told Noah, but this was her mother after all. "I'm going back to Nashville."

Her mother took a moment to digest this information. Her expression remained neutral, as if she were keeping her reaction from Emma. "How does Noah feel about this?"

"Well..." Her gaze dropped to the blue-and-yellow-flowered table cloth. "He doesn't know yet."

"But didn't you see him last night?"

Emma nodded. "It wasn't the right time."

"Emma, you need to find the time. He needs to know, sooner rather than later."

Ding.

Emma reached for her phone. It was a text from one of the performers. "I have to go. I have a show to put on."

"But you'll talk to Noah, right?"

"Yes, Mom. Don't worry. Everything will be all right." At least she hoped it would.

Noah would understand her decision, right? It wasn't like she'd ever promised to remain on the island. And now that his offer for his dream house fell through, he could come to Nashville to visit—or stay.

———*ele*———

He hummed along with the music as he worked.

Noah couldn't remember the last time he was in such a good mood. And it had everything to do with his date with Emma last night. He'd been fighting his feelings toward her for so long but he was finding that giving into them wasn't so bad. In fact, it was quite the opposite.

He recalled the sweetness of her laughter. He loved to entertain her and watch as her eyes sparkled. Not only was she fun to be with, but she was also great to just sit next to in silence and watch a movie. He could definitely get used to spending a lot more time with her.

In fact, he'd considered asking her to dinner tonight, but then he realized the concert would run until late. But there was always tomorrow night and the night after that.

She'd even inspired him to work on some of his woodcarvings. He recalled doing them as a kid and wanted to do something special for her. He'd revived his old skills. He had been surprised how the skills came back to him without too much effort. The hardest part had been finding the specialized tools he needed. But thanks to the internet, he found what he wanted.

He was hoping to have his surprise for her finished soon. He was thinking of giving it to her after the concert on Sunday—maybe over dinner. And then he planned to ask her if they could try running together again. It wasn't so much fun when he was alone, but having Emma as his running partner would change things. They could train together for the 5K in the fall.

As he was making his way to the stage for one last adjustment, he spotted Emma off in the distance. It was mid-morning and the first time he'd spotted her alone. He made a detour in her direction. Her back was to him, so she didn't see him coming.

He stopped right behind her. "Good morning."

She spun around with a smile on her face. "Good morning to you."

Acting on instinct, he leaned forward and planted a quick kiss on her lips. When he pulled back, her eyes were opened wide, as though the kiss had caught her off guard. Was it too much, too soon? He hoped not.

"Someone is in a good mood today," she said.

"I am. I watched this movie last night and it was the best."

She arched a brow as a smile lifted the corners of her mouth and puffed up her cheeks. "So it's the movie that has you in this good of a mood?"

"Of course," he teased. "What else would it be?"

She laughed as she shook her head. "Then I suggest you watch that movie more often."

"Oh, I definitely plan to watch it regularly."

She continued to smile at him. "Do you even know the title of it?"

He paused. As a matter-of-fact he didn't. He'd been totally and utterly distracted with the woman who had been sitting next to him on the couch. "Do you know the title?"

She shook her head. "Someone had me laughing with stories of his childhood."

"I guess we'll have to watch a bunch of movies until we find it. We could start tomorrow night after the concert. What do you say?"

"Well...um, I don't know."

"It's okay. I know you'll be tired after the big weekend. We can get together Monday or Tuesday."

He wasn't picky. He just knew he wanted to spend a lot more time with her and get to know her much better. He felt as though he'd been waiting all of his life to find her and at last it was all working out.

❧

She had to tell him now.

Emma dreaded what she was about to do. This thing between them was so new and delicate that she hated to leave the island. And yet she needed her career. It was a part of her—a part she couldn't live without and still be happy. She hoped Noah would understand. But would he?

Unsure about his response, she hesitated. Maybe she could put it off a little longer. Maybe tonight when they had a little time alone. And yet she knew that putting it off any longer would just make things worse. She had to tell him she was leaving. And she had to do it now.

"I should let you get back to work. We can talk later." Noah turned to walk away.

"Noah, wait." When he turned back to her, her stomach knotted up with nerves. "There's something I need to tell you."

He studied her for a moment. "What's the matter?"

"Nothing. Not exactly." There was a part of her that was so excited about her meeting with the record label, but it was offset with the knowledge that she wouldn't be able to see Noah every day.

"What's going on, Emma? Whatever it is, you can talk to me."

And that was part of the problem. She didn't want to lose the connection they'd made. Would he feel the same way? Or would he write her off when she left?

"I've heard from my agent." She tightened her grip on the clipboard she was holding. "Actually, he's here on the island."

"He came here to talk to you."

Emma nodded. "He wants me to go back to Nashville."

Noah rested his hands on his trim waist. "What did you tell him?"

"I told him I had a concert to oversee."

"The concert is over this weekend, what about after that?"

"Well, he told me that he'd set up a big meeting with one of the biggest labels in Nashville." She smiled but when he didn't smile back her smile faded away. "The meeting is this coming week."

"So that's it?" His gaze searched hers. "You're just leaving?"

"Noah, we both knew I couldn't stay here forever." The admission was hard for her because she didn't want him to disappear from her life. In the two weeks they'd been together, she'd come to feel like he'd always been a part of her life.

"The last I knew, you didn't even know if you wanted to go back."

And as much as she loved this island, it wasn't her future. Bluestar would forever have a special place in her heart, but she knew no matter how hard it was to leave, that it was the right thing for her to do. Though she would be back to visit, just not as often as she'd like.

"I just need you to know..." Her voice caught with emotion.

"You just want me to know that you have bigger and brighter plans than life on the island." His gaze grew dark, but before she could decipher if it was pain or anger, he blinked and the look was hidden behind a wall that had suddenly formed between them.

"It's not like that."

"Go chase your dreams. I have work to do." He turned and strode away.

"Noah, wait." She wanted to go after him, but what would be the point? Because in a way, he was right. She was going to chase her dreams. The only problem was that he'd somehow become part of that dream, and by leaving the island, she was leaving a piece of her heart behind.

She didn't know how to have her dream career and the man she cared about. She'd been working toward being a singer since she was a kid singing into her hairbrush in front of the mirror. Did she have to choose between her career and maintaining a meaningful relationship with the man she felt as though she'd known her whole life?

As she stared at Noah's retreating back, her vision blurred with a rush of tears. She blinked repeatedly. She couldn't fall apart now. She had a concert to oversee.

"Emma, this looks amazing."

She turned to find Aster, Sam, and Nikki walking hand-in-hand toward her. They were all wearing smiles. Their happiness was a balm on her aching heart.

There were hugs all around. When Emma pulled back, she looked at her brother and Aster. "I didn't know you two were flying in today."

"We caught the first flight available," Sam said.

"We were so anxious to get home." Aster smiled.

"We missed you," Nikki said. "Huh, Auntie Em?"

"Definitely. How are you doing?"

"We're good." Aster glanced at Sam. "Aren't we?"

He nodded his head. "We're doing great."

Emma couldn't help but think of the saying about what doesn't break you, makes you stronger. It looked like Sam and Aster had come through a dark time in their lives, and it had made them stronger.

Her gaze strayed to the stage where Noah was climbing a ladder. She worried that wasn't going to be the case for her and Noah. He was so upset with her that he wasn't even willing to consider making arrangements so they could continue seeing each other.

"We wanted to thank you for all you did," Sam said, "with Nikki and Dash. I'm sorry that you had to go through all of that."

"Don't feel bad. It, thankfully, worked out for everyone." She did not want to rehash the incident with Dash and how scary it had been.

Aster glanced at Sam. "Should we tell them?"

He nodded. "Go ahead."

"Tell us what?" Nikki asked.

"I'd like to know the same thing," Emma said. By the way they were both smiling, she was certain it was good news. At the moment, she would take all the good news she could get.

"We set a wedding date." Before Aster could say more, there was a squeal of delight from Nikki.

"That's wonderful," Emma said. It was another reason for her to return to the island. Her gaze strayed to Noah as he stood on a ladder replacing a light. But would he be her date to the wedding?

"Can I be in the wedding?" Nikki asked.

Aster nodded. "I was hoping you'd be my flower girl."

Nikki smiled and nodded. "Can I get a new dress?"

"I think we can manage that," Sam said.

"Yay!" Nikki hugged Aster and then pulled back. "Does this mean I can call you Mom?"

Aster's gaze moved to Sam. He smiled and nodded.

Aster's eyes filled with happy tears. "I would love that."

Emma watched as all three of them hugged. They made such a beautiful family. She couldn't help but feel a tiny bit jealous. Would she ever know that sort of happiness?

Emma swallowed past the lump in her throat. "So when is the wedding?"

"We don't want to wait," Sam said. "It's going to be in August."

"August?" Emma surely hadn't heard her brother correctly. "You mean August of next year?"

"No," he said. "August this year. You know the month after next."

"Wow. That's soon."

"I'd have had it sooner," Aster said, "but your brother convinced me that your family would want a little time to make plans."

"Well, yeah," Emma said. "This will be Mom's first kid getting married. She's already so excited."

Emma put on a happy exterior but on the inside, she was still reeling from Noah's resistance to the idea that they could have a long-distance relationship or figure out some other arrangement.

"Did we interrupt you?" Aster asked, drawing Emma back from her meandering thoughts.

"Uh, no. We were just going over some final details before the concert begins. Bluestar is so excited about this event. It has drawn a lot of tourists from the mainland. It's going to be a huge hit."

"Thanks to you."

Emma shook her head. "I didn't do anything special. This was your brainchild. I just followed the plans you laid out. Would you like to take over?"

Aster shook her head. "I couldn't do that after everything you've done."

"Why don't you two work together?" Sam suggested.

Emma and Aster looked at each other as though gauging the other's reaction. Then Emma said, "I'd like that if you're up to it."

"I'd love it. I thought my brain was going to turn to mush while I was stuck in that hotel room with nothing to do."

"Then we'll let you ladies get to work. Nikki and I are going to visit her grandmother." Sam took Nikki's hand in his, and then they were off.

Emma set to work explaining a few of the changes that had been made to the day's lineup. She pushed her thoughts about Noah to the back of her mind. She would have to deal with Noah later. Maybe by then she'd figure out a way to fix things between them.

But this concert wouldn't wait for her broken heart. After all, the show had to go on. Lucky for her, she'd learned how to compartmentalize her emotions when she'd been out touring. But this was going to be the longest day of her life.

CHAPTER TWENTY-SEVEN

S HE WAS LEAVING.
And he would be alone again.

Later that day, Noah was still at the concert. So far three bands had played to a huge crowd. At the moment, they were taking a break between bands. The lighting engineer had asked him to stick around for a little while since one of their crew was late. He'd reluctantly agreed.

For the past several hours, Noah couldn't stop thinking about how Emma seemingly put her career ahead of their relationship. Had he read more into their time together than she had?

It wasn't like they'd made each other any promises, but he still thought they were starting something—something serious—something lasting. Had he been the only one to think this?

"Easy, man," Greg said, drawing Noah's attention.

He stopped what he was doing to glance at his friend. "What?"

"That screw you're tightening, if you keep turning, you're going to strip it."

Noah glanced at the screw that was supporting one of the lights. He removed the screwdriver as he grumbled under his breath. He climbed down the ladder.

"I'm not even supposed to be here." He wished he was anywhere else.

Greg's brows drew together. "What's up with you?"

"What are you talking about?"

"I'm just wondering what happened to the friendly guy I've been working with these past couple of weeks because you might look like the same guy, but you sure don't act like him."

"I... I'm just tired. This was more work than I was planning to do."

"Then you'll be pleased to know the other guy showed up, so you can go now."

"Good." He had no idea what he was going to do, but it didn't include sticking around there.

"Mind telling me what's going on? Because it's more than just working late." Greg studied him. "It's woman trouble."

"What?"

"I've seen this look before. You're fighting with Emma, aren't you?"

"No. We're not fighting. She, ah... She announced she's leaving."

"Oh." Greg's brows rose high on his forehead. "So that's it."

"What's that supposed to mean?"

"You're worried that you're going to miss her."

"I didn't say that."

"You didn't have to. It's written in that frown you're wearing. Did you try to work something out? Maybe if you ask her, she'll stay here."

He shook his head. "She has her mind made up. She's going back to Nashville for some big meeting with a record company."

"And did you consider going with her?"

"No." The answer was short and quick.

"Why not? Did you even talk to her about this? Or did you just get mad and leave?"

The way Greg said it made him see his reaction differently. He'd mishandled it. Emma didn't say that they were over. She'd said she was going back to Nashville. But he'd been so caught off guard and defensive that he hadn't been able to see that they still had options to continue to see each other.

"No." Noah rubbed the back of his neck.

"Maybe you should go talk to her." Greg walked away.

Noah put his tools away. All the while he tried to think of what to say to Emma. Would she even want to speak to him?

Buzz-buzz.

He wasn't in the mood to talk to anyone. Still he reached for his phone. When he saw his real estate agent's name on the caller ID, he pressed the phone to his ear. "Hello."

"Noah? It's a little hard to hear you."

He raised his voice. "Sorry. I'm at the concert on the beach."

"Oh. I see. I called because I have news for you."

"You've found another house for me to see."

"Not exactly. The financing for the Merriweather house fell through, and they let me know before it hits the market. So if you want it, I need to know right away."

"I want it." He didn't even have to think about it.

"I thought you'd say that after speaking with your girlfriend."

"My girlfriend?" He was confused.

"Um, Emma Bell called me. I thought she was your girlfriend. Anyway she called to see if there was anything she could do to find you a house. I told her the market was limited, but she let me know how much you loved the Merriweather house."

"She did, huh?" His thoughts turned to Emma. He was touched by her thoughtfulness.

"Do you want to go with the same offer?" she asked.

He told her to bump up the offer a little. He didn't want to lose the house twice. She told him that she'd submit the new offer.

Now he had a reason to speak to Emma. He would thank her for putting in a good word for him.

His gaze moved to the sea of people. Trying to find her wouldn't be easy, but he wasn't one to give up easily. He started to make his way through the crowd.

It took a while to find her. But at last, he spotted her off to the side of the stage. She was speaking to someone. He picked up his pace so she wouldn't get away.

He wanted to apologize for overreacting to the news that she was leaving. He hoped they could work something out because he didn't want her to disappear from his life. She brought such light and beauty to it. She made him see things differently—like his woodcarving.

He hadn't carved wood in years, but when he tried to think of something special he could do for her, that was what came to mind. And though he wasn't sure about it in the beginning, once he started to carve out a design, he found he still enjoyed the process. It gave him pleasure as well as relaxed him. He probably wouldn't have reacquainted himself with that type of work if not for her. Eventually, he'd tell her that but not before he finished her special project.

He was almost to her when her heard Emma say, "JT. W-What are you doing here?"

"I came for you. We need to talk."

This was JT? Noah came to a halt. His mind raced with all of the reasons that JT would be there. And Noah didn't like any of the answers.

"Not now, JT," Emma said. "I'm working."

By now a hush had fallen over the crowd as they all turned to watch what was going to happen. Noah should turn away. He should leave. And yet his feet wouldn't move. It was as though they were cast in concrete. He just stood there watching in horror, as though it were a fast-moving train headed straight for him, and he was helpless to move away.

JT reached for Emma's hand. "Em, I'm sorry. I will spend the rest of my life making this up to you. Just say that you'll come back to Nashville."

There was a long pause. "I've given it a lot of thought. And I've decided to go back."

There was an audible gasp from the crowd that jarred Noah into motion. He turned on his heel and almost ran into the people crowded behind him to get a picture of the famous couple. Whereas he wished he didn't have their image emblazoned upon his mind.

Emma wasn't just leaving Bluestar—she was going back to that two-timing jerk. Red-hot jealousy burned in his gut.

The air seemed to grow thinner, and it was hard for him to get a full breath of air. He needed to get away from this crowd—away from Emma and JT. How had he misread everything?

CHAPTER TWENTY-EIGHT

EVERYTHING HAD FALLEN APART.

Sunday morning, Emma woke with a headache. She told herself that it was all of the loud music yesterday and not drinking enough water, but the truth was that she'd been wrestling with what had happened with Noah yesterday.

Maybe she hadn't handled things quite right. Had she let him think she was staying on the island for good? She didn't think so. So then why did Noah look like she'd just betrayed him?

Emma didn't want to go the concert today. And thankfully, she didn't have to. Aster was now up to speed on everything and had offered to handle the event that day. Emma was more than happy to be off the hook.

She couldn't believe JT had the nerve to show up on the island. Did he really think they'd just kiss and makeup? That was never going to happen.

When she'd told JT that she'd made the decision to move back to Nashville, she'd made it perfectly clear that he wasn't to call her or to stop by her place. She wanted absolutely nothing to do with him.

Between dealing with JT's sudden appearance and Noah's disappearance from her life, she was not feeling the best by the end of the evening. Not having any appetite, she'd gone to her room as soon as she got home last night. She'd been there ever since. But she couldn't hide in her room all day.

A shower had helped her feel a bit more human. Her mother checked in on her with worry written all over her face, as she'd heard about JT's surprise appearance at the concert. Emma assured her mother that she was fine, but she just wasn't up for answering questions. She needed some time alone to clear her thoughts.

She grabbed her backpack with her notebook and pen. With no particular destination in mind, she rushed down the steps and into the kitchen where she came to a halt. Aster was there, sharing some coffee with her mother. They both turned to her with concerned looks.

Her mother was the first to speak. "Are you feeling better?"

Emma nodded, even though her head still hurt.

Aster sent her a tentative smile. "Good morning."

Emma wasn't so sure there was anything good about it. But none of that had anything to do with her future sister-in-law, and so she forced a smile to her face. "I'm surprised to see you here."

"I wanted to say hi to your mother before I head to the beach. I also wanted to speak to you, but if you aren't feeling well, I can go."

"No. I just had a little headache last night. I think it was all of the loud music, but I'm fine now." She didn't want Aster and her mother to worry about her. "Do you need me to help out today?" She didn't want to go to the concert, but if Aster needed her assistance, there was no way she'd turn her down.

"Yes. But it's not what you're thinking."

"Give me a sec." Thinking she was going to need some reinforcement for whatever Aster had in mind, Emma poured herself some coffee and then added a little milk and sugar. In the background, Aster and her mother were chatting about the concert. Emma took a big sip before heading over to have seat at the table. "Okay. What do you have in mind?"

"Well, first I want to thank you again for all you did. The concert went off without a hitch, and I've heard nothing but great things about it. And that is thanks to you. Now I have one last favor to ask of you. And if you don't feel like doing it, just say so. I won't be upset at all. It's totally up to you."

Emma took another drink of coffee. "You've got me curious now. What's the favor?"

"Will you be the final act today?"

Emma immediately shook her head. "Thanks, but no."

Her mother gaped at her. "Emma, why not?"

"Because I don't want a sympathy request."

Her mother's brows drew together. "I don't understand. Why do you think this is sympathy?"

"I think I understand." Aster looked straight at Emma. "I'm sorry I didn't ask you to perform in the beginning, but when I was planning the event, you were out on tour and so busy that I didn't want you to feel pressured to drop everything. But I'd be honored to have you do the final number of the evening. There's no pressure. Just think about it." Aster took her now empty mug to the sink before turning back to them. "And now I need to get going."

They said their goodbyes and wished Aster the best of luck today.

"That was so nice of her," her mother said. "You should do it."

"I don't think so. I don't even know what I'd perform."

"Sing one of the songs you sang on Songbird-. Everyone will love it."

Emma wanted to think that after all of this time, she'd moved on from her Songbird appearance. She wanted to be seen as a more experienced singer. But was that true? Or was she just fooling herself?

Knowing her mother was going to keep pushing this until she agreed, Emma chose her words carefully. "Let me give the idea some thought. I'll see you later."

"Okay, sweetie. If you need anything, I'll be here."

On second thought, Emma decided to take her guitar with her. And out the door she went with the early morning sun on her back, she pedaled north to the pier.

She was relieved to find no one there. She could finally take her first full breath. Once she made herself comfortable on the pier, she pulled out her guitar and started to play. The song that came to mind was the one she'd been working on at the beach with Noah and Nikki. It still wasn't quite finished. She reached for her notebook and turned to the page with her lyrics. And she set to work.

She didn't know how much time had passed as she finished the song and wrote out the music. It felt good to be creative. She just wished Noah was around to hear the finished song because in the end, it was about him.

"Emma?"

She turned and spotted Summer stepping onto the pier. "Hi. What are you doing here?"

"We had a coffee date this morning, remember?"

"Ugh. I totally forgot. I'm sorry. I've just had a lot on my mind."

"So I've heard."

Emma set aside her guitar. "How did you find me?"

Summer sat down near her. "It wasn't hard. After checking at the beach and then your mother's house, this was the next logical spot. This is where you always went when something was weighing on your mind. So what's going on?"

"You mean besides the fact that my agent showed up on the island to announce that I have a big meeting next week with a record label. And then I told Noah that I'd decided to go back to Nashville, and now he's not exactly speaking to me. Oh, and then there's the part about JT showing up at the concert last night and thinking he could sweet talk me into going back to him."

"Wow. Huh. That is a lot."

Emma leaned back. "Tell me about it. The only thing that would be worse was if Noah knew that JT was here."

"As a matter of fact, he does."

Emma sat up straight. "What? But how?"

"Well, it seems that Greg told Lucy, who told Birdie, who told me that apparently Noah was going to speak to you when he happened upon you and JT. He heard JT asking you to take him back and then he left."

"Oh, no. What am I going to do?" She closed her notebook and shoved it into her backpack. "I need to talk to him."

Summer placed her hand on Emma's arm to slow her down. "Greg tried last night after Noah left, but he didn't want to talk. Maybe he just needs some time."

"But what if he thinks I went back to JT? Nothing could be farther from the truth. There's nothing JT could say or do to make me change my mind about him."

Summer seemed to give the idea some thought. "Maybe you need to show Noah how you feel about him."

"And how am I supposed to do that if he wants nothing to do with me?"

"There has to be a way."

They both grew quiet as they pondered the options. Emma's mind raced. She didn't want to leave Bluestar with things in shambles between her and Noah after all they'd gone through to reach the point where they were friends—no, more than friends.

"I don't know," Emma said. "I'm out of ideas. Maybe I should just sing the finale at the concert for Aster and then head to the airport."

Summer's eyes widened. "I didn't know you were performing."

"I wasn't until this morning when Aster showed up and asked me. She told me there was no pressure, but I just feel like I should do it. And now that I've finished a new song, I can try it out and see how people respond to it before I play it at my meeting with the label heads."

"Oh, a new song is exciting. What's it about?"

Emma paused. "It's a love song."

Summer's face lit up. "It's the perfect way to let him know how you feel about him."

Emma gasped. "How'd you know?"

Summer shook her head as she rolled her eyes. "Everyone on the island knows except you and Noah. Otherwise, why would he be so upset about you leaving? Once he hears it, he'll know it isn't JT that has your heart. It's him."

Emma's face grew warm. "How am I supposed to play it for him? It's not like he'll be at the concert."

There was a glint in Summer's eyes. "He'll be there. Leave it up to me."

Emma's stomach shivered with nerves. What if she got up on the stage and sang this love song to Noah, and he rejected her? Then she would once more be publicly humiliated on top of having a broken heart. But if there was a chance of winning him back, she had to take it.

CHAPTER TWENTY-NINE

HOW COULD HE HAVE been so wrong about Emma? Sunday afternoon Noah had closed himself off in his woodshop with the radio playing in the background. He had asked himself that question over and over again. He hadn't eaten since Saturday morning, and he was running on very little sleep.

Sure, they'd had a rough start, but he'd thought that was all behind them. He'd thought they'd formed a strong relationship. And then there was the scene with her and JT.

Every time he thought of her with that two-timer, his gut knotted up. Why would she go back to JT? Was it the media attention? Was she hoping JT would help launch her career?

It didn't matter the reason; she was out of his life. He ran the sandpaper over the twelve-by-twelve-inch square of wood with a carving of the ocean and the sun. In the sky was written I love you.

He'd been planning to give it to Emma, but now he didn't know what he'd do with it. He shouldn't have even finished it, but he wasn't one to leave projects partially finished. And it gave him something quiet to do in the early hours of the morning when the rest of the island was sleeping.

Buzz-buzz.

He didn't want to talk to anyone. He silenced his phone and tossed it on the workbench. He turned his attention back to the woodcarving. It was time to stain it.

On the radio one of Emma's songs started to play, and he found himself listening. She was good—really good.

He recalled how her face lit up at the concert. By being around music, she was in her element. Unlike his prior career, Emma found her job to be meaningful and satisfying, even if it meant she had to live away from the island and to travel a lot. Not that this revelation was useful to him now.

He hunted through his various shades of stain, trying to decide which would look the best. He wasn't sure why he was putting so much effort into something he'd never give away. But maybe one of his clients would see it and want it for their significant other.

What shade would Emma like? Light or dark? As soon as he realized the direction of his thoughts, he halted them. It didn't matter what shade Emma would prefer.

Frustrated, he just grabbed a can. As he moved to the center table, he glanced at the name of the stain: maple syrup. It was a rich enough color to draw out some of the plaque's finer details without washing out the image.

Knock-knock.

He paused and didn't say a word, hoping whoever was on the other side of the door would go away.

"Noah, I know you're in there." It was a woman.

He couldn't readily put a face to the voice. Still, it didn't matter. He wasn't in the mood to do business or anything else.

Knock-knock.

"Noah, I'm not going anywhere."

He inwardly groaned. The fastest way to get rid of her was to answer the door. He walked over to the barn door and pulled it open. He was met with a friendly smile. It doused his agitation.

It took a moment for him to put a name to the face, but then it came to him. This was Summer, and she owned the yoga studio. He also knew she was friends with Emma. Surely she wasn't there to find out what had happened between him and Emma. If so, he was going to end that conversation quickly.

He cleared his throat. "What can I do for you?"

"There's a problem at the concert."

He hadn't expected that response. "What sort of problem?"

"It's something to do with the stage, and they need you there right away."

"What happened?" His mind raced through all of the different scenarios. "How serious is it? Did the stage collapse?"

"I don't think it's that serious, but Greg will meet you there. I have to go." And with that she walked away, leaving him to wonder what could have gone wrong.

He didn't waste time. He grabbed his toolbox, turned off the lights, and headed for the door. He swung his toolbox into the back of his cart and took off toward the beach. There weren't any parking spots. He ended up double-parking.

He wasn't sure what he was going to find. Knowing he was going to have to make his way through a large crowd, he decided to leave his toolbox for now. It wasn't until he was making his way from the parking lot and down the steps to the beach that he realized there was a band performing.

If there was a problem with the stage, why would they let anyone on the stage? He was confused. Was it possible Summer had been wrong? He glanced around for her, but didn't see her anywhere.

The song ended and the band's lead singer thanked everyone to tremendous applause and whistles. And then the lead singer asked everyone to wait for a special announcement. There was no problem there.

Still, he was there now. He might as well make sure there was nothing else wrong. He slowly made his way toward the stage. He recalled Summer mentioning that Greg would be there. He scanned the crowd for his friend. With Greg's great height, he was easy to spot.

As he stepped toward Greg, Aster took the stage. "Weren't they wonderful?" After another round of applause, Aster continued. "And now I have a special guest who is going to wrap up this show. Most of you know her. She's Bluestar's rising star...Em Bell."

Noah didn't think it was possible, but the applause was even louder. Emma stepped onto the stage with her guitar. He didn't want to be intrigued, but he couldn't pull himself away.

Emma stepped up to the microphone. "Thank you for having me. What I'm going to play for you this evening is a new song. And as you can see, I don't have my band with me. So it's just going to be me and my guitar. I wrote this song on one of the most perfect days of my life—a day at the beach—a day I'll never forget as I spent it with two of my favorite people."

Was she talking about the day she'd spent with Nikki and him? Was that what she called a perfect day? Because it had been a perfect day for him too.

A cheer went up from one person in front of the crowd. They were obviously a big fan of Emma's.

As Emma started to play her guitar, Noah stepped up beside Greg. He leaned over to him. "Hey, what's the problem?"

Greg turned to him with his brows scrunched together. "What are you talking about?"

"Summer came to my woodshop and said I have to get here right away because there was an emergency—something about the stage."

Greg shook his head. "I haven't heard anything." Then he shushed him and gestured toward Emma.

She started to sing about a summer breeze and swaying trees. Her voice was beautiful. It had warmth and depth. It drew his attention and as she sang, he forgot he was upset with her. For that specific moment, he focused on her words.

"I didn't want to like you.
And somehow you knew.
I didn't want to need you.
But like the rolling tide...
You kept coming back.
And now I know it's true...
I love you."

Again, a fan called out. This time Noah got a look at the person. It was JT. Jealousy burned in Noah's gut. He'd heard enough. He was ready to leave.

He leaned toward Greg's ear and said, "I have to go."

Greg reached out and grabbed his arm. "Just wait."

"I don't need to hear her sing a love song to another guy." No matter how much he enjoyed the sound of her voice and the bouncy tune.

"Trust me."

By this time Emma was back to the chorus again. Noah crossed his arms. As soon as she was done with the song, he was leaving. He didn't care what Greg had to say.

His gaze moved between her and JT. He could see JT grinning because he was the subject of her song. But as she sang the chorus this time, the words were slightly different.

"I didn't want to like you, Noah."

A chorus of gasps washed over the audience.

Noah focused all of his attention on the lyrics. Had she said what he thought she'd said?

"I didn't want to need you, Noah."

JT looked angry as he turned and stormed off. Buh-bye.

Emma's gaze met Noah's, and it was as though she were singing the song just for him. His heart pounded in his chest. She picked him? She loved him?

"But I just can't deny it.

I love you, Noah. Now and always."

Greg elbowed him. "I told you it was worth it to stay."

To a standing ovation, Emma bowed and then made her way off the stage. A crowd of fans rushed her. She stopped to sign autographs.

Noah stood there waiting for her. There was no way he was letting her get away again. This time he had his head screwed on straight—well as straight as it could be when the woman of his dreams announced to the world that she loved him.

Greg turned to him. "It looks like my work here is done."

"What do you mean your work?"

"Summer asked me to keep you here until Emma finished her song. She didn't provide any details, but I knew if it had something to do with getting you two back together, that I was all in. So now I'm off. Enjoy your evening." Greg chuckled to himself as he sauntered off.

Oh, he was going to enjoy his evening a whole lot.

"I'm sorry to make you wait." Emma's voice drew him from his thoughts.

He turned to her. "I didn't mind. It was a beautiful song, almost as beautiful as the woman who sang it."

Her cheeks took on a rosy hue. "Thank you."

"Did you mean it? What you said in the song?"

"Yes, I meant every word."

It was all the confirmation he needed. He didn't know where the future was going to take them but as long as they were together, he would be happy.

ele

Did he feel the same way?

Emma stood there in front of the man she loved, unsure if he truly felt the same way about her. She willed him to say those three words, but instead he was quiet. What was he thinking?

Her heart pitter-pattered as her stomach fluttered with nerves. As the silence dragged on, her insecurities grew. Had she misread the whole situation? Was he about to let her down gently?

She would ask him, but at the moment her mouth refused to cooperate with her mind. Her tongue stuck to the roof of her mouth. What did she do? Stand there and wait for his letdown? Or should she move on?

His gaze met and held hers. "Will you come with me?"

She wasn't sure where he wanted her to go, but as she glanced around, she noticed people watching them. Some people had their phones out and were taking photos of them. Someplace more private would definitely be better for this conversation.

She nodded her head.

He took her hand in his. His grip was warm. His hand was rough from working with wood. He was quiet as they made their way to the parking lot. It was there that he guided her to his cart.

They weren't the only ones leaving the beach. There was quite an exodus, so they spent a little while slowly making their way past Beachcomber Park. It wasn't until he turned south on Main Street that she realized where he was taking her—to his woodshop. Why there?

As though he could read her mind, he said, "I've got something to show you."

She instinctively knew it was something important. But what could it be?

He pulled to a stop in front of his woodshop. They both got out. She couldn't take it any longer. She had to know if he cared for her too.

She stepped up to him, hoping her voice didn't fail her. "Noah, if you don't feel the same way, just tell me. There's no point in dragging this out."

He reached for her hand again and gave it a squeeze. "Just give me another moment and you'll have your answer."

She nodded. Just a little longer.

They entered the shop, and he turned on the lights. He stepped up to the table in the middle of the room. He reached for a twelve-by-twelve-inch piece of wood.

He held it to his chest as he approached her. "I didn't have time to finish this, but I made it for you."

"You did?"

He nodded and handed her the solid piece of wood. When she turned it around, she was floored by the delicate work and the beauty of the seashore. But it was the words at the top that caught and held her attention. It read: I love you.

She read those three words over and over again. Her vision blurred with tears of happiness. Then she raised her gaze to meet his. "You made this for me?"

"I did." He gently took the plaque from her and placed it on the table. Then, he placed his hands on her waist and pulled her toward him. "I love you, Emma Bell. I don't know when I started to fall for you. Maybe it was when you took my coffee at The Lighthouse Café or when you challenged me to go running with you, but somewhere along the way, you gave me back the joy in life that I had been missing. You made the sunny days brighter. And you reminded me that there's more to life than my career."

Her hands slid up over his shoulders and wrapped around his neck. "I did all of that?"

He nodded. "And more."

"And you helped me see that I couldn't give up on my dreams. I don't have to choose between my passion and my love." Her gaze searched his. "We will find a way to make this work, won't we?"

"We most definitely will. And there's something else you should know."

"What's that?"

"I bought the Merriweather house. It seems someone put in a good word for me, and when it came back on the market, I was given the first opportunity to buy it."

Her smile broadened. "That's wonderful."

"Is it? I mean now I can't move to Nashville full time. I have a house that needs some attention so it can be a loving home."

"I'll split my time between being here with you and in Nashville."

His eyes filled with concern. "Are you sure you want to do that. I understand how meaningful your career is to you. I don't want to stand between you and your singing. You're so amazingly talented."

A big smile pulled at her lips. "Thank you. And you won't be. Coming back to the island with you and my family gives me the balance I need to create new material and to breathe."

His gaze searched hers. "Are you sure?"

"I'm positive. I love you."

"And I love you." He pulled her closer and pressed his lips to hers.

Where there was love, there was strength. It might not always be easy but together they'd find a way to make it work. Because her heart would always lead her home.

Epilogue

New Year's Eve

D REAMS REALLY DO COME true.
Maybe that should be a line in her next song.

Emma couldn't stop smiling. On her tour bus, six miles outside of Dallas, she sat across the table from Noah. So much had changed in the last seven months.

She had signed with Cades Records. They had big plans for her career. And as her agent would say, "The sky's the limit."

Noah had started a new online business, selling his wood art. She had helped him set up his virtual storefront. And the best part was that he loved what he was doing.

His wood art gave him the ability to move between Nashville and his new home on Bluestar Island. They were happier than they had ever been.

She'd just finished recording her first album that included the song she'd written for Noah, and it had been well received. And tomorrow she was the opening act for a huge country singer. The tour was kicking off in Dallas.

She was so excited and nervous. It was going to be a sold-out show. She'd never sung to so many people. It was going to be a new and exciting challenge.

She stared at Noah as he worked on hand carving a twelve-by-twelve-inch square with the image of a bear.

Just then the bus hit a bump in the road, bouncing them in their seats.

"I don't know how you do it," she said.

"Do what?" Noah paused and looked over at her.

"I don't know how you carve while we're on the road. Aren't you afraid of ruining the piece?"

He shook his head. "Nah. If anything a gash or nick just adds more character to the piece."

She smiled and shook her head. How was she supposed to argue when his wood art was selling faster than he could create it? In fact, they'd started a waiting list.

"It's beautiful," she said.

"Thank you. I'm just surprised you don't mind the mess."

She'd cope with the wood chips if it meant she could spend more time with Noah. They hadn't talked about marriage yet. They were both taking their time, but when they talked, they'd refer to the future this and the future that. Wedding bells would ring for them eventually. Of that she was certain.

When she looked at Noah, she saw her future. He was the person she wanted next to her throughout life's adventures. He was and always would be her best friend.

Noah reached across the table, wrapping his hand around hers. "Are you happy?"

She smiled and nodded. "I didn't know it was possible to be this happy. I love you."

"I love you too."

Want to read more about Emma and Noah? Sign up for my newsletter and receive a Bonus Epilogue.

Get your bonus epilogue HERE.

EMMA'S ANGEL FOOD CAKE

INGREDIENTS

1 ¾ cups egg whites (let stand until room temp)
¾ granulated sugar
1 cup powdered sugar
1 ¼ cups cake flour
¼ tsp salt
1 tsp cream of tartar
1 tsp vanilla
½ tsp almond extract

1. Preheat oven to 375°
2. Separate eggs (approx. 10 jumbo) and let stand for an hour or two until room temp
3. In a food processor grind the granulated sugar for 1 minute (if you grind too long, the sugar clumps)
4. Combine powdered sugar, cake flour, and salt. Set aside.
5. In a large mixing bowl, using a whisk attachment, beat egg whites until frothy THEN add cream of tartar
6. Whisk until peaks are soft. NOT hard!

7. Add vanilla and almond extract. Whisk until mixed.

8. Gradually add the granulated sugar into the egg whites. Whisk until combined. DO NOT over whisk.

9. Fold in dry mixture a little at a time.

10. Pour in an UNGREASED pan.

11. Bake @ 375° for 30 minutes.

AFTERWORD

Thanks so much for reading Emma and Noah's story. I hope their journey made your heart smile. If you did enjoy the book, please consider...

   - Help spreading the word about Rising Star by writing a
review.

   - Subscribe to my newsletter in order to receive information about my next release as well as find out about giveaways and special sales.

   - You can like my author page on Facebook or follow me on Twitter.

   I hope you'll come back to Bluestar Island and read the continuing adventures of its residents. In upcoming books, there will be updates on Emma and Noah as well as the addition of some new islanders.

   Coming next will be Summer and Greg's story!

Thanks again for your support! It is HUGELY appreciated.

Happy reading,
Jennifer

About Author

Award-winning author, Jennifer Faye pens fun, heartwarming contemporary romances with rugged cowboys, sexy billionaires and enchanting royalty. With more than a million books sold, she is internationally published with books translated into more than a dozen languages. She is a two-time winner of the RT Book Reviews Reviewers' Choice Award, the CataRomance Reviewers' Choice Award, named a TOP PICK author, and been nominated for numerous other awards.

Now living her dream, she resides with her very patient husband and two spoiled cats. When she's not plotting out her next romance, you can find her curled up with a mug of tea and a book. You can learn more about Jennifer at www.JenniferFaye.com

Subscribe to Jennifer's newsletter for news about upcoming releases, bonus content and other special offers.

You can also join her on Twitter, Facebook, or Goodreads.

Also By

Other titles available by Jennifer Faye include:

THE BELL FAMILY OF BLUESTAR ISLAND:

Love Blooms

Harvest Dance

A Lighthouse Café Christmas

Rising Star
Summer by the Beach

WHISTLE STOP ROMANCE SERIES:

A Moment to Love

A Moment to Dance

A Moment on the Lips

A Moment to Cherish

A Moment at Christmas

TANGLED CHARMS:

Sprinkled with Love

A Mistletoe Kiss

GREEK PARADISE ESCAPE:

Greek Heir to Claim Her Heart
It Started with a Royal Kiss
Second Chance with the Bridesmaid

WEDDING BELLS IN LAKE COMO:

Bound by a Ring & a Secret

Falling for Her Convenient Groom

ONCE UPON A FAIRYTALE:

Beauty & Her Boss

Miss White & the Seventh Heir

Fairytale Christmas with the Millionaire

THE BARTOLINI LEGACY:

The Prince and the Wedding Planner

The CEO, the Puppy & Me

The Italian's Unexpected Heir

GREEK ISLAND BRIDES:

Carrying the Greek Tycoon's Baby

Claiming the Drakos Heir

Wearing the Greek Millionaire's Ring

Click here to find all of Jennifer's titles and buy links.